BURNT TONGUES

BURNT TONGUES

Edited by Chuck Palahniuk,
Richard Thomas, and Dennis Widmyer

TURNER PUBLISHING COMPANY

Turner Publishing Company
Nashville, Tennessee

www.turnerpublishing.com

Burnt Tongues

Cover design and Illustrations by: Rachel Jablonski
Book design: Tim Holtz

Library of Congress Cataloging-in-Publication Data Available
Upon Request

9781684425341   Paperback
9781684425358   Hardback
9781684425365   Ebook

Printed in the United States of America
17 18 19 20 10 9 8 7 6 5 4 3 2

CONTENTS

THE POWER OF PERSISTING: AN INTRODUCTION

Chuck Palahniuk

My favorite books are the ones I've never finished reading.

Many of them I hated the first time through: *The Day of the Locust*, *1984*, *Slaughterhouse-Five*. Even *Jesus' Son* occurred as something so odd that I balked and set it aside. High school spurred me to hate *The Great Gatsby* and the stories of John Cheever. I was a fifteen-year-old pimple factory. How was I supposed to swallow the embittered disillusionment of a thirty-year-old Nick Carraway? Growing up as I did, in a trailer house sandwiched between a state prison and a nuclear reactor, Cheever's genteel world of country clubs and commuter trains seemed more make-believe than the Land of Oz.

After a few years of such false starts, I picked up an almost-forgotten copy of Bret Easton Ellis's *The Informers* and read it cover to cover in one sitting. Since then I've bought copies to give to friends, copies and copies, with the caveat: "You're going to hate this at first . . ."

Not to be a name-dropper, but I had dinner with Ellis, and referring to *Fight Club*, he asked me, "How does it feel to have a good movie made from one of your books?" He was also referring to the film adaptation of his book *Less Than Zero*, which everyone disliked at the time. Oddly enough, I recently watched it—The Bangles singing "Hazy Shade of Winter," oh, the skinny neckties and huge shoulder pads, oh, the pleated pants—and I wept, it was so moving. Part of that effect was the nostalgia. But part was my becoming smart or old or open enough to appreciate stories that aren't exclusively about me.

Young people want mirrors. Older people want art. If I couldn't see myself, my world, in Cheever or Gatsby, I rejected them.

To illustrate my point in another way, I didn't always wear eyeglasses. Through my first three years of school, I cursed the idiot who'd hung the clocks so far up on the walls. Really, what was the point of putting a clock so high that no one could read the time? The same went for basketball hoops. The game involved heaving a basketball at something almost invisible, it was so far off. This was a pointless game invented by lunatics.

But at the age of eight I got my first pair of glasses, and suddenly the world made sense; clocks were no longer a blurred smudge of white near the ceiling. The inexplicable swooshing sound that came when someone scored a foul shot—I realized it was a net I'd never been able to see hanging below the hoop. There were some headaches at first, but I adjusted.

The good news is that we all grow up. Even I grew up. Every year, I open *Slaves of New York* or *The Day of the Locust* or even *Jesus' Son* and enjoy it as if it's a wholly different book. Of course, it's not the book that's changing. It's me.

I'm the one who still needs rewriting.

Don't we all?

For the sake of argument, I hereby reject first impressions of "good" or "bad." Over time, readers will remember strong writing; time passes, and the reader changes. What's considered tasteful and readily acceptable to one era is easily dismissed by the next, and while the audience for bold storytelling might start small, as time passes it will continue to grow.

A hallmark of a classic long-lived story is how much it upsets the existing culture at its introduction. Take, for example, *Harold and Maude* and *Night of the Living Dead*— both got lambasted by reviewers and dismissed as distasteful, but they've survived to become as comforting as musty back issues of *Reader's Digest.*

We return to troubling films and books because they don't pander to us; their style and subject matter challenge, but to embrace them is to win something worth having for the rest of our lives. The difficult, the new and novel establish their own authority. The impulse of young people is to complete ourselves as quickly as possible—with the objects we can easily acquire, with fast food, and to fill our heads with printed/downloaded/secondhand information as if we'll never need to buy, eat, or learn another thing until we die. Reaching that goal is, in itself, a kind of death. By middle age our lives are burdened with cheap, easy everything. Like Nick, the narrator in Gatsby, most of us are trapped within our hastily built selves by the age of thirty.

By middle age we're striving to declutter and to diet. Oh, if only I could get cranial liposuction to extract all the trivial facts still crowding my brain.

Think of every movie you treasure. On closer inspection, there are still parts of each story that you fast-forward through and parts you rewind to watch over. These parts change as your moods shift, but the extreme is what endures. What we resist persists.

To give credit where credit is due, that last line is something they used to teach in the oldest training. At least that's where I first heard it. Nonetheless, it bears repeating.

What you resist persists.

The worst thing you could do is read this book and instantly enjoy every word. This book, the book you're holding, I hope you gag on a few words—more than a few. May some of the stories scar and trouble you. Whether you like or dislike them doesn't matter; you've already touched these words with your eyes, and they're becoming part of you. Even if you hate these stories, you'll come back to them because they'll test you and prompt you to become someone larger, braver, bolder. Among the writers I've known at the beginning of their careers—in workshops or classes— their most common weakness was an inability to tolerate any lasting, unresolved tension. Beginning writers will shy away from escalating and maintaining discomfort in a story. They'll set the stage for glorious potential disasters—but quickly sidestep them. Most of these writers come from shitty backgrounds. Nothing drives a person to the secret, internal world of writing fiction as effectively as a miserable childhood, and after those early years of coping with erratic parents or violence or poverty, the smart kid has no tolerance whatsoever for further conflict. Such a kid develops a skill for smoothing out upsets and avoiding confrontations. Imagine an airplane bouncing down a runway, never going faster than thirty miles per hour, never staying airborne for more than fifty feet. Now ask yourself: Would you take such a flight from Los Angeles to New York? Unless writers can come to embrace and live with suspense, their work will always stay flat.

Among the rewards of writing fiction is the opportunity to reacclimatize yourself to discomfort but in the best possible way. You're no longer that child victim. You get to create and control the conflict. Over weeks or months, you heighten the tension, and ultimately you get to resolve it. On the other hand, your reader is expected to experience the finished product in a fraction of the time you took to create it. It's no wonder some books take as long to consume as they did to produce. It might've taken Fitzgerald a couple of years to write *The Great Gatsby*, but it took me over a decade of rereading it before I could empathize with the narrator's heartbroken tone. Whether you take days or years to read them, these stories wouldn't be in this book without the community of writers created by Dennis Widmyer, Mirka Hodurova, Mark Vanderpool, and Richard Thomas. For over a decade they've led an online support system that has given writers from around the world a place to workshop their fiction, to meet fellow writers, and to improve their storytelling. Subjected to the feedback of hundreds of peers, these stories have survived and improved. Even my own suggestions didn't ruin them.

One of my favorite writers Joy Williams once said, "You don't write to make friends." I fully agree, but somehow you do. You do make friends along the way.

I hope you love their stories. Some I already love; some I'll love in the future. Tastes change. If you want instant gratification, look in a mirror. For the rest of my life a different me will pick up this book again and again, read every page, and never feel as if I've finished it—because I, myself, am never finished. Eventually, you and I, we'll both love it—all of it. These stories can show us new worlds like a dozen pairs of eyeglasses. The future is always a headache at first.

FROM THE EDITORS
The Genesis of Burnt Tongues

When I think back to the original workshops that generated the stories for *Burnt Tongues*, I remember so much excitement. There was a hum, a buzz, partly from just being around Chuck I think (one of the nicest guys in the industry, so generous) but also because we felt like we were building something different here. The work was transgressive, for sure, edgy and unsettling.

So much has happened in my own life since then—I've run a magazine (*Gamut*) and published books (*Dark House Press*), got nominated for major awards (Bram Stoker, Shirley Jackson, and Thriller award), published 150+ stories, as well as three novels. These stories STILL rock me to my core. I think this work prepared me to edit anthologies like *Exigencies*. I don't think I could have accepted a tale like "Ceremony of the White Dog" by Kevin Catalano, if I hadn't read stories like "Dietary" by Brandon Tietz, or "Heavier Petting" by Brien Piechos, or "Charlie" by Chris Lewis Carter. These stories upset me, but like any good horror story—shouldn't they? These tales pushed my buttons, they made me think, they made me angry. The opposite of love is not hate—it's indifference. It's impossible to be indifferent when reading these stories. I'd rather you throw this book across the room then just shrug your shoulders.

Another thing that's exciting, in looking back, is seeing how many of these authors have gone on to publish more stories, or write novels, some getting agents, nominations for awards, etc. While I didn't nominate EVERY story in this anthology, quite a few came from my recommendations as a moderator in the workshops—maybe 75% I'd say. So seeing somebody like Fred Venturini break out—*The Heart Does Not Grow Back* at Picador, and *The Escape of Light* with Turner Publishing—it's inspiring. Neil Krolicki got work into *Thuglit*, Tyler Jones into *Dark Moon Digest*, Amanda Gowin into *Gutted: Beautiful Horror Stories* (a Bram Stoker nominee).

There are some films that have changed me as a writer, a person, and those experiences stay with me, whether it was *Oldboy* or *Hereditary* or *Martyrs*. They haunt me with their imagery, their reach, their originality. It's the same thing with these stories—the clench of my guts as the tension builds, the sickening sensation that this is not going to end well, the emotion of these tragic stories, as they unfurl in all of their horrible glory. They are as powerful now as they were when we first published them. Buckle up . . . and don't say I didn't warn you.

Richard Thomas
Co-Editor
Burnt Tongues

LIVE THIS DOWN

Neil Krolicki

You pour the one part bath salts into the two parts pesticide, and how long you've got depends on which website you trust. Corine hits Play on her iPod, and we're not supposed to make it past song six. Her Cruel World playlist. From her phone, Dana sets her Facebook status to: "Dana is sooooo out of here." She taps out her final Tweet: "XOXO, All is forgiven . . . Just kidding." Line one of Corine's final blog entry says: "Feel terrible, everybody. Blame yourselves." This is the opener we voted in; of the two runners-up this one was the most, like, melancholy.

You didn't know what any of these sites said until you chose Japanese to English and clicked translate. Even then it was mostly a mess to read, but we got the gist. This recipe, the internet said it's proven and reliable. It made this way of killing yourself sound like a compact sedan, which makes sense because Japanese people invented this whole deal. Japan is way chill about suicide. You lose your job, all your money, can't feed your kids, and everybody's cool if you want to sit in your car while it's running in a closed garage. If you want to shoot yourself in the mouth or jump off, like, a really tall building. Or if you want to mix up a couple chemicals that shouldn't be mixed and lock yourself in a room with it. They're way fine with that. It's honorable and stuff.

We were never down with the whole bullet or building thing because then everyone at your funeral can only cry around some fancy vase with the neatly packaged, burned-up you inside. Your mom and stepdad only have to look at a photo of you from a sixth grade dance recital in a pretty frame. No one was going to get off that easy.

The anchor chick reporting on Japan's Detergent Suicides a few weeks ago, she didn't give you a step-by-step, but she gave you enough to Google. "Hundreds of Japanese citizens taking their lives by mixing this brand of bath salts (shown top right) with this brand of lime sulfur–based pesticide (shown bottom right)."

Cops in Japan would pull down one how-to site, and five more would pop up. From the country that builds all the little gadgets that make your life easier comes this way to make your death easier too.

Easy. Peasy. Japanesey.

So, way, way before you get to mixing, you're snagging your mom's Visa number and booking a killer suite on the highest floor of the Ritz-whatever downtown. You're telling the dude at the front that your parents are checking in later tonight and it's totally fine if he gives you the room card. You and the two friends with you are just going to hang out. Watch Pay-Per-View.

In the room, you jump on the four-poster bed. You open the curtains and take a sec to look down on everybody before you start pulling the yards of clear plastic out of Dana's suitcase.

P.S. This next part takes longer than you think.

One of us stands on the back of the luxury porcelain toilet, holding the edge of this shower curtain stuff up to the ceiling in the bathroom. The other tears off an arm's length of this silver tape with her teeth and smacks the edge down. Overlapping and taping long sheets so it covers everything: the inset quartz sink, the diffused glass light fixtures, the marble flooring.

Everything but the eighteen-jet tub.

Doing all this prep work to make a condom of the bathroom with three girls sealed up inside, this is a total bitch. But if you aren't planning on killing a hotel full of dogs and cats, if you're not shooting for a mass evacuation with every guest yakking violently all the way to the hospital, then the airtight bubble thing is pretty crucial.

Taped to the outside of the bathroom door is Corine's sign with the clip art skull that says: Poison Gas—Do Not Enter!!! So any housekeepers letting themselves in tomorrow morning don't go opening this bathroom without those rubber jumpsuits with built-in gas masks. Dana says we should have typed it in Spanish too.

The handles are too small for Corine to get her fingers through, so it's Dana and me lifting the heavy jugs out of the roller suitcase and tipping them into the tub. The label has pictures of ants and beetles, all with bright red circles around them and slashes through the middle. Corine starts turning the boxes of bath salts over the tub, shaking the pellets until the first box is gone. Then the second and third. We suck in our last clean breath before Corine pokes the jets-on button. Then she hits Play on the iPod, speakers on either side, with the same thick finger.

You've seen Corine on the internet, and if you haven't you don't go to Watson Middle School. Only, there everyone calls her Pussy Lover, not Corine. The video you saw online, the one that got posted and re-posted and emailed and forwarded times a million, Corine's always said it's fake. To the lunchroom table of jackasses laughing and licking their lips she screamed, "It wasn't what you think! I would never do that!"

But they'd chant: "Pussy Lover! Pussy Lover!" A whole lunch period doing slurp sounds and meowing.

This is why Corine eats lunch off campus on the stack of newspapers waiting to be recycled at the Safeway three blocks from anyone who'd call her anything. Away from anyone who'd see her three roast beef sandwiches, her sack of Doritos, four chocolate snack cakes, and diet soda.

The kid outside Corine's house that night with the video camera was filming his buddies chucking rolls of toilet paper over her roof. Knotting it up in her trees. Spreading white-tipped matches on her lawn so the next time it got mowed there'd be a fire. With the night-vision setting that made everything green and glowing like an X-ray, he shot them pumping mustard into her door locks. Recording every giggle as they slid the garden hose into a basement window well and turned it on. It was when he zoomed in on them smearing white shoe polish on her living room window that he caught Corine inside at that exact wrong moment.

Even Corine admits that the video really does look like she's lying on the living room couch without a shirt or a bra. That you could be looking at two sets of glowing Persian cat eyes hovering around her bare rack, with their little sandy tongues darting, if that's what you wanted to see. But she's only holding Sheeba and Sam-Sam. There's no peanut butter or syrup involved, like everyone says. There totally isn't. A girl can hold her cats, can't she? What's on that video is misleading. It's a lie.

This is the defense Corine's sticking to, even with the tub in this bathroom fizzing and bubbling like those little packets of six-hour energy boosters do in water. Only the tub jets aren't churning up guarana or taurine or caffeine. It's hydrogen sulfide gas. There should be a science credit in this for me. You think of it oozing over the tub in thick waves, like the dry-ice clouds that crawl over a punch bowl at Halloween, but it's not like that. You sort of only know it's doing anything because the air starts to taste like you're rolling a nine-volt battery around in your mouth.

Dana leans over the tub for a sec, then jerks back. She says, "Ugh, it's doing something," batting at her eyes all fast. Fanning her adorable little nostrils poked in her cutesy nose, bolted to her perfect stupid face.

Pick any trophy from the glass cabinets just inside the school doors—track, soccer, basketball, state champs, national champs—and you'll find the name Dana Vecchio engraved under all the little gold people frozen in sports poses. Coaches from the high school showed up to her games, and they'd tell her what her future would be. Dana and me, we never even talked till after this last winter break when her entourage suddenly had a lot more openings.

The boy Dana tied herself to since first semester had this party. He's the guy whose parents will go on weekend trips without hiding their liquor because he's got a lot of As and touchdowns. Being with him, being seen with him, this upgrades Dana to queen of the sports parasites. So here she is partying like a queen should, downing hard lemonades and slippery nipples until her bad-idea meter doesn't even blip when jock-number-whatever tells everyone to pile into the hot tub outside.

The recommended capacity for this hot tub, whatever it was, they were over it by a lot. Dana says it was a mash of bodies in bras and underwear, sloshing out buckets of foamy chlorine water while they passed around bitter shots. And there the whole time, smashed right up against her in the bubbling tub of feet and tits, was her guy, with smiles and Jäger.

This is what made her stupid for him, this smothering attention. The way he smuggled her into his basement bedroom all those times so he could suck on her neck. The way he was always so careful on top of her and the way he offered to mop her down with a warm, wet towel after he'd pulled out on her stomach. He's a big believer in the honor system: "The more on her the better." Dana's bar for chivalry is pretty low. Yes, it was the shots. Yes, it was the hard lemonades. But Dana says when her man started sneaking his fingers into her underwear, she didn't care that they were both smushed up against everyone there with them in that hot tub. Making out.

Totally getting it on.

Until somebody screamed.

Until some guy said, "Aww, Jesus!"

Then smiley boy wasn't kissing her, and she opened her eyes. All around her in the water was a cloud of crimson, thick enough to tint the light underneath red as Valentine's Day, blossoming out.

Some girl yelled, "Oh, my God!"

Her boyfriend's fingers pulling really quick out of her made a bigger explosion of red, with stringy webs of chocolate syrup and pearl globs floating up and sloshing into the tub filter.

Her wet teammates tried to mash their way out, splashing rust-colored water on one another. Red bits gushed all over them. Inside their eyes. Inside their screaming mouths. Fingers clawing and drunk bodies falling over the edge to the frozen concrete.

Everyone inside the house, packed into her boyfriend's shower, his parents' shower, his little sister's shower, they gagged and spit and knocked heads fighting for the water nozzle.

Outside, by herself, Dana sat in a half-empty tub of chlorine water and blood. Crying. It's not nice to laugh.

The next day, Dana's gyno-doc called this an inevitable miscarriage. For serious, I'm not making this up. But it was anything but inevitable to Dana, who had no idea she'd been drinking her baby retarded and Down syndromey for the past twelve weeks. Didn't know she was sending little kidney bean Dana's birth weight farther down into the gutter with every toke and beer bong she hit. Now, her doc didn't say any of this was the reason her mommy parts cleaned house, but she didn't say it helped, either.

Dana's name on those trophies doesn't mean much after this. Maybe there's some number of state championships you can win to make everyone forget about the time you shot chunks of your undercooked kid all over them, but probably not.

As the death cocktail rumbles in the tub, Corine pulls out her phone. Wants to take a picture of the three of us together before we're not together anymore, but there's no way. Not with me. She says, "Sorry" and "I'm totally sorry." Those cruddy little phone pics, they can ruin lives. Ask my ex-boyfriend Trevor. Ask everyone he knows.

Trevor would drive down from the high school at lunchtime to pick me up in his topless Jeep. I'd pull myself in by the roll bar really slow so everyone watching, every girl who wasn't dating a more mature guy like me, could boil in jealousy for a sec. Behind the sub shop, didn't let him kiss me with tongue, let him go up my shirt, I'd smell the breakfast sausage and syrup on him as he leaned over me in the seat, fishing for my bra hook. The varsity wrestler in him was always pushing for the panties, and I'd have to say, "Eeeeeasy, killer." Pulling his fingers from my zipper, I'd have to say, "Gear down, big shifter." He'd feed the pink head of his boner through his jeans, and I'd have to say, "Pump the brakes!"

Enough times of "respecting my boundaries" and Trevor stopped showing up for lunch. Stopped taking me home after school. I'd be stuck on the piss bus with all the bitches smirking at me like someone who didn't know they were dumped. This wasn't okay.

He didn't answer my texts until the one with the picture attached. When I held my camera phone to my bathroom mirror reflecting me in the first stages of slutty: glossed-up pouting lips, tousled hair, and some midriff. You know, classy.

Trevor texted back: im not convinced.

Slut bag: Phase 2 meant losing my shirt completely and popping the top button on my jeans.

Click. Send.

His text said: UR getting warmer.

The next part is not my smartest move, true, but it was either firing off some pictures of me, minus a bra, with my jeans pulled down, or it was back to going out with guys at my school. Back to movies at the mall and hanging at Cinnabon and our parents driving us everywhere. I mean, come on.

Click. Send.

So, the last thing I want to happen is what happens first. These pics traveling like they tell you STDs travel. Trevor giving them to two friends, who give them to two friends and on and on. Until a mostly naked, porned-up me pushing my chest together is on every guy's phone at the high school I'm going to next year.

P.S. Carrying around a topless me in your phone, emailing it to your entire contacts list, plastering it online, this is called child pornography trafficking. It's a felony.

This is what the cops tell every dude, packed in and chained to all the seats inside a bus with steel mesh over the windows. Every guy who got pulled from fourth period and herded onto this long blue tanker with the sheriff's seal on the side, waiting outside the doors of the high school. Cell phone companies have to tell the cops when they run across "potentially exploitive content."

Me screaming at the cops, me stomping and crying and saying that no one forced me to take those pics, that they were my idea, meant exactly squat.

This is every guy I'd ever want to date. The older brother of any guy I'd ever want to have take me to the prom, with a criminal record because of me. An entire male student body having to attend court-ordered sex addiction groups, having to register as sex offenders on the federal database. Having to check in biannually with caseworkers until way after they graduate.

Would you like to know how many girls appreciate some skank turning their boyfriend into a pedophile? It's zero. All these girls who'll want nothing to do with me next year, just like the girls this year.

If you don't count the scrape of steel wool down your throat when you inhale, the Death Balloon Bathroom is pretty painless. The internet was right on.

From our Indian-style circle we're slumping against the toilet, against the steps to the jetted tub, the plastic on everything crinkling and bunching up. If the song playing is number five or seven, we've all lost count. We're breathing through dried-up mouths packed with cotton, and it's not like we're tired, but our eyes are shut.

The coughing just happens. Our lungs jerk when we suck in another deep breath and try to hold it, so we didn't do anything when Dana's hacking fit started. We kind of expect the choking and the gagging part, but we don't expect the stream of wet pasta that shoots out of her throat and splashes off the wall, all hot. Before Dana even wipes the bits off her lips, Corine's leaning forward, hurling her lunch out past her teeth in a thick spray.

All I want is to breathe my toxic gas in peace. To punch my own ticket, like, gracefully and stuff. Apparently, this is too much to ask.

What's in my stomach chainsaws up the walls of my throat and arcs violently into the pool of last meals piled on the plastic. Dana's rigatoni. Corine's fried chicken. My veggie burrito. The last things we expected to eat in this life mixed up and running together, dripping from our hair.

P.S. This wasn't on the internet. No heads-up that said, "Before you bite it, be ready to puke like a fire hose."

Dana's doubled over, holding herself, when the second wave of Corine's heaves surge up and plaster the back of her head. Dana's lunch, part two, gushes through the fingers she's clamped over her lips, and I'm right after her, hurling and screaming like some invisible linebacker is Heimliching me. The little ribbons of blood swimming around in the cakey muck, it's anyone's guess who it came from. Fat tracks of tears cut down Corine's face, pooling on her lips and swirling in with the long strands of spit hanging from her chin. As Dana rakes back the soaked clumps of brunette hair from her face, her hazel eyes are wide and panicked.

This is not what those Asians described at all. Not peaceful.

Not serene. Not fast.

Another wrenching yak detonates in my stomach, and Dana's pulling herself up, her feet slipping in the hot mess. Before I can spit out the clumps of barf in my mouth enough to scream, "Don't!" Dana's shoving her head through a hole she gouged with her fingernails. Clawing at the edges to slip her arm through and open the bathroom door.

I shout, "Wait!"

But she's slithering out the opening headfirst, sliding into the bedroom, like a baby being born on a river of stomach butter. I'm yanking Corine's soaked hoodie with my whole body.

"You can't give up!"

Corine pushes me off as she spreads the tear with her shoulders, wiggling her wide torso through until it plops onto Dana in the bedroom. They're both hacking and smeared solid with lung gravy.

On my butt with my heels together, I keep booting the sticky parts of them jammed up in the door until I can shut it again. Standing. Even for the second it takes to twist the lock, it makes the floor spin and my legs fold in at the knees. My cheek hitting the fancy stone floor covered in plastic, covered in puke, creates a loud clicking sound, and there's blood in my mouth.

At the door, the girls are pounding—and whatever they're screaming, it sounds miles away. Today was the last time I would eat breakfast. The last time I'd see my mom. The last time I'd hear this song. This was always the plan.

Heaven isn't me waking up in the arms of my dead Gram-Gram. It isn't clouds and Jesus and hugs. It's way-too-bright lights and some dude keeping your eyelids back with rubber-gloved fingers. It's yelling and needles poking into your arms and lots of people sticking their face in your face, asking Sesame Street questions.

"Can you tell me what day it is?"

"Can you tell me what two plus two is?"

"Can you tell me what state we're in?" For angels, they're pretty stupid.

Later, when you know this is a hospital, you're laid out in a room and it's dark outside the blinds. There's a guy with, like, eight pens jammed in his shirt pocket and a dick for a nose shuffling in, telling you you're lucky the chemicals you mixed were never fatal.

Fucking internet.

This hospital psychiatrist, Dr. Pen Collector, says we could have sat there all night and the worst that would have happened was the puking. A super, mega headache.

Fucking Japan.

Dr. Dicknose keeps his voice calm and steady and low, and I'm back in the guidance counselor's office two weeks ago, fielding the same psychosocial assessment questions.

"Do you sometimes feel like you have no hope? That nothing's going to get better?"

My ass is back twisting in a scratchy upholstered chair in the holding area outside the counselor's door, parked across from two other girls counting the squares in the carpet pattern. We all had the same pink note that pulled us out of class requesting a "little talk." We knew each other, but we didn't. I told the big girl that what people were saying about her on that video with the cats was totally bullshit. To the sporty brunette girl, I said, people need to shut up about the hot tub thing, that none of those jock tool bags had any right to judge her.

The two girls looked up at me, and they smiled.

Dr. Dicknose is in full-on passive interview mode. If I had anything left to barf, it would have come up when he starts in with the tell-me-how-you-came-to-feel-this-way spiel.

We should have done the toilet cleaner and ammonia. Or the bleach and weed killer.

Past the doc assessing my future suicide risk, past my mom pacing in the hallway, there's a little brown man wheeling a cart stacked with spray cans and scrub brushes. With the spray bottle he's misting doorknobs and room numbers with something bright like raspberry Kool-Aid.

The doc asks if there's ever any conflict in my home life.

Somewhere in this hospital Corine and Dana are getting these same questions. Already we're the girls who couldn't even kill themselves right. Our suicide notes are getting printed and passed around for laughs. Pasted and forwarded to infinite address books.

The doc asks if I've ever been on any antidepressants. The quiet brown guy keeps spraying, keeps wiping.

The kids at Watson, they'll only be surprised now if we *don't* kill ourselves. Our out-of-nowhere shock value is totally blown. Around the school there'll be calendars where you can put money down on which date the Misery Triplets will try again. You can bet on the method. Dana, Corine, and me will have in-boxes chock-full of helpful tips like: "A gun in the mouth is always effective" and detailed instructions on tying a foolproof noose. Helpful diagrams included.

The doc says, "Think of all the friends you'll leave behind to suffer."

I'm wondering how hard it is to, like, swap the clear fluid in my IV bag with whatever toxic disinfectant that raspberry Kool-Aid is. Not that hard, I bet. Simple, probably.

Easy. Peasy. Japanesey.

CHARLIE

Chris Lewis Carter

The shelter is closed, but someone knocks anyway, three
quick raps against the door pane, a panicked knock. "Hey," a
man shouts. "Is anybody in there?"

Three more raps. "I need help!"

The sudden noise sends dozens of high-strung animals
into a frenzy. Shabby dogs bark and paw at their cage doors.
Ancient cats with mangy fur yowl incessantly. The entire
back room becomes a cacophony of bitter howls and clang-
ing metal.

Three more raps.

"There's a fucking car still on the lot! I know you're in
there!" Shit.

He isn't leaving anytime soon, so I hit the outside lights
and part some of the door's blind slats with two fingers.
Whoever it is, he's plastered the opposite side of the glass
with fresh red smudges that obscure most of my view. All
I can make out is a long shadow that connects to a pair of
penny loafers.

I try more slats until I see a large man wearing a brown
overcoat and a matching fedora standing on the stoop. He's
cradling a twelve-pack of Budweiser with one arm, careful to
keep pressure on the sagging cardboard bottom.

"Finally," he says, crouching slightly to meet my eyes. "Open up. It's an emergency!"

I mouth the words *We're closed*, but that doesn't faze him. "You don't understand. They tortured her," he says. "Her eye, it's . . . Jesus, I thought you people were supposed to be humane."

The kennel ruckus has died down. Through the door, I hear the Budweiser box meow. It sounds strained.

Pitiful. Desperate. Shit.

A few moments later, we're both standing in the tiny administrative office, which is cluttered with stacks of paper-work and spit-coated chew toys. Polaroids of smiling children holding secondhand pets line the walls. The air reeks of urine and stale kibble.

The man lowers the box onto my desk and pulls back the flaps. He sucks air through his clenched teeth, then reaches inside and lifts out a ragged mass of black fur, slick with blood. "Oh, Christ. Look what they've done to her." He runs a hand along her glistening back, and she turns in my direction.

"Oh, Christ," I echo.

It's a miracle she isn't dead already. Along with the gouges in her back and sides, her right eye is dangling from its gore-caked socket. Just a bloated sack of blood vessels with a hole punched directly through the cornea.

She sneezes, and a tiny cloud of red mist plasters onto the front of my smock.

My hands begin to feel ice-cold. "Un-fucking-believable." But it's not the cat's face that rattles me. I've seen it all over the past seven years. Every day, animals are brought to this shelter looking like hell, the victims of abuse or neglect—severed ears and cracked teeth, snapped tails and crushed paws.

No, what gets me is the pattern on top of her head. There's a large white splotch, a fat star with rounded corners that travels halfway up the back of her ears.

Just like Charlie.

She even looks about the right age. This is a cat near the end of her life span, with or without the help of a brutal beating.

She stares at me through her one good eye—a pale blue orb surrounded by thick red crust—and the memories twist through my mind, clear and sharp as splinters of glass.

"I found her near the park on Greenwood Avenue," the man says. "Some little fucks were stabbing her with sticks. You can help her, right?"

I rub my forehead and try to realign my thoughts. "Sorry, sir. We're just a shelter. We aren't responsible for medical treatment. She'll need to see a vet."

He begins to stroke the cat's head. Even now, in what must be total agony, she leans into his fingers and purrs. "And they'll help her?"

I stare as the man rakes droplets of blood through the white splotch, dyeing it a faint shade of pink. "Sure, but she definitely needs surgery. Probably cost you a few hundred bucks."

He looks at me as if I've just asked for his wife's bra size. "Jesus, man, I don't want to adopt her. I just wanted to save her from those little bastards."

The cat nuzzles his open palm. He shuts his eyes and takes a deep breath. "What's going to happen to her when I leave?" I explain that the shelter typically covers the medical expenses of non-sponsored strays, provided the injuries aren't too severe and the animal is a reasonable age. But in

this particular case, we'll likely recommend the vet eutha-
nize her with an injection.

Sodium pentobarbital. Quick and painless.

Putting it so bluntly makes me sound like a dick, but
my hands are tied. We're overcrowded as it is, and hardly
anyone will adopt a cat her age, much less a deformed one.

Because that's the sad truth about shelters: they aren't
really about rescuing animals.

Not even close.

They're about vanity. For twenty bucks and a character
reference, we're the perfect choice for anybody with a bud-
ding messiah complex.

People don't just come here to adopt a pet. They want
a good sob story to tell friends and family. How they alone
were caring enough to give a poor, mistreated stray a
chance at a regular life.

But here's the catch: the story can't be too good. Too
good usually means extra work or—even worse—a family
pet that looks gross.

They want the slightly malnourished tabby, not the
completely blind American shorthair. They want the German shepherd with the crooked ear, not the Border collie
with explosive diarrhea.

Everybody wants to play savior, but no one wants to
own the animals that truly need saving.

The cat mews, as though she fully understands the
situation. She looks at me again with that pale blue eye
of hers.

Charlie's eye.

"Can't you at least perform first aid?" the man asks.
"Something to ease her suffering?"

I want to tell him it's too late, that we both know anything I do will just help him, not the cat, feel better. But watching this guy hold her tight against his chest, gently scratching the star-shaped splotch, I say, "Yeah, sure."

The man nods, then exhales, which causes his chins to ripple. "It's a pretty fucked-up world when kids get a kick out of doing something like this."

"Don't worry. They'll regret it one day," I say. Then, without realizing it, I add, "Even if they never meant to hurt her." The man narrows his eyes at me. "Does this look like an accident to you? Those little fuckers were . . ." He pauses, then says, "We're not talking about the same animal anymore, are we?"

Shit.

I haven't spoken about Charlie for fifteen years, but something about this mangled look-alike drags the words out of me. She is a feline priest ready for my confession.

"My sister's ninth birthday party," I say.

Jessica was a little brat who always wanted the best of everything. Our parents barely made enough to get by, but they somehow managed to turn our backyard into a glorified carnival. They rented a miniature pony and a bouncy castle and had hundreds of those big, foil-covered helium balloons tied to everything. As I explain this, I tug a fresh pair of latex gloves from my pocket and work them over my hands.

"We weren't exactly what you'd call friends," I say. "In fact, we hated each other. Jessica loved to make fun of my glasses and crooked teeth every chance she got."

I pull half a dozen Kleenex from a box on the desk and dab them against the cat's back and sides. Deep red blots bloom across the wads of tissue.

"We had just watched Jessica open about a hundred gifts—toys, games, enough clothes to fill two closets. Any normal girl would have been thrilled, but she sat on the lawn with her arms crossed and her lips puckered. There she was, wearing her princess tiara and a little red sundress, sulking like she'd got nothing but odd socks."

The cat sneezes again. Another mist cloud drifts to the floor and sprinkles onto a rag doll with tufts of stuffing poking out. It gets thrown in the trash along with my gloves and the Kleenex, which by now are all soggy with blood.

"That's when our parents came parading out of the house with a cardboard box," I say, sliding on a second pair of gloves.

Mom made a big deal out of announcing how there was one more gift for their special birthday girl. Everyone crowded around Jessica as she ripped open the flaps and started squealing.

The man grunts. "Let me guess. A cat?"

"A kitten," I say, then grab the shelter's first aid kit from the desk drawer. "No more than eight weeks old. She reached inside the box and pulled out a tiny ball of fluff. It was solid black, except for a white splotch on top of its head."

The man squints, then his eyes grow wide with comprehension. He traces one bloodstained finger along the outline of the cat's now-pink splotch but says nothing.

"Jessica named her Charlie right there on the spot, then hugged our parents and said that a kitten was the only thing she'd ever wanted. After that, she paraded Charlie around the yard and let all the kids pet her."

Well, everyone except me.

I take a small pair of scissors from the kit and slide the garbage can underneath the cat. She purrs while the sticky clumps of fur that cover her wounds are snipped away.

"When it was finally my turn, Jessica skipped up to me and said that ugly boys didn't get to pet Charlie. The other kids laughed, and I ran off toward the picnic tables in tears. Meanwhile, Jessica gave Charlie to Mom and went to play inside the bouncy castle with everyone else."

Another set of gloves go into the garbage, replaced by a new pair. I grab a needleless syringe and a bottle of hydrogen peroxide from the first aid kit.

"I tried telling Mom what had happened, but she never sided with me over my sister. She said that Jessica was just being her usual silly self and not to take jokes so seriously. To prove there were no hard feelings, I could watch Charlie for a few minutes while she and Dad went inside to get the cake. Before I could say anything, she dropped Charlie in my lap and headed for the house."

I fill the syringe with peroxide and pull another wad of Kleenex from the box. "She must have been agitated from being handled so much. Because when I tried to pet her, she dug her claws so deep into my hand that it bled."

With each squirt of peroxide, patches of white froth bubble up from the cat's fur. Streams of pink-tinted solution drain into the Kleenex.

"Even Jessica's stupid kitten didn't like me, and that really set me off. Both of them needed to learn that I wasn't going to be pushed around anymore. And that's when I noticed just how many helium balloons were tethered around the wooden slats of the picnic tables."

The man removes his fedora and fans himself while I put on my fourth set of gloves and grab a roll of gauze from the kit. "I stuffed Charlie into the front pouch of my sweatshirt and began snapping the colored ribbons that held the balloons in place. I gathered up maybe two dozen of them, big and silver, all of them saying, Happy Birthday, Princess in block lettering. Crouched behind the tables, I knotted the ribbons together at the top, then tied a huge slipknot at the bottom. My dad had taught me how to make one earlier that summer on a fishing trip. The thing about slipknots is that the harder you pull, the tighter they become."

The man shifts his weight, then glances at the door. We both know he can leave, that no one is stopping him from walking out of the office, out of the shelter, but he isn't moving.

Perhaps he's fascinated that a stranger would share his deepest secret because of an old, mutilated cat. Or maybe my story is the verbal equivalent of a car crash, and he can't help but rubberneck for just a little longer.

Either way, he's staying until the end.

"The other kids were playing in the bouncy castle across the yard, and our parents were nowhere in sight. It was the perfect opportunity. I pulled Charlie out of my pouch and threaded her midsection inside the slipknot, then climbed on top of a picnic table and yelled, 'Hey, Jessica, look who I've got!'"

The man swallows a lump of air. He extends his trembling arms, allowing me to wrap thin, white ribbons of gauze around the cat's body.

Before long, Jessica tumbled out of the bouncy castle and stared in my direction. Sometimes I wonder how it must have looked from her perspective: seeing the brother she had always tortured perched on a picnic table with her new kitten strapped to a cluster of balloons.

"She started running across the yard," I say. "She was screaming, 'Charlie! Put her down! Charlie!'"

The man almost sounds like he's purring now. His lips are an airtight seal, and a groan swirls in the back of his throat.

"I never intended to hurt her. It was just supposed to give Jessica a scare. The sight of her kitten dangling in midair for a few seconds should have been enough to keep her from picking on me ever again."

That was the plan, anyway.

The gauze is taped, and I ease myself against the corner of the desk. The words are pouring out of me, fifteen years' worth of guilt spilling out into the tiny office.

"For a moment I thought it wouldn't work, but Charlie was no heavier than a stuffed animal. When I released my grip, the balloons jerked her into the air. She started crying and thrashing around, but that only made the knot tighter."

"Oh, dear Jesus," the man says.

"By now the other kids had piled out of the bouncy castle and were pointing and shouting at the sky. Jessica slipped on a pile of pony shit and landed face-first on the lawn. It was total chaos—enough to convince me that my point had been made. But when I reached up to grab Charlie, my hand felt nothing but empty air."

The office is completely silent. Even the cat seems to be hanging on my every word.

"The balloons had sent Charlie too high, too fast. She was already more than an arm's length away and drifting farther by the second. Even when I jumped with everything I had, my fingers just brushed the tips of her tiny paws. There was nothing I could do except watch her float away. She passed by our second-story window, bounced off the satellite dish on our roof, and sailed clean over the house."

I stare at the blood-flecked floor and shake my head. "Want to know the hardest part? There was a second, right after I let her go, when she looked straight at me with those sad, blue eyes. I can still picture them, clear as day."

The man wedges his lips between his teeth. He's still cradling the cat like a child, stroking her head with shaking fingers. "When our parents finally came running out of the house to see what all the fuss was about, I jumped off the picnic table and bolted out of the yard. I couldn't bring myself to look up at the sky anymore, but I could still see the shadow of those balloons on the ground. Even after I ran for half a block, there it was, gliding across the sidewalk. Almost like it was following me."

The man exhales in a wheeze, as though the climax of my story had robbed him of the ability of breathe. Then he says, "So, what happened?"

I tap the lid of the first aid kit, and it falls shut. "My parents offered to buy Jessica a new kitten, but she didn't want one anymore. I was grounded for a year, and we never had another family pet."

"And Charlie?"

"That's the thing. No one ever found her body. Not the local shelters, our neighbors, or me during my own constant searches. She was a ghost. Part of me has always wondered if she survived. If maybe she became just another stray that would somehow end up here. I know that probably sounds crazy."

"Not at all. So do you actually think—could this really be her?" He offers me the cat like he's performing the end of some ancient ritual.

I lift her from his bloody hands. "Thanks for listening," I say. "But Charlie is dead."

The man crinkles his brow, then stuffs a hand into the pocket of his overcoat and removes a business card. "Here," he says, tossing it onto the desk. "Let me know what happens to her, okay?" He takes one last long look at the cat and sighs. "Jesus Christ," he says and turns to leave. "What a world. What a goddamned world." His voice echoes through the hallway, then the front door slams and stirs up another chorus of animal noises.

I stand there, holding the cat, feeling her warmth against my arm.

"Charlie," I say, slipping the phone receiver from its base and jabbing a few numbers with my free index finger, "is it really you?"

Someone picks up on the other end.

"Hello, Doc?" I say. "It's Roger. Sorry to call you so late, but I've got a personal emergency this time. It's about my cat."

And Charlie purrs.

PAPER

Gayle Towell

He had big hands. Kyle doesn't. Kyle's hands are small—
about the same size as mine but his fingers are a little longer.
But him, he had big hands. And the skin on his hands had
a weird pattern to it. The little crosshatch lines you see on
your skin when you look close—his went deeper.

And he was hairy. Really fucking hairy. He would climb
off me, and in the sweat on my stomach would be dozens
of his curly black chest hairs. Now, Kyle has a total of three
hairs around his right nipple, two near his left, and that's it.

The smell of him—his sweat mixed with that cheap
cologne he would wear.

He never said, "I love you." He would always say, "You
know I love you." And I must have been fucking brainwashed
because I believed it.

Yes, me, Jane, the great prodigy, the smart one, was young
and stupid. Naive. Jane could marry an older man when she
was twenty because she was smart like that. He could pin her
arms up over her head, pinch the wrists so tight together it
would leave bruises. He could fuck her dry and make her bleed.

And this was happiness.

She'd give him a blow job not because she wanted to but
because he'd have her hair tight in his fist and hold her face
over his dick.

And this was marriage.

I won't marry Kyle. Even if he asks, which he hasn't, because clearly marriage is just a piece of paper you sign.

Kyle's hovering over me now in our bed, naked. "Why is it all the areas I like to touch make you cringe? 'Don't kiss the nipples,'" he mocks. "'Don't kiss the neck. And for the love of God, don't go anywhere near the crotch.'"

"Those are the rules," I say. "You know the rules."

"But you're just lying here"—he kisses my forehead— "with nothing on but your skin"—he kisses my cheek—"here in our bed"—he kisses my lips—"and I can't help myself." He goes for a nipple.

But I'm quick. I block him with a hand over each one.

He's smiling at me through stringy blond hair hanging in his face. He's been growing his hair out. For me. Because I said it would look good like that.

I reach up and tuck it behind his ears. Force a smile back. "I've got to get up early tomorrow."

He sighs his same old, tired, not again sigh, looks over at the bedroom door, and gets out of bed.

"Where are you going?"

"I'll come to bed later."

"Are you mad? Don't be mad. Please don't be mad."

He leans over and pulls the blankets up to my neck. Runs his skinny fingers through my tangled black hair. "Hey, did you feed the fish today?"

I shake my head.

Day two at my new job and there seems to be some unspoken etiquette in the women's restroom. The previous visitor always leaves a large unrolled paper towel segment ready for the next person. Waiting for me after I wash my hands again this morning is a segment of paper towel ready for my use, and I tear it off. I put my hand on the lever to unroll more but don't.

I'm still in new employee training all day for two more days after this one. They hired a dozen of us at once and have a full schedule of mysteriously acronymed sessions for us to attend. At this point I'm not even sure what my job entails. My title is Actuarial Research Analyst. Not an actual actuary because this wasn't exactly the plan, and hence I haven't taken any actuarial exams. The fact that I was a thesis away from a PhD took a backseat to the three terms of statistics and the one business class I had taken as an undergrad. So much for grad school.

In the conference room the lights are dimming, brightening, dimming, brightening in decaying oscillation about some ideal equilibrium. Our team trainer is fine-tuning the dimmer switch, trying to get the lighting at the right spot where the PowerPoint stands out, but it's still light enough for everyone to take notes.

This first presentation is an overview of New Employee Success Training (NEST), which is apparently different from yesterday's New Employee Orientation (NEO). After the overview, we're being sent to another room with three fold-out tables lined with eight-by-eleven pictures. Pictures of famous works of art. Photographs of well-known places. Close-ups of everyday items. We're asked to walk around silently and pick the picture that we feel represents us in our new work environment.

Later I'm explaining to my seat neighbor that I feel this eight-by-eleven close-up of a face with an acupuncture needle in the cheek represents how new employment is about being vulnerable to something potentially painful in the hopes it will make you better in the end.

My seat neighbor Karin (that's Karin, not Karen, and indeed she felt the need to dot the *i* on her name tag with a heart) has chosen a picture of smiling children holding hands because the new job is about learning and teamwork. Karin thinks she's my buddy because we're the only women in the room, but honestly, all we have in common are our vaginas and our tits.

I'm in a stall in the bathroom at break time, hiding out, trying to kill the time alone. I pull a pen out of my pocket. On the side of the giant toilet paper roll stuck on the wall to my left, I draw a circle. I draw a smiley face inside the circle. Next I add a stick figure body and stilettos that reach just to the bottom edge of the roll. A triangle dress, long hair, and a bow on her head complete the ensemble.

After washing my hands and tearing off my paper towel, I unroll, leaving approximately twelve inches of towel ready for the next person's use.

Kyle says he had a dream. A weird dream. He was trying to save me, but he couldn't find me. I was through some sort of invisible portal. I tell him he plays too many video games. He says, no, serious. The weird part, he says, was that he knew if he could only access the fourth dimension, he would get to me. It was one of those dreams where you know something, even though no one's told you and you can't see it. He was standing in sand. There were five pebbles in the sand evenly spaced in a circle. He says he drew in the sand with a stick. Drew lines connecting each of the pebbles to each of the other pebbles.

"A complete graph," I tell him.

"Huh?"

"That's a complete graph—when you connect each vertex to every other vertex."

"Oh," he says, "well, anyway, that's how I got to the fourth dimension."

At work, my stick figure woman on the toilet paper roll has lost her feet. She is now just the triangle of her dress, arms, and head. A bow in her hair and a smile. I pull the pen out of my pocket again and draw a quote balloon coming from her mouth. In it I write: Oh no! I feel like I'm being used! But she still has that stupid smile, so I add Tee-hee!

We're sitting around the big table in the conference room, and anytime someone looks my way all I can think about is how my sweater's too big and I didn't wash my hair this morning. Two hours into database programs overview and there's this feeling like my heart's beating faster than it really needs to. This internal panic coming from nowhere, this feeling that anyone in the room might attack at any moment and I should be ready to run—every time my chair so much as squeaks, it turns up a notch.

At lunchtime, since they've finally assigned us offices, I hide out in mine. I sit under my desk because it's nice down here. It feels safe. In my own little world eating a sandwich while everyone else hangs out in the lunchroom and gets to know each other. The standard, "So where did you go to college and where are you from originally?" and such. Though by today they've probably moved on to dietary restrictions, family lineages, and favorite sports teams.

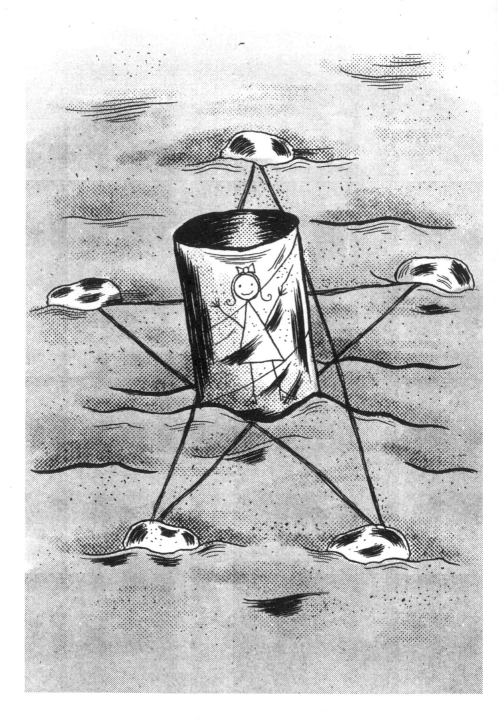

The only really annoying thing about being under here is that I can't quite sit upright. My choices are slouching forward with my neck making a forty-five-degree angle or reclining back against the wall, but the wall—they went a little overboard texturing the paint—snags the back of my shirt. But it's worth it. This space is worth it.

I finish my peanut butter and jelly right as there's a knock on the door. Three hard taps. It could be Karin, but it sounds like a guy knocking. I hold my breath. My door's not locked, so whoever it is might come in and see me like this. I count out sixty seconds in my head before exhaling again. Whoever it was must be gone, but it's left me feeling like I did in the conference room again. I hate this feeling. My hands are even shaking.

There's still twenty minutes left for lunch, so I take the pen out of my pocket. On the underside of the desk I draw Kyle's five rocks as dots. I connect each point to every other point. The result is a pentagram inscribed inside a pentagon. I scribble over it.

I draw three points and connect each of them. This is simple. It's a triangle. In topology they call this a 2-simplex, sort of the fundamental prototype of two-dimensional space. I draw four dots and connect each dot to every other dot.

This one's trickier to see, but it's a tetrahedron squished down into two dimensions. A 3-simplex. Fundamental proto-type of three-dimensional space. Imagine taking four triangles and gluing all their edges together to make a closed figure. Squish it flat, and you've got the picture I've just drawn.

Five points connected to each other in this way is a 4-simplex. Fundamental prototype of four-dimensional space. Kyle's subconscious is genius. Imagine taking five tetrahedrons and gluing all their faces together. You can't do this in three-dimensional space , but if you could, you'd have a 4-simplex. Project that 4-simplex into two-dimensional space, and you have an inscribed pentagram.

I walk in the door to the smell of garlic, and Kyle's in the kitchen draining pasta. He made dinner. A nice dinner. And he hates cooking. If I don't make a meal, he lives on cereal. We have this whole line of cereal boxes on top of the fridge, each with about a bowl's worth of stale cereal left in it. You know—you don't want to eat the scraps at the bottom of the box, but throwing it away would be a waste of food, right?

"Hey," he says, "how was day three?"

I say, "You've been busy."

He says, "Sit, sit. Food's almost ready, then I want to hear all about it."

A glass vase with red roses sits in the middle of the dining room table. That floral shop smell of flowers and packaging and I remember working in my grandma's flower shop back in high school. My first job. Back before college. I touch the soft petals and pluck one off. I sit and rub the paper-thin petal between my thumb and forefinger and wait for Kyle.

He comes over with a steaming plate in each hand. Sets one down in front of me and the other in front of the seat next to me. He turns the lights down, sits, and smiles at me, his stringy hair hanging in his face again. I reach out and tuck the loose strands behind his ears. He expects me to say something. I pick up my fork and start poking around the pile of pasta with it. He watches me a moment, then does the same. I tell him that thing he drew in the sand in his dream was really a four-dimensional figure. Halfway through my meal, I get out of my seat and walk over to turn the lights back up.

Kyle watches, his mouth hanging open just a bit and the skin between his eyebrows all bunched together.

I get a piece of paper out of the desk in the living room and pull the pen out of my pocket. I sit back down and shove my plate to the side, click the pen open, and look up at him.

His lips are pursed. He's waiting.

I give him a topology lesson. I show him how to see the squished tetrahedrons. Tell him how really the space around it is the interior of that last tetrahedron and is kind of where the fourth dimension lies.

He says he knows. That's how it worked in his dream. He says he didn't get to tell me the end of his dream.

The end of the fourth and final day of orientation and my toilet paper girl is just a head. A bow on top and a smile still. She's upside down today, so I spin her back to upright. Today she gets a new quote bubble: See, ladies? This is what happens when you let it go too far! When I dry my hands, I unroll some paper towel again. This time I fold the end of it into a point like they do with the toilet paper in hotel rooms.

On my way out of the building I pass by one of the big meeting rooms. The door is open, and one side of the room is nothing but a huge window overlooking the city. No one's in there, so I go in to have a look. We're ten stories up, and I can see all the way across the river. Can see where the highway leads down to my exit.

I flinch when a voice behind me says, "It's hard to find women working in the field who are actually qualified."

I turn around, and it's the team trainer guy. Not more than an arm's length behind me. He must be mistaking me for someone else. I'm probably the least qualified new hire here by their standards.

"Sorry. I, uh, didn't mean to startle you." He motions to the window. "Nice view, huh?"

I nod and turn back around. I point. "I can see where I live from here."

"Yeah, you can see a lot of things from here." And he must have stepped even closer because there's the hot humidity of his breath on my neck.

I'm scared to turn around now. Maybe it's my imagination. Or he's just trying to look over my shoulder and see where I was pointing. Ignore it, real or not, and it will go away, right?

But I'm frozen.

Hot breath on my neck every time he exhales.

Staring at the river. Watching the cars move through the traffic lights.

Hot breath on my neck. Frozen.

He says, "Well, I guess I'll see you tomorrow."

I manage a nod, and the breath leaves my neck. I count out sixty seconds before turning around again.

It's near midnight, and neither of us has been able to sleep. Kyle is curled up facing away from me in bed hiding his hard-on and resentment. It's been two weeks since Kyle and I have made love. Fucked. Done the deed. Whatever name you want to give it.

I throw the blankets off and sit up at the edge of the bed.

Kyle turns the lamp on and says he doesn't get it. "What did he do to you, Jane? What did that asshole do to you?"

For whatever reason, it's always weirded me out that Kyle uses my name when he talks to me. The asshole he's speaking of, my ex, he'd always call me honey. I used to think that was somehow special. Now I kind of think it just meant I wasn't really me. I was honey.

"I'm sorry. It's the job. I'm worn out."

"Don't lie," he says.

I flinch at his words. Subconscious response. I give myself away.

"You think I would ever hurt you?" The look on his face. That I would flinch at his words. "I'm serious," he says. "Talk to me."

I tell him, "I hate my job."

"That's not what this is about."

"It's true. I hate it. I wish I'd finished my PhD."

Kyle sighs. "I never did tell you how my dream ended last night."

"You did. You found the fourth dimension," I say. "You know I was going to work on dimension theory? Now I fucking enter shit into databases for a living."

"That wasn't the end of the dream," he says. I look him in the eye. "Sorry. Sorry you've had a rough week at the new job."

"Why are you sorry? It's not like it was your fault."

"I know."

"I feel like a has-been already, and I'm not even thirty yet. I don't know what I'm doing with my life."

"Nobody does. Nobody does."

"What is the point in the end?"

"Does there need to be one?"

"So, how did it end, then? Your dream?" I move to sit cross-legged in the bed facing Kyle, who's now sitting up, leaning back against the headboard.

"It was about you, you know. I had to find the fourth dimension to get to you." He looks right at me.

I pull my T-shirt over my head and throw it to the side. "Go on."

"I drew the lines in the sand, then I somehow just slipped into elsewhere and you were there. But. You were bald. You had no hair. And no clothes."

"Why do you stick around?" I say. "Why do you even put up with me?"

"Because I want to. And you know, I don't think I've ever wanted anything more. Why are you here with me, Jane? Why do you stick around?"

I get up on my knees and slide down my underwear.

Kyle says, "What are you doing?"

I don't really know why or where it's coming from, but I've got that knotted, anxious feeling in the center of my chest again. That feeling like I'm going to cry, but I've swallowed it. My hands are cold, numb. My mouth shakes; my voice shakes when I speak. "Tell me the rest of your dream."

Kyle grabs the blankets and drapes them around my shoulders. Stares down at my breasts a moment before he pulls the blankets tight around me, hiding them from view.

"You had a knife in your hand. In my dream. A big sharp blade. I think you had used it to cut off your hair, because you had a fistful of your hair in your other hand. You gave me your hair. You said, 'Hold this for now,' and you closed my fingers around it. Then you walked away from me and stepped onto this flat rock. You turned around and looked down at your stomach, rubbing your fingers over it. Still holding the knife in your other hand. You lifted the blade, and I said, 'What are you doing?' You said, 'It's got to come out, and this is the only way.'"

I shrug the blankets off my shoulders. "What's got to come out?"

Kyle has gone from looking drowsy and irritated to full alertness. He's sitting all the way upright now and not leaning back against the headboard anymore. He's watching my face so closely I can't bring myself to look at him for more than a passing glance because those green eyes of his are too much.

"I couldn't get to you in time." He reaches out and traces a line down the middle of my belly. "You stabbed your stomach, sliced down the middle, and your guts—your intestines—just fell out onto the rock."

"I would never do that."

"Well, you did in my dream."

My eyes burn, and soon they'll be wet enough that my eyelids won't hold in the tears. I suck in air, hold it for a count of ten, let it out slowly, but each exhale shakes more than the last.

Kyle says, "I turned away, but you said, 'Look at it. You've always wanted to know what's inside.'"

Kyle's hand on my chin turns my face right toward his, and I can't avoid his eyes anymore. And his eyes—they're red around the edges too.

"Then you dropped the knife and fell to the ground. Crumpled like paper."

MATING

Tony Liebhard

Squirrels spend months preparing for winter, gathering nuts and hiding them in various locales, hoping to hoard enough grub to last until spring. Only problem is, sometimes they forget where they stashed their snacks. In rare events, even the smartest, most hardworking rodents starve to death.

All that time and effort for nothing.

Staring at the last question on the Animal Behavior mid-term today, I have total empathy for all the squirrels lying dead in trees somewhere.

For two weeks I memorized lecture notes, studied flash cards, and participated in study groups. But nothing prepared me for the only essay question on the entire exam. Worth ten points out of a possible hundred. And 10 percent of the freaking grade. The difference between an A or a B. What might drop my GPA and keep me out of vet school.

Describe the mating habits of bluegills.

With the rest of the exam completed, I sit and watch the clock, trying to recall anything aquatic. Half a semester worth of material and Dr. Penn decides to ask us about something that wasn't even in the PowerPoints. The bluegills thing was just some rambling tangent he went off on one day in class. The rant was so random I probably didn't even jot down any of it in my notes. Though I should've known better than to disregard it. When a professor who calls himself Aquaman gives you a test, you should expect at least one question will be about fish.

Even if I did write it down it wouldn't have mattered. Odds are I wouldn't have read about it last night when I was cramming anyway. I barely had time to look over the important stuff, let alone the insane yammering of some vet school reject.

I wish I'd never found that damn cell phone.

Yesterday was immortalized in ink inside my planner. 8–10: calc. 10–12: research. 12–1: lunch. 1–3: Vertebrate Ecology. 3–12: study for doomsday. An hour break was scheduled in the evening to walk dogs at the Humane Society, one of my many duties as Pre-Vet Club president.

Somehow Vert Eco ended early. There was a new gap in my schedule for a quick nap. Half asleep, I began walking home. Just as I passed the Social Sciences Building, a distorted version of "Brown Eyed Girl" by Van Morrison erupted from a row of bushes.

Following the sound to the source, I looked beneath branches of pine needles until the music stopped. Sunshine reflected off the pink metallic case of a cell phone hidden among pinecones. I grabbed it off the ground, and the touch screen lit up.

The wallpaper said "Lexi's phone" and was littered with animated hearts.

She had eight missed calls and twenty unread text messages.

In the middle of trying to figure out how to unlock the keypad, the phone started vibrating. I almost dropped it.

"Brown Eyed Girl" began playing again. The screen said, Incoming . . . Vanessa.

I tried to decline the call but somehow hit the wrong button and wound up accepting it instead.

"Oh, my God," a girl said. "It's about freaking time you answered your phone. Are you that hungover?" She paused. "Lexi?"

"This is not her," I said.

"I'm sorry," she said. "I must've dialed the wrong number."

"No, you didn't. This is Lexi's phone."

"Well," she said, "can I talk to her?"

"I'm sorry but you can't."

"Why not?"

I went into detail about how I found Lexi's phone on the ground on the way home from class and so on and so forth.

"Oooooooh," she said.

"If you happen to see Lexi or talk to her," I said, "will you please tell her to call her phone? That way we can figure out a place to meet so I can give it back to her."

"Sure thing." A lighter flicked, followed by a long exhale. "You know, it's really nice of you to, like, go through all this trouble to give her phone back."

With the phone pressed against my ear, I started walking home again. "Anybody else would do the same thing."

"Oh, whatever," Vanessa said, with a prolonged exhale. "People suck."

"They can."

"You know," she said, "you sound kind of hot."

In nature, animals often use sound to attract mates. Birds and insects croon unique melodies to lure in the opposite sex. Dolphins can seduce each other from miles away with the right tune. Even an ugly bird can mate if he sings pretty enough.

I said, "You ever sit outside on a hot summer night and hear crickets chirping?"

Vanessa exhaled a long one and laughed. "Yeah, why?"

"Do you like the way they sound?"

"Um, yeah, sure. It's kind of pretty."

"You ever see one?"

The conversation ended with me asking her one more time to please pass the message on to Lexi.

After the Animal Behavior midterm today, I stop in the biology research lab and open my lecture notes. A skim through the material reveals no trace of anything bluegill related. Of all the things Dr. Penn could've quizzed us about, he had to pick the most insignificant nonsense and make it worth the most points on the test.

After flipping through the notes a few more times, I give up and begin collecting data for my research project about the role of scent in mating. In theory, each animal has a special fragrance they use to attract the opposite sex. With just an odor, they can entice a mate, sight unseen. These natural perfumes that animals emit are called pheromones.

Scientists have long wondered if this same phenomenon exists in humans. Although there's no conclusive evidence to support this theory, a study once showed that strippers who were actively ovulating made the most tips. Strippers who were on the pill, which prevented ovulation, made significantly less money. Fat, ugly, skinny, gorgeous—looks didn't matter. Was there some invisible chemical at work? And, if so, in a world where physical appearance matters most, could other senses, such as smell, help an unattractive person find a mate?

In my apartment last night, I sat alone in the living room scanning the Animal Behavior study guide. Class notes were spread across my desk, and I didn't smell pheromones. All I smelled was barbecue grilling outside.

Sunlight crept through the blinds on my living room window the way waves carry sand pebbles to the shore. It was such a beautiful day yesterday, and I was stuck inside studying, trapped in a learning cage, while other people sat outside drinking, laughing, and barbecuing. Enjoying the weather. Enjoying each other. Enjoying life.

I looked at my lecture notes and glanced outside. I keep telling myself after every test that I'm going to start going out and meeting people and having fun. Too bad every time one test ends, another begins.

I take a break from collecting research and open my planner. 12–1: ace the midterm. 1–2: research. 2–3: lunch. 3–4: Pre-Vet Club emails. 4–10: study for calc test on Monday.

All this studying doesn't even matter anyway. No matter how hard you work, you always seem to get a curve ball like the bluegill question thrown at you. Sometimes you wonder what the hell the point is. Sometimes you wonder why you even want to go to vet school. It almost isn't worth it.

Almost.

Summer after sophomore year, I interned at one of the best zoos in the country. I took care of everything from bats to giraffes. I didn't get paid jack, but it didn't matter. I loved every second.

My favorite part of the internship was working with a three-legged tiger named Peggy. She just had her first litter of cubs, two little boys called Fuzz and Buster.

The cubs spent most of their days chasing each other around the exhibit. Once in a while Peggy would hobble around using her lone front leg as a crutch. The cubs usually used this as an opportunity to join forces and take her down. After two weeks, they had it down to a science: one swept the front leg while the other jumped on her back.

This routine would go on until Fuzz and Buster tuckered out. During naptime the cubs used Peggy as a pillow in a way that shielded her stub. From this angle, she looked like any other tiger. They looked like any other family.

As the cubs slept, Peggy licked their burnt-orange coats clean and watched over them diligently. The way she looked at them as they slept, you knew she would do anything to protect them. Even with only one good paw. Even if it meant she would have to sacrifice her own life to keep them safe. Witnessing that kind of unconditional love was a miracle of nature.

Moments like those are what made me want to become a vet.

Secretly, I always hoped some of that love would extend to me.

The larger black arm on the clock in the front of the lecture room did its job full force today. Tick. Tock. Tick. Tock. My heart raced. I wrote down, "The mating habits of blue gills," and erased it at least fifty times.

This is what being a nice guy gets you. Instead of studying last night, I spent most of my time acting as a receptionist.

Lexi's cell phone kept ringing as I tried reading the Animal Behavior notes. Every few minutes, another song played. Her phone was a handheld jukebox.

"Single Ladies" . . .

Incoming . . . Adriana.

"Girls Just Want to Have Fun" . . .

Incoming . . . Madeline.

"I Kissed a Girl" . . .

Incoming . . . Escalade. Everybody wanted to know:

Is Lexi there?

Why do you have her phone?

One girl even said, "So, do you know how I can get ahold of her?"

Worst part was I had to answer every call, just in case it was Lexi. A guy can't get anything done in these conditions. You can't memorize material for a test with a phone going off every two seconds. If I knew that trying to give Lexi her phone back was going to be that big of a pain, I would've let it rot in the bushes.

I thought about shutting it off until I was done studying but decided to leave it on, because if I lost my cell phone, I would want someone else in my position to do the same thing. Sometimes you need to do an act of self-sacrifice for the greater good.

A vampire bat will vomit blood into a roostmate's mouth if it is too sick to hunt.

A pregnant tiger will chew off her own leg when it's stuck in a trap to keep her unborn offspring safe.

A reclusive nerd will hit the Accept button, donating priceless minutes of study time, just so some spoiled brat can get her texting machine back. This is the opposite of Darwin. Extinction of the nicest. Suicidal altruism.

There was a delightful period of silence last night. I raced through the notes, scribbling additional information in the margins based on the material in the textbook. My studying momentum was building and . . .

Lexi's cell vibrated again. "Unbelievable" by EMF blasted from the speaker. The screen said, Incoming . . . Madison.

I sighed and answered the phone. Madison asked, "Is Lexi there?"

"Sorry," I said, "but she can't come to the phone right now."

"Why not?"

"Because," I said, "she's tied up in my basement."

Click.

After research today, I pass by a group of people handing out flyers on campus. I keep my nose buried in the Animal Behavior notes, which still show no trace of anything bluegill related. While I'm skimming the section about sexual dimorphism, this girl with a nose ring homes in on me like a hummingbird to nectar.

"Hey," she says, "haven't I seen you at the Humane Society?"

"Um. Maybe."

"Yeah." She looks me up and down. "You're always walking dogs."

"So?"

"So, that's pretty cool."

I keep my face planted in the notes. "It's all right."

She flips a few renegade strands of blonde hair away from her robin's egg eyes. The hair and eye color everybody wants, even though both traits are recessive. "I'm sure you already have plans for the weekend," she says, offering me a flyer, "but if you're looking for something to do . . ."

I politely decline. "I'm super busy this weekend."

"Well, if you manage to find some extra time . . . ," she says, slipping a red flyer into my Animal Behavior notes.

I sigh and read the headline. "Animal Allies?" Their mission statement is to promote the well-being of all living creatures. "I'm the president of the Pre-Vet Club. Why haven't I heard of you?"

She keeps forcing flyers onto people. "We're kinda new." The flyer advertises a wine-tasting fund-raiser at the Humane Society. All proceeds will go toward purchasing claw caps for cats at the shelter.

I close my notes. "Claw caps?"

"They're caps that go over a cat's nails so they can't scratch stuff," she says. "It's basically a humane alternative to declawing."

"I didn't know declawing was inhumane."

"As president of the Pre-Vet Club, you of all people should know. It's like getting the tips of your fingers chopped off."

"I guess I never thought of it that way."

"I never did, either, until I started working as a vet tech." She grabs another stack of flyers off a nearby table. "If you're in the neighborhood walking dogs tonight, you should stop by."

"I'd like to," I say, "but I need to study for a calc exam."

She puts her hands on her hips. "It's Friday."

"Calc doesn't take a day off."

"Well," she says while handing out flyers, "neither does animal cruelty."

The beautiful music you hear in the clouds is usually male birds telling others to stay away. Chirp, chirp, this is my territory. Tweet, tweet, that's my girl. How such a lovely sound can be interpreted as a threat is a mystery to me. But after a night full of squawking yesterday, I think I'm a bit closer to understanding the secrets of nature.

Some calls should be ignored.

Some calls were never meant to be answered.

Picture a lukewarm spring morning. Dewdrops in the grass. The sound of running streams. A turkey walks through the woods, enjoying the day, letting his beard hang. Suddenly, he hears a female calling. He struts toward her, giving her a gobble back, letting her know he's looking to hook up. She keeps gobbling, and he follows the sound, unable to resist the allure of her song. Her sweet serenading leads him out into an open area of the woods and . . .

Boom!

He gets shot by a hunter dressed in camo holding a turkey call. You can learn a lot from nature.

Lexi's phone chirped. Another new text message.

I opened my living room window. Sunlight poured inside, illuminating everything. Rays of light reflected off the pink metallic case of Lexi's cell.

Nobody knew that I found her phone. If I threw it back outside, nobody would know the difference. It could've been some other poor schmuck's problem.

Altruism, schmaltruism.

I ran across the living room and snatched the phone off my desk.

It wasn't my fault Lexi was irresponsible and lost the damn thing. Who cared if she ever found her stupid phone anyway? Let some other nice guy finish last.

Survival of the fittest all the way, baby.

I brought my arm back, ready to chuck the stupid thing out the window and . . . it started vibrating.

"Party in the USA" by Miley Cyrus began to play.

Incoming . . . Destinee.

I clenched the still-vibrating phone in my hand, staring at the screen. With the light shining in through the window, I took a deep breath, clicked the Accept button, and muttered, "Hello?"

"Who's this?" a girl said in a bitchy tone.

"I don't know. Who's this?"

"The owner of the phone you just answered."

"Lexi?"

"Oh, my God, he knows my name."

A girl in the background said, "Maybe he's stalking you." Simultaneously, both girls said, "Cah-reepy."

I ground my teeth and squeezed the phone, trying to crush it. I pretended to throw it out the living room window twice.

"Why do you have my phone?" Lexi asked. "Did you, like, steal it or something?"

"Long story short," I said, rubbing my forehead and taking a deep breath. "I was walking home from class today, and I found your phone. I just want to give it back to you. Can we meet somewhere so I can do that, please? I'm really too busy to be dealing with all this."

"Where'd you find it?"

"In the bushes outside McCloud Hall."

"Oh, my God," Lexi said. "It must've fallen out of my purse when I stopped to pee on my way home from the Beta kegger last night."

"I see . . ."

"So let me get this straight," the girl in the background said. "You just found her phone and you wanted to give it back to her?"

"Yep. That's all I wanted."

Both girls said, "Ooooh, that's soooo nice."

"Most guys wouldn't do something like that for a complete stranger," Lexi said.

"Yeah," her friend added. "Most guys are assholes."

"Whatever." I paced across the living room. "Can we meet somewhere so I can give you your phone back?"

"I've got a tanning appointment soon," Lexi said. "But after that we could meet up."

"It has to be within the next hour," I said, looking at my planner. "I have to walk dogs at the Humane Society soon."

"Aww," both girls said in unison. "Puppies." Except they said it like "poopies."

I held the phone away from my ear.

The girl in the background said, "Oh, for cute!"

"Yeah, they're super-duper adorable," I said. "What time can we meet?"

"I should be done tanning in about a half an hour," Lexi said. "Then I'm signed up for an elliptical at the gym." She paused. "We could meet at the gym in thirty mins."

"I'm kind of on a tight schedule."

"If for some odd reason I'm not there on time," Lexi said, "one of my bestest guy friends is working the front desk. Just drop the phone off with him."

"All right. Sounds good."

"Okay, then, see you soon," she said. "Thanks for finding my phone."

"Oh," I said, looking at my gigantic pile of notes. "No problem."

Before hanging up, Lexi said, "Hey, one more thing."

I sighed. "Yeah?"

"What's this I hear about me being tied up in your basement?"

Nowhere in my planner does it say: reread the Animal Behavior midterm notes to find out if we ever really covered anything about bluegills. But this evening, when I'm supposed to be studying for my calc test, that's exactly what I'm doing.

I bet Dr. Penn loved every minute of it today as he sat behind his desk at the front of the auditorium, scanning the crowd, smiling. Aquaman in his faded blue San Diego Zoo sweatshirt. The letters in the logo cracked from decades of washing. His hair like a vulture's nest made exclusively of gray strands. He looks out at us every day and sees the future he never had. Just because he wasn't good enough to get into vet school doesn't mean he should take it out on the rest of us. Half the garbage on the exam was irrelevant. When a family brings a dog in to be neutered, the difference between hibernation and torpor won't mean jack. I mean, the mating habits of bluegills?

Seriously!

I don't want to wind up like him, some middle-aged college professor with a tan ring finger. Today in my living room, no cell phones ring. Outside, coeds nap on towels, blanketed by the sweet grace of sunshine. Nothing but the sound of fun.

I shut my Animal Behavior notes, and a piece of red paper falls out, landing on the floor. In black letters it says: Five Good Reasons Not to Declaw Your Cat. Below this there is an X-ray of a human hand with the fingertips separated from the knuckles. The bottom of the flyer advertises a wine-tasting fund-raiser tonight at the Humane Society hosted by Animal Allies.

After reading one last snippet of notes last night, I made a few PB&J sandwiches and engulfed them on the way up to campus. Last week, I had brought a digital recorder to Animal Behavior and taped the lecture. While I drove around trying to find a parking spot, it sat in the passenger seat playing with the volume cranked. Almost every stall was full. One pay meter was open. I hopped out of my car and tossed in two quarters. I had fifteen minutes to find Lexi and give her phone back.

Before locking my car, I sprayed on cologne. The wind picked up as I walked across campus.

I held the cell phone tightly and flipped through the photo gallery. Ever since I talked to Lexi, I was dying to match her voice to her face. It's our curious nature to follow a pleasant sound to the source. No matter what it takes. If we don't see who is behind the beautiful music, it will drive us insane. We will always be left wondering.

We are all the turkey in the woods.

I scrolled through the pictures on Lexi's phone. Every snap-shot had the same group of girls posing eagerly for the lens. A brunette was front and center in every photo. On Halloween she wore an orange satin nighty with black stripes that clung to her body like static electricity. The edges of her costume were lined with black fur. She had black leather boots zipped up to her knees. A pair of furry tiger ears sat upon her dark brown hair with white high-lights. Even her eyes had the eerie yellow-brown glow of a cat's.

Before I reached the gym, it started drizzling. Raindrops pelted my face as the wind gusted. When I met Lexi, I was going to let her know how much trouble I went through just so she could get her stupid phone back.

I had the speech practiced in my head.

I walked across campus in the cold rain just to give this back to you. I have to walk dogs in T-minus thirty min-utes, and since I had to take precious time out of my day to deliver the phone that you lost back to you, now I'm not going to get to eat dinner. I have a slight glucose headache building. I'm short a week's worth of sleep. And I'm out fifty cents because I had to park at a pay meter. When she tried to offer me a reward for finding her phone, I was going to be this big hero, a knight in shining armor, and say, No, that's okay. Keep it. You don't need to give me money. I was just trying to do the right thing.

The opposite of Darwin.

Her heart would melt, and she would thank me. Walk-ing up the concrete path to the gym, I thought, Maybe she'll hug me. Maybe she'll give me her phone number.

Maybe she' ll ask me to come to a party sometime.

I'm going to start meeting people and going out and having fun. I took a deep breath and opened the door to the gym.

No girls were standing in the front entrance. Not a single one from any of the pictures on Lexi's cell. The only person there was a guy sitting behind a desk.

With the phone in my hand, I walked over to him. "Hey."

The guy behind the desk looked up from his laptop. "Hey. Can I, uh, help you?"

"This is going to sound weird, but I think I have your friend Lexi's cell phone."

"Oh." His eyes went wide. "Yeah, she called and said you might be stopping by."

"Well." I handed him the phone. "Here you go."

The guy grabbed it and smiled. "Okay, I'll make sure she gets it."

Part of me was relieved to have the damn thing out of my life. But part of me also wanted to stick around and wait for Lexi. To see what she really looked like. To at least get a thanks. But I had to get going. Pre-Vet Club was scheduled to walk dogs soon. I needed to cram for the Animal Behavior midterm. Study for a calc exam on Monday.

One test ends. Another begins.

I exited the gym and walked down the sidewalk. Lexi's voice played in my head. The pictures on her cell phone swam behind my eyes like exotic fish trapped inside an aquarium.

Streetlights magnified raindrops as they fell to the cement. I turned around to look through the window at the front desk one last time.

And there she was.

Lexi, wearing a black short-sleeved shirt with Siberian tiger pajama pants. Her dark brown hair with white stripes pulled back into a ball. Her golden halo gaze.

Panthera tigris in the flesh.

The guy behind the desk stood up, smiled, and gave Lexi her phone.

She started jumping up and down and screaming. She threw her arms around him, and he embraced her back.

They began mock slow dancing in a circle, and I swear, for one second, the guy from behind the desk locked eyes with me and grinned.

Sitting here alone in my apartment, I read the Animal Allies flyer and think about last night. Outside in the cold rain, the light from inside the gym illuminated everything out in the darkness.

And I remember.

The last question on the midterm.

The one about the mating habits of bluegills.

In order to lay eggs, fish build nests just like birds and reptiles. In the aquatic kingdom, however, males build nests instead of females.

A dominant male bluegill, for example, will build dozens of nests during spawning season, hoping to attract a mate.

There are times when even the fittest need to go the extra mile to reproduce.

When a large, dominant male bluegill finishes making craters in the sand, he picks a central location and guards his turf, chasing away all other males who dare enter. Thus the smaller, weaker male bluegills are forced to hide in the weeds and watch the ritual from afar like losers sitting alone in the bleachers during a slow song at a high school dance.

Day and night, the dominant male protects his nest, and all his labor finally pays off when a female shows up to spawn. As soon as the deed is done he kicks her out and goes right back to defending his territory, all while fanning his tail to aerate the freshly fertilized eggs.

Only one thing ever lures him away. Another hot female looking to spawn.

The second he leaves his nest all his hard work goes down the drain when a weaker male zips in and re-fertilizes the eggs.

Nature's equivalent to a drive-by shooting. They call these fish sneakers.

Right now, sitting in the horrifying silence of my living room, no birds chirping or phones ringing, I could recite the mating habits of bluegills from the lecture verbatim.

But in the essay section on the Animal Behavior midterm I wrote down nothing.

On my desk the red Animal Allies flyer dwells among the pages of lecture notes like the hourglass on the belly of a black widow. I check my watch. The wine-tasting event is about to begin. I shut all my books, including my planner. For the first time since the midterm, I look at the clock, cognizant of every passing moment as I grab my keys and head for the door.

MELODY

Michael De Vito Jr.

Just the smell of Melody makes all the hairs on my neck lift off like rockets.

At night, we squeeze close—her back to my front. The milk chocolate and the hard candy shell. Her body sticks to mine, and my friend, he gets stiffy pressing on her thighs— so smooth and shiny in the night-light. Inhaling the vanilla and brown-sugary sweetness she uses—there are no words. We hold close. Never letting go.

The first time I breathed in Melody's pretty smell, she stood behind her register at the ShopRite.

Her hair, brown as caramel candy, slid off her shoulders like the roaring rapids. On her shirt, you could only see the letters *ODY* and *KS*. And I stood there like a contestant on *Wheel of Fortune*, snapping my fingers soft near my trousers, trying to talk out the words.

Right then was when she stopped checking out groceries and grabbed some spray stuff off her register. She sprayed her wrists and rubbed them to her neck.

That's when I could see the shirt. Oh—Melody Rocks.

A road sign pointing straight to the heavens. The air became vanilla, like in an ice cream shop. On my tongue, syrupy brown sugar.

When my turn came up, all I could think was—use the skin stuff to win Melody. So instead of checking out, I ran to go get her as many bottles as anybody could carry. On the way, I almost knocked over my neighbor Mrs. Lowder, who said, "Slow down!"

But all I could do was snap my fingers for Melody, a name you could just say out loud over and over.

In the pretty smell aisle, I discovered the vanilla brown sugar picture right away and grabbed up eight bottles. Only six made it to the conveyor belt. Butter fingers. I dropped them down with the Peter Pan crunchy peanut butter and the Ajax scrub pads and the WWE magazine left from before.

Mrs. Lowder saved my place in line for me. Like a place for me in heaven. And I took it back. Stood straight in front of Melody. Well, she—she just looked up and said, "Hi!"

Her eyes bright as blue Tropical Skittles, Melody said, "This will keep you busy for a while."

That was when I handed her three of the vanilla brown-sugary bottles. And because I knew this was my moment to say something, I looked down into Melody's big, big eyes and just came right out and snapped my fingers to the words—Will you be my girl?

Melody—she turned her eyes away. She took the bottles. "Oh . . . thank you. Yeah. See you later."

I snapped my fingers—Yes. Picked up my goodies and headed for the door. Yes—see you later, Melody.

The cars in the street screeched to a stop when I walked across. One of the drivers yelled, "Effin' a-hole."

From behind me, Mrs. Lowder hollered to be more careful. At the apartment, waiting for later, I played the Jet band and lip-synched in front of the mirror. Banging my feet on the floor to the da-da-da of the drums. While I chewed handfuls of Tropical Skittles, my tongue got as green as the wrestler man George "The Animal" Steele's.

I went *"rarrgh"* at the mirror, then stuck out my tongue just like The Animal.

Finally it was later, and I had to—had to—get back. Melody, she stood alone then, spraying down vegetables. Melody and her Colgate smile said, "You're back." And then she shot the red peppers. "Of course!"

"Of course" meant my chance. So I went for one of those candy apples they keep in with the fruit and dropped down to one knee. I raised the bright candy to Melody. And guess what? She accepted it. With such grace—like Vanna White.

And that's how Dougie and Melody became an item. Because love—love will make you do things you didn't know you ever could. Love brings you to your knees.

On the way out of the ShopRite that night, Mrs. Lowder was falling down with her groceries. She saw me leapfrog the guard posts and asked if I would be a doll and use some of my brute strength to help her with the bags. After winning Melody, well, I just picked up Mrs. Lowder and her bags and ran her right across the street. Because love—love makes you strong. All the while Mrs. Lowder's belly jiggled and her boobies bounced as she hollered, "Oh, Dougie, please, you big jooch. You're going to hurt yourself."

Mr. and Mrs. Lowder live below my apartment. Whenever I visit they are always so good to offer me sandwiches with Oscar Mayer bologna and even some Coors beer. I don't have enough in the bank to buy a computer, so they let me use theirs when I need to give the looks to the internet.

On the internet there's a place where you can get
everything Melody. For a surprise, I got us "I ❤ Melody,"
"100% Melody," and "Property of Melody" T-shirts. As soon
as they come in the mail, Mrs. Lowder helps me wrap them
up in paper that's orange like mango tangelo Tropical Skittles. When I give them to Melody her mouth makes a big *O*.

I snap my fingers hard to the word—Surprise!

So now, at night, we wear them together but don't ever
wear any undies. Makes it easier to push on each other. Melody, she wears the "100% Melody" one almost every night.
Her bottom presses against me like a balloon. And my "Property of Melody" gets the crusties from my friend who Melody
lets go inside. After I goop in there, she lets me squeeze her
tight as can be, and my brute strength makes the goop ooze.

Every morning, wake-up time comes to repeats of the
same song over and over on the CD player alarm clock.
Looping my tie right over left, then through the middle in
front of the mirror, I don't dig for boogers. Because Melody
is sleeping. Then it's one and two into my brown suit jacket.
I turn to Melody and snap "You're my girl!" when I leave.
Blowing her a kiss from the door, I tell her later we will spray
down the vegetables together at the ShopRite. Of course, I'm
always sure to wave good morning to Mr. Lowder who sits
outside with his paper. I snap my fingers near my trousers to
Melody's name and walk over the hill to the office.

There, the staff, they play lots of pop music. While I sit
in the cramped seat with my files all together, the day takes
almost forever. Love does this to you—makes you feel an
hour without Melody is a day.

The manager, Mr. Man-with-all-the-answers, finally
checks my files. He says, "In the alphabet *E* comes before

M, Dougie." He pushes his glasses up his crooked nose and looks more, saying, "You've never made a mistake like this one. You'll have to do them over."

My trousers tear up the backside when I sit back down. The rip sound makes everyone look. So I tear up some papers and try not to dig for boogers.

If you could believe it, just then on the radio comes Jet band—"Are You Gonna Be My Girl?" I'm rocking back and forth because this is my wake-up melody. Get it? My wake-up melody.

The manager man, he bangs his hands in the air along with the song. He picks up the phone, hits one button quick, and says, "Hey, baby! How's my girl?"

Doing my files over, I stroke the handle of my desk phone. But Mrs. Lowder says distance makes love grow stronger.

Then the manager man curls his finger for me to come back over. "Are you through?"

And I snap my fingers to the word *yes* as I knock my knees to the music. Standing in front of his desk, I tap my feet. A picture of his girl is on the desk.

He watches me watch the picture and says, "Beautiful, ain't she?"

I snap my fingers—not as sweet as my Melody. Or Vanna White. Then I push my finger into his picture.

Mr. Answer Man catches pretty good. He puts the picture back in place, then waves at the door. "Douglas, these will do. Why don't you get going for the day?"

Walking as if my torn pants are on fire from purgatory, I hurry out of the office to get to Melody. Car horns blast as loud as a wrestling ring bell, and I can't even hear myself snap, Melody, Melody, Melody.

Mrs. Lowder walks on the other side of the street. She hollers over, "Please be more careful, Dougie."

Waving hello, I rush on to the ShopRite. And that's where I find my girl near the stockroom talking with another girl who pretends to be like Melody. People who imagine being somebody else are not real people at all. But good people believe in all people.

When Melody turns to me, she lifts her hands high in the air and drops them down quick. "There you are!"

I get down on one knee and open my arms wide—Here I am.

When I start to stand, the faker girl stomps by and pushes her elbow into my chest. She bounces off me like The Brian Kendrick does off the wrestling ropes. Except I catch her up fast before she falls. Then with her nose turned up all snooty, she says to Melody, "What are you doing with him?"

When Melody reaches up high to touch my shoulder, my face turns as red as strawberry Skittles. She says, "He's my happy knight in candy armor."

Faker girl is not nice when she says, "More like middle-aged balding gorilla in the same old suit."

But Melody puts her small hand in my big one, and we go to spray down the vegetables. As we walk to the front, we pass the candy apples. Melody, she claps and says, "Remember that?"

And I pledge allegiance and snap to the words—How could I ever forget?

So we spray down the peppers and tomatoes. And then we hold hands all the way to the door. I leap on the electric pad making the door glide open. Boy, does Melody like to laugh.

She plants a kiss on my forehead. "So I'll see you later then, yes?"

I snap my fingers to the words—Of course.

On the way out across the street, I smile big for Mr. and Mrs. Lowder. The car horns blast, and real quick I stop digging for boogers.

From the window in the apartment, I can see clear across to the ShopRite. Melody, she helps every single person bag groceries. Always careful with double bagging and she never puts the Clorox bleach in the same bag as the Land O'Lakes eggs.

Pat and Vanna have special contestants on tonight— twins. Great company. Together we buy vowels, but try and try as I might, the contestants always beat me to the answers. At midnight my eyes weigh in at two hundred and sixty-five pounds. Melody tiptoes in the apartment 'cause she doesn't want to wake her playful tiger, and I play dead as she comes over to kiss me off to sleep. Her hand goes right to her heart every time I leap up and hug her.

Gotcha!

In front of the mirror by the closet, I help Melody strip off her dirty work clothes. I raise her hands up high in the air as she gets into her "Melody Rocks" T-shirt. And then I use my brute strength to carry her to bed. Back-to-front we do, pushing and pressing and moaning. I snap—I love you, Melody.

When I squeeze too tight sometimes Melody loses wind. There is just no stopping our laughter when she pops one out. We cry ourselves to sleep.

On Saturday the wake-up song comes too fast because on Saturdays Melody goes to work early. I help her get up and make us mugs of Nestlé hot cocoa. I open the door for her and give her a salute.

Mr. Lowder calls up to me from down below, "Good morning."

And I give him a good morning salute too.

Around lunchtime, I put together some bags of Tropical Skittles to bring to Melody for a treat and start to climb into my suit.

I check on Melody's workday from the window. The sky's so bright and blue I can only ask why I am so lucky to be in love with Melody.

But what I spy out my window today makes me ask another question. She's sitting on a car in the parking lot. She's not alone. Hey, Melody—I bang on the window—why are you with another man? She's leaning up against him. Hugging. Kissing his forehead.

No time to get my pants on. I have to—have to—get down to the ShopRite and get Mr. Driver Man away from my Melody. As I take the stairs two at a time, Mr. Lowder almost gets run over.

"Dougie, where are your pants?" He grabs for my arm. "You get back here right this instant."

But I push him down to the floor and leap over him.

Melody turns around when she hears the glass door to the building break into a zillion pieces. She puts her left hand into her pocket and pulls out a phone as I run toward her with just my shirt and undies on.

A car screeches but still hits me. But I bounce off the window and slide from the hood like the champion Tommy Dreamer and just keep running.

All the while, Mr. Lowder's screaming from behind, "Come back, Dougie!"

But the ShopRite—the ShopRite is home base, and when I get there, I don't even know what to say. So I bear-hug the kissing Driver Man and throw him to the ground.

Melody screams, "Stop!"

But I grab dirty Driver Man by his hair and make my big hand into a fighter fist and punch him three times in the eye. Then like The Animal Steele, I put him into a full nelson. I swing my body flat on his and slap my hands down on the pavement three times.

I win Melody back again.

Mr. Lowder pulls at me. "You can't do this. You can't." Because I know I won, I let loser Driver Man go.

And now the siren sounds that started far away roar closer, and then the police car screeches right in front of the ShopRite. Two policemen come out from the car.

I give them a salute.

One of them asks, "Who is Melody?" Snapping my fingers, I point to Melody.

She throws up her hands and screams, "Get back!" Then Melody tells the policemen, "Dougie just walks around the store in the same brown suit every day. He's always giving me things. But he's never been aggressive. He never says a word."

I stick my hands under my armpits when Mr. Policeman asks my name.

And from behind me, Mr. Lowder says, "Douglas Lowder."

He always ruins everything.

He says, "Our Dougie would never hurt a fly."

That's when Mr. Dirty Driver Man moans, "I'm not even hurt. Just keep that gorilla away from my girl, and I won't press charges."

The police, they ask my father where we live, and he points at the apartments across the street. Mr. Policeman, with his radio making voice noises, says, "Let's walk you both home then so we can take a look around. Make sure you're not going to hurt anyone else. Is that okay, Dougie?"

I snap a yes.

On the way over, Mr. Lowder tells him that my mother wants me to be as free as possible. They rent me the apartment, but they live right downstairs. He tells them I have a job through a special state program.

Mr. Lowder says, "One of us always follows him around to make sure he's safe. Douglas may be slow, but his love and kindness are genius."

We go up to the apartment with Mr. Policeman. He says, "Have a seat, Dougie."

He flips through my WWE magazines and takes some Tropical Skittles from the candy dish. I play freeze while he peeks through the windows and around the doors. He stops when he gets to the closet. And I start knocking my knees.

He helps Melody out of the closet by her hand. She's wearing her "100% Melody" T-shirt and no undies still. I'm snapping my fingers to Melody's name now.

My father bows his head like in prayer and says, "Well, we had to give him something. He was humping all the pillows."

Mr. Policeman just shakes his head and speaks into his radio, "There's nothing here. It's clean. Well, sort of."

Mr. Policeman holds Melody by a finger. The rest of her hangs bent on the floor. He goes to leave and hands the finger to my father. "Probably want to get rid of this," he says.

Mr. Lowder shakes his head and drags Melody away, saying, "Be a good boy, Douglas. Come down for dinner in an hour."

When the door closes it's just me on the couch. Just me climbing out of my suit jacket and spraying the vanilla brown-sugary goodness on my wrists so I can rub them to my neck.

I press the clicker for the TV and put a pillow in front. After too long *Wheel of Fortune* comes on so I stop digging for boogers. I don't get any of the puzzles until the bonus round. That's when I beat the clock. Snapping my fingers to the words—If you love somebody set them free.

F FOR FAKE

Tyler Jones

Most of my life I've been pretending to be someone else.
I just wasn't doing it well enough to draw any attention.
About three years ago I was walking through Powell's City
of Books in Portland, Oregon, searching for a leather-bound
limited edition of Theodore Arden's novel *Cautioners*. An
employee was a few feet away stocking the shelves and
replacing books that had been taken down and abandoned
at various points in the store. I could feel him watching me.
At first I was offended, thinking he was making sure I didn't
steal anything, but when I glanced in his direction he quickly
looked away, almost as if he were embarrassed. As I tilted my
head to read the spines, I saw him staring at me again. This
time I was sure he wasn't suspicious, at least not overtly so;
he appeared fascinated, stunned.

I turned to face him, and he didn't look away. There was
a moment of silence, neither of us willing to speak first.

Finally he cleared his throat and held out a book.
"Excuse me, sir. Would you be willing to sign this?"

It was a first edition copy of *Minor Keys*. I signed it.

I signed it the way I'd practiced for twenty years, natural in the way that only signing your name can be. I didn't
stall or put thought into it. He handed me a pen, and from it
flowed the long scripted letters of the name Don Swanstrom.

It looked exactly like the autograph in a copy of *Minor Keys* I'd seen on an internet auction site just a week earlier. The winner was a buyer from Japan whose top bid was nearly twenty thousand dollars.

I gave him back the book, and his hands were shaking. "I can't believe you're here," he said. "I've read all your books more than once. You've changed my life; you are the one that made me want to be a writer."

I smiled and nodded my appreciation. "Thank you. I'm glad you like them."

"Can I buy you a drink if you're not busy?" he asked.

"Thanks for the offer, but I have to get going, and I'd be grateful if you didn't mention I was here until I'm gone."

I'd written actively since high school, finishing eight novels, forty-two short stories, three screenplays, and one or two intended for the stage. None of them were published. I received the same rejection letters over and over from literary agents. My stories were criticized as being unoriginal and bland. My style was called "a watered-down imitation of Don Swanstrom." I was accused of plagiarism, and I have to admit that may have been true in some of my earlier novels. I was obsessed with the man—I thought he was a genius, a wordsmith whose work rivaled the brilliance of Shakespeare.

I read and reread Don Swanstrom's entire bibliography every year, sometimes chronologically and other times based on what season I first read the book in. For example, I read *Steel and Glass* during the winter of 1988, the year it came out, and to me it will always be a winter book. I remember sitting in the ski lodge next to a large window overlooking the slopes. My friends were careening down the mountain while I was inside, biting my nails and holding my breath as I turned the pages. I was lost, transported into another world. I couldn't believe this was the work of a young man— both of us born in the same year—because he displayed a maturity and wisdom that was beyond his age. A part of me was jealous, angry that I couldn't focus enough to write something even half as good as *Steel and Glass*.

During the summer of 1992 I read *Paper Tigers* twice, right in a row. I finished it, turned back to the first page, and read the whole thing again, this time taking notes. It's hard to explain to someone who's never had the experience—the unmistakable, life-altering moment when you read a book and realize that someone out in the world has read your mind and put into words all the thoughts and ideas crashing around inside your own head. For me, it was like Don Swanstrom was my doppelgänger, a more articulate and self-aware version of myself.

Swanstrom didn't write plot-based novels with linear timelines. His books were ideas set in an almost recognizable world but one that was slightly off-kilter. One of his biggest criticisms was that his characters never felt like real people, and this was something I loved about his work. Each person in a Swanstrom novel represented a philosophical point of view, a way of processing events and information. When these people spoke it was in hyperintellectual phrases that had virtually nothing to do with who they were. Swanstrom's characters were simply meant to represent opposing arguments to whatever theme he was exploring. Most of his work involved conspiracies and secret machinations, those hidden wheels that cause the modern world to turn.

Of all his books, *Exit Lights* means the most to me, particularly because of where I was in my life when I read it. I was going through my second divorce, and my two children refused to smile or acknowledge my presence, which led me to believe their mother was telling them lies about me. I had been working for a publishing house, writing the summary paragraphs that are put on the back covers of books to intrigue a potential buyer. Working there was like a slap to the face. I thought being in the industry would open doors for me, but I soon learned that everyone was a writer. Everyone had a novel or two under his belt, and it was torture to watch coworkers have their works published and leave the cubicles for the college circuit to read from their self-indulgent novels about wealthy young men chasing drugs and women.

I watched as my life slowly veered into dissatisfaction. It all felt like it happened in slow motion over a long period of time, but in reality it took only five months.

First, the publisher downsized in response to the financial crisis, and my job was deemed unnecessary. I couldn't find work anywhere, and my wife finally decided she couldn't live with me any longer. Worst of all, I had no energy to write, and whenever I tried it was simply an exercise in futility. A painful reminder of how ordinary I really was.

Some beliefs die hard, and when they shudder their last breath, it shakes your insides like a million butterflies are trapped in your chest. A feeling like dying, like fear, like falling. What's left over is who you really are. And when that person emerges, it's sometimes surprising but more often disappointing.

Exit Lights was released on Tuesday, January 29, 2008. I didn't feel like reading it at the time because novels had always been an escape for me, and now that real life was so dramatic I didn't think I could bring myself to care about something invented. But after the first chapter I was hooked. I read that book in a fury, devouring and ingesting it. I read it the way some people read the Bible—to tell me who I was and what life means.

It seemed that Swanstrom and I both lost our ability to write at the same time, maybe even at the exact same moment. He had always come out with a new novel every two years, like clockwork. But since *Exit Lights*, he'd released nothing. I could only conclude that the man was suffering from an extreme bout of writer's block, and this fact caused me no small amount of anxiety.

When your life is reduced to nothing more than a series of small defeats, you begin to look forward to any break in the monotonous routine of dragging your weary carcass to and from whatever dead-end job you find yourself trapped in. This is what Swanstrom's novels were for me. After reading his newest book, I would spend the next year and eleven months eagerly awaiting the next one.

It wasn't enough for me to just have the books. I wanted to know everything I could about the man who wrote them. Swanstrom never gave a single interview, so I scoured every newspaper and magazine for profiles about him. Every time he released a new book extensive articles were written about the complex messages hidden in his dense prose. But Swanstrom was always untouchable, just out of reach. You see, Don Swanstrom was the literary world's greatest recluse. Virtually nothing was known about him beyond a few private letters that had sold at auction for over seventy-five thousand dollars each, and even in those letters he was obviously guarded.

Only one photograph was known to exist, a candid picture taken during his senior year of high school and printed in the yearbook—he was notably absent in the portraits section, a bold script over the space his image should have occupied saying, Picture unavailable. It was all we had, that one photograph of Swanstrom smiling in the bleachers of what must have been a football game. Though not conventionally handsome, his face has a seriousness that's present even while he's smiling. The eyes are deep set, his teeth somewhat crooked. There is no outward indication of the brilliant mind or inexhaustible creativity.

He looks like anyone.

The concentration, the devotion required to be absent from the world for so long is staggering. I understand vanishing for a year or two, but it's been over twenty-five. At that point it takes on an almost religious fervency, a piece of performance art that is as much about political protest as it is about personal disappearance. Like those Buddhist monks who lit themselves on fire in Saigon. It's a magnificent, terrible, and confounding statement about the world. The only conclusion one can reach is that society is unfit to be lived in; therefore, the physical body must either be banished or exterminated.

After leaving the bookstore, I was exhilarated. I went straight home to study my facial features in the bathroom mirror. The resemblance was something I had never seen until then, but like they say, you never know how you look to someone else, how they perceive you. I held up the yearbook photograph next to my face and smiled, copying Swanstrom's smile. It was uncanny how alike they were.

Maybe the similarities had evaded me because I was never smiling when I looked in the mirror. Whenever I saw myself it was as the broken-down, depressed failure I knew I was, but to see myself through another's eyes had opened up new possibilities and horizons. Another reason perhaps is because I had built Swanstrom up so much in my mind that I had never before searched for any similarities in our appearances. But when I looked at his picture and my face, it was as though he had aged right before my eyes and was staring at me from behind the mirror.

Some decisions are like standing at the edge of a precipice with a parachute strapped to your back. It's doubtful the fall will kill you, but in those seconds before the leap is an imperfect moment of clarity, an understanding that the decision, once made, cannot be undone. This is how I felt as a plan began to take shape at the back of my mind. I breathed slowly in and out, measuring my breaths in time to my heartbeat, hoping that the metronomic quality of one would steady the other. Once I stepped from the ledge into open space, there would be nothing between me and the ground. I would be isolated, suspended like a marionette without strings, hovering above another life.

To set the plan in motion would require immediate action, no second-guessing. I was bound to fail, but I was hoping that my failure would allow for some sort of auxiliary life, not the one I wanted but better than the one I had, an afterlife of sorts, something taking shape after the death of what I was living. Yes, Icarus fell to earth after flying too close to the sun, but what a glorious fall it must have been. Almost worth the flaming wings tied to his arms, waving helplessly in a shower of cinders and sparks, before beginning the long fall back to earth.

Staging the "break-in" wasn't hard. I had an office at my house that was used for all my writing, personal and professional. The room was a paper museum; there were copies of every book I had written a summary for, and after twenty years the total was close to four hundred. There were also the manuscripts of everything I'd ever written, stacked carefully and filed in large boxes. A lifetime's worth of writing—my heart, my soul, my existence.

Everything in that room was already listed in my insurance documents, and were they to disappear it could be validated that the room did in fact house thousands upon thousands of pages. What they were, exactly, no one could say, but the irrefutable evidence of lost or stolen work could not be denied.

I tore through that office like a madman, leaving nothing untouched. I opened every drawer and filing cabinet, dumped supplies all over the floor, pulled my degrees down from the wall, and ripped open envelopes from phone and cable companies. By the time I was finished, the room had been ransacked, destroyed. I took everything of value, mainly the manuscripts and screenplays, to a storage unit on the outskirts of town and called the police to report the robbery. After that I made three more calls—to the insurance company, the local newspaper, and the Channel 6 news station.

The following day the front page of the *Oregonian* read, World Famous Reclusive Author Breaks Silence after Home Invasion.

Within hours my house was surrounded by news vans with satellites spinning atop the roofs, cables and wires snaked across the lawn.

Men and women covered in makeup stood in the grass, rehearsing their lines while cameramen set up their equipment. Inside, I watched the spectacle on television. Watched what was happening just outside.

A man wearing a yellow rain slicker with the Channel 12 logo on the breast said, "Reclusive author Don Swanstrom is as famous for his novels as he is for maintaining his privacy. Last night that all changed when his home was broken into by an apparently obsessed fan who made off with years' worth of work and several uncompleted novels."

A woman, trying to keep her blonde hair from blowing into her face, said, "Any scrap of paper with his handwriting on it was stolen. Phone bills and envelopes that bore the alias he had used all these years were taken. Although the loss is tragic, it has compelled Swanstrom to finally come out into the open to plead with the thief to return his work and grant him and his family their privacy once again. We'll keep you updated with the details as they become available."

Everything in life is temporary, and I knew that the news attention would last for only a week at most. I had to take full advantage of it until the façade crumbled and truth won out. I anxiously awaited the response of the real Swanstrom, who I imagined was locked inside a bunker, quietly churning out novel after novel, hiding from the wolves. He had to address this; there was no way he could ignore it.

Late in the afternoon I was in the middle of my third interview with the press, explaining again my reasons for coming out into the open, how I was tired of the mentally disturbed fans who were determined to find me, when my lawyer, Kelly Davis, whispered in my ear that Swanstrom had issued a statement through his literary agent calling me a fraud.

I had anticipated this. I was not disappointed because I hadn't expected the game to go on indefinitely, not in this day and age with computers and databases and electronically saved documents. But it takes time to gather information and only seconds to make earth-shattering claims that the press has to jump on just in case it all turns out to be the real thing. They can't let the news slip past them, even if it's made up. It's easier to retract headlines and apologize than it is to wait and hope the story is verified. The world will keep spinning, and no twenty-four-hour news organization could survive unless a certain percentage of all reported stories were erroneous.

What all the news channels and I both knew was this: even if my story of the break-in turned out to be a lie, there was a secondary story waiting behind it. Who was this man, and why was he pretending to be a famous author no one has ever seen?

Just think, after every mass shooting that takes place in America, there is a week or so of news coverage about the victims, then the focus shifts to the perpetrator. It's a natural progression of interest. Once we know everything about those who died, we want to know about the person who killed them. By five o'clock that evening I was sitting in a CNN trailer outside my house, listening to a producer explain how the show would be conducted while a young woman applied powder to my face. I wore an old gray sport coat, a flannel button-down shirt, and although I didn't need them, a pair of black eyeglasses purchased from a thrift store. I was unshaven, and my eyes were bloodshot—I was the very image of a camera-shy genius.

The interview was to be conducted in my living room with the stone-faced news anchor and me seated on either side of the fireplace. He shook my hand quickly and without much enthusiasm while looking over a list of questions. I felt certain he'd never even heard of Don Swanstrom, let alone read one of his books. I took the opportunity to close my eyes and fall back inside my own story, into the lies I'd recited to myself over and over until I believed them. By the time the producer started counting backward from ten, I was no longer myself.

I was Don Swanstrom.

I stepped into the role I'd written, the fiction I was living. My own memories disappeared, and I saw things that had never happened. I could picture the house where I, as Swanstrom, lived, the office where I worked. I instinctively knew the extreme measures I took to avoid detection. When the red light of the camera turned on, I was ready.

I answered every question without a single pause, withholding certain information because I wasn't suddenly an extrovert after all.

The interviewer asked if I was concerned about the literary agent claiming I was a liar. The agent who claimed to represent the real Swanstrom.

I laughed. "If he's real, where is he? It's just a faceless voice. Probably a fan upset that I don't fit whatever image he had of me."

Then at the very end, I looked into the camera and spoke directly to the thief, begging him to return the stolen manuscripts so I could finish them and give the books to him as completed works.

That night my sleep was interrupted by dreams of Swanstrom looking at me with disappointment, shaking his head, and asking me why I did this to him. I woke up, saying, "I thought you of all people would understand."

Early in the morning the phone started ringing incessantly. I ignored it the first couple of times and then finally picked up. It was Kelly Davis.

"We need to talk," he said, "immediately."

I watched through the window as his Mercedes pulled into the driveway and he stepped out. A former high school athlete, Kelly looked like an overweight linebacker stuffed into an expensive suit. A suit now so wrinkled and creased it appeared as though he had slept in it. As Kelly walked to the door, he waved away reporters and brushed past microphones, ignoring shouted questions about his client's identity.

I opened the door for him and locked it once he was inside.

His face was a mask of anger and sleeplessness. "Are you seeing this? When I agreed to represent you I did so under the premise that you would be honest with me, that you would divulge any information pertinent to your defense and protection. Look me in the eye, and tell me that you haven't lied to me."

I looked away.

"Do you realize how this makes me look?" he said. "You think just because I'm a lawyer I don't have any integrity, that I only want publicity? Is this a stunt? Because I'm telling you, Don, if it is, I want no part of it. You tell me the truth, and I'll walk away right now without calling the cops."

I motioned to the kitchen. "Do you want some coffee?"

Kelly said, "This is serious. You cannot claim to be someone you're not without consequences."

I described everything to him, leaving nothing out—he deserved to know. I explained how Swanstrom had lost his gift, how it disappeared somewhere in the fall of 2007. I told

Kelly that everything I'd done was to give the man a plot, one that he was obviously in desperate need of.

Kelly sat at the table holding up his head with his hands, sighing like all his breath was leaving him at once. "I can't believe this."

I showed him Swanstrom's picture. I asked him if he'd ever been mistaken for his hero, for someone he idolized. He said no. I asked him what he would do in my situation, if someone sees in you a man that everyone is searching for but cannot find. According to the news, there had been a surge in the sales of Swanstrom's books since my unveiling.

I said, "Who does that benefit, Swanstrom or me? I came out so he wouldn't have to. I took a bullet for him."

My lawyer pointed out that I had fired the shot.

"True," I said, "but I still took it."

Kelly was lying on my couch with a cool washcloth on his forehead, running through his options while I watched the circus outside.

"A lawsuit has been filed against you," he said. "Whoever this 'faceless voice' is, he can afford attorneys better than me."

"What proof has he offered?" I asked. "How do we know that he's the real Swanstrom?"

Kelly sat up and pointed at me. "If it's Swanstrom, he doesn't need proof; he has the truth on his side. He is who he says he is. Truth is like a lion. It doesn't need to be defended when it's attacked—you just let it out of its cage. What do you have? Stories and lies, nothing more. And I think you know this. I think you've known all along that this could only go so far. You just wanted to see how far and how much you could gain before it fell apart."

I said, "What have I gained?"

"Your face is all over the news, man. Some people would die to have their name uttered by a famous news anchor or to be interviewed on a major network. You've had both in the last two days—you can't tell me that's nothing. You'll be written about—granted it will be as a psychotic fan, but you will be written about. You could probably even write a book about this and sell a million copies."

Something clicked as the last of those words left his mouth, and he looked at me with an expression I could not name.

Kelly and I spoke late into the night over sweating glasses of whiskey and ginger ale. I let him in on every plan and begged him to trust me. I convinced him that I was not crazy and I had thought through every contingency.

"You're already in this thing too deep to just walk away," I reasoned. "At least see it through to the end."

By dawn I'd worn down his defenses, and Kelly agreed to my insane proposition. He left through the back door and walked three blocks to the nearest gas station where he called a cab. Once at his office, he filed a countersuit against the other man claiming to be Don Swanstrom.

Swanstrom refused to become visible, but he did conduct a phone interview with Larry King that was the beginning of the end. When I heard the man's voice, calm and soothing, thickened by years of cigars, there was no doubt in my mind who he was. It was the voice of the man who wrote the novels that changed my life, that educated me and shaped the way I saw the world. It was the voice of a sage, a prophet. I felt overwhelmed as he told Larry he felt sorry for me. He said I was obviously disturbed—twice divorced, estranged from his children, failed writer—and I was under a great amount of stress and shouldn't be judged too harshly. Swanstrom said he felt sympathy for me but would still press charges.

Even though I knew in my heart that he was who he said he was, he had still offered no definitive proof. I conducted more interviews with journalists and reporters, calling the interview with Larry King "an orchestrated piece of live cinema utilizing the talents of a voice actor."

Swanstrom fired back in another telephone interview, sounding exhausted and frustrated, that he would not forfeit his privacy in order to disprove a liar.

I continued to push, further insulting him with every interview and magazine profile. Although I had heard his voice, I wanted more. I wanted to see his face just once, to see his eyes, his wrinkles, his hair. I wanted to see if time had caused us to look more, or less, alike.

I stood my ground for three more days, countering every attack from Swanstrom with more bold lies and accusations. He lamented the fact that a man who wished to remain unknown could not do so in a world overrun by technology and devices. "Just show your face on television for five seconds," I said to another expressionless news anchor. "That's not going to make you any less unknown. Five seconds, that's all it will take. If you have the nerve to call me a liar, at least have the guts to back it up."

Unfortunately, I got my wish the very next day. I watched it live on the news as a gurney was wheeled through the front door of a modest Colorado home while a woman stood inside weeping into a handkerchief. The body was covered in a sheet, but I could make out the slight frame of a man lying motionless beneath it.

A few hours later a photograph was aired, a black-and-white portrait taken only two years prior that showed the same Swanstrom from the high school picture appearing older and wiser. Deep wrinkles surrounded his light eyes, which sparkled in spite of his severe expression. I felt weak when I saw his face. Though I was standing still, my heart was beating like I'd been running at a full sprint. We didn't look anything alike. I looked like an older version of the young man, while he looked exactly like himself.

Carol, Swanstrom's plain, soft-spoken wife, explained that her husband had died of a heart attack brought on by high blood pressure and cholesterol.

"It was the stress that killed him," she said in tears. "That awful man who put him through this should be imprisoned." She vowed that she wouldn't rest until I was exposed, and I believed her.

That night I slept in fifteen-minute increments, waking up each time from the same dream. A dream in which millions of pieces of burning paper were falling from the sky.

The next day I turned on the news and heard my true name being spoken.

Earl Curtis Willard III—the name of a fake and a liar.

As I walked to the car in handcuffs, blinded by camera flashes, I asked Kelly Davis to retrieve my manuscripts from storage and burn them.

There was a combination of sadness and relief in his eyes, but he nodded and said, "Of course."

I regret that I couldn't be there when he did it. It would have been like a funeral.

Seven years seems like a long time for pretending to be someone else, but the court considered it identity theft with the intention to profit from another's name. I didn't fight the sentence; it seemed fair to me.

Only a couple of months after I was taken to a minimum security prison I got a letter from a well-known literary agent who offered to represent me if I ever decided to write anything. My early work was a pale imitation of Swanstrom's unique style, but now that he is no longer alive the world is in need of someone like him. His death has created a void, an indentation in the universe that I intend to fill.

At the end of the day, your life is just a story. If you don't like the direction it's going, change it. Rewrite it. When you rewrite a sentence, you erase it and start over until you get it right. Yes, it's a little more complicated with a life, but the principle is the same. And remember, don't let anyone ever tell you that your revisions are not the truth.

As of this date, I've sold contracts for three of my novels, and one screenplay is in development for a film. My agent assures me that once I am released, I have a bright future ahead of me. Every day I receive letters from people who think of me as a martyr, some kind of flawed hero.

I did what I did, but I stand by it. It's not easy to find an audience anymore—sometimes you have to let the audience find you. Maybe someday people will read my books not just out of morbid curiosity but because the words speak to them.

Maybe a lonely young man will be inspired to write something of his own. More than anything I'm looking forward to the day I can leave this place and see the spine of my own novel on a shelf in the bookstore where I was first asked, "Would you be willing to sign this?"

MIND AND SOLDIER

Phil Jourdan

Plant had fingers crusty with dried mud, and he pressed
them against each other to twirl a blade of grass in circles.
Sometimes the world lets men prove themselves at the cost
of their selfhood: Plant's sense of time and space had dis-
solved into a mess of colors and shades, memories of days in
the jungle, trying not to set off traps, living to be a hero, and
falling asleep a wounded baby. This was the world to him,
the flux, the dizzying fullness for which there existed medication. Any faith in justice or honor had been poured out of
him, and bravery, that thing you need on the battlefield and
off, had dried up, prune-like, and discarded. There was more
comfort in playing with a blade of grass than in the arms of
his wife or in the smile of his son.

For some, in respectful neighborhood gossip, this was
proof enough that he had fought the battle and must be
left to brood. But to that curious boy from next door, Raul,
Plant's collapsed mind seemed to hold some allure of which
Plant himself had not even an inkling.

He'd heard his wife scolding the kid for coming too
close to her poor injured husband, but Plant wasn't quite
bothered by Raul's visits. Reduced to permanent and mad-
dening immobility, sitting on the porch all day only feet
away from the creaking wheelchair, the soldier even took

some semblance of pleasure in seeing Raul make his careful, clumsy way toward him.

A peculiar pleading look in the boy's eyes: eagerness and fear. His mouth was open, but he said nothing. He sat next to Plant, and together they looked out onto the street.

"Hey, Raul," Plant said.

"Hello, Mr. Vanderloo."

The boy's lips were thick and dark, but the rest of him, his skin and palms, were light, an ugly pale. There was something soft about him, a wimpy sadness in his movements. Perhaps a mere effect of the general blurriness through which Plant saw the world. He'd heard Raul described as intense, odd, clumsy. Maybe so. But in these moments they shared, the kid seemed less clumsy than improbable. The whole person of Raul: not right, not obvious, an unsettling thing to a man trained to find traps in implausible places. Raul's big body and small limbs, his negroid lips, as Plant's wife called them, his curly, dark hair that just touched his eyebrows, and the deep voice that seemed to crawl out of his mouth like a beetle. Everything about him was likeable and scary, even terrifying because of the chilly quiet in his eyes. So it was no wonder Plant tolerated Raul's visits. It was a trip into the weird.

"How you doing," Plant said.

"I'm okay."

"You come here to see Gordon?"

"No, sir."

"We're not in the military, Raul."

"No, Plant."

"So what's happening?"

"I need advice."

"What about?"

"Well," Raul said, staring at the blade of grass in Plant's hand, "I'm telling you this because it's you that I trust the most for some reason."

"Yes," Plant said and handed him the blade of grass. "You can tell me. I'm not going anywhere." He pointed down where there was no heavy, healthy leg. "Eh?"

(And as was prone to happen once or twice a day since he'd stopped swallowing his medication and started feeding it to the dog in secret, his mood dropped like an egg falling to the granite. He couldn't explain it when it happened and could not bear to think of it when it passed. But he felt his insides solidify, and he grew a little too aware of those missing parts, the leg, the two testicles—two of them, lucky man—the skin of his buttocks. What a filthy, raging, disgusting mess he was. What a treat. What an embarrassment for everyone concerned, his wife with the unceasing care, his son with the admiration. The constant admiration, the father to be proud of. The country, the entire country grateful. Plant was missing chunks of his body, but everyone was so fucking grateful. And this kid was asking for advice.)

"Advice on what?"

"I think I'm in love with someone." Raul tilted his head at him. "A girl, of course. I think I love her so much that it's starting to make me sick."

"Sick?"

"In the head."

"You need to watch over your body and get yourself sorted out before you go chasing after girls. There's plenty of time for girls."

"You don't understand, sir . . . Plant. I'm feeling sick. Physically sick."

"Physically sick."

"With love."

"With love. Yeah."

"I get queasy. Not in a good way. I want to vomit."

"You get the feeling you're about to puke out everything you like about her, like it's a kind of poison, right. It's scary. I understand it," Plant said and covered his mouth with his dirty hand. "But I'm telling you, you can't . . . well . . . you can't . . . Who is this girl?" He put his hand on his knee and gripped it.

"I couldn't tell you that."

"Hmm. It's embarrassing to say."

"I was thinking maybe you could give me some tips."

"What for?"

"I need to have her."

"Have. Good word."

(You know, Plant wanted to say, when I was over there fighting little gooks and getting my fucking limbs blown off in the name of a place I've never felt a part of anyway—oh yeah, you don't have to feel at home when you're here or any-where; you don't have to love where you are ever, ever—there wasn't much time for romance and girls. But you did have to ejaculate. Yes. As if there could be war without semen somewhere in the balance. So you know what we did? We fucked what we found. We found whores to fuck. And some-times we didn't pay them. That was when we were lucky and they were lucky and there was no battle to fight. Deep in the jungle, there weren't any whores. You had to learn to love your blue balls for weeks on end or take advantage of nearby villages, where you could just grab a pretty girl and stick yourself inside her, your knife at her neck. It's nice to like somebody across the street. It's nice to have a crush.)

"You know what that teaches you about romance?"

"What . . . what teaches who about romance?"

(And these old fucked-up hands of mine, crusty with all this mud from picking at pretty flowers and twisting grass until it's nothing but dead matter—back then—you know this. You can sense what this is, what I'm telling you, because when you don't get her, when you can't impress the girl, you'll want to go to war. Where you can mean something to someone, and hey, your whole country will fuck you if you go to war. But my hands are as dirty now as they were then, of course. Being at home doesn't change that. Putting myself, not so delicately, into them. The women. You know what that would be back here, that action? Your mother would call it rape and would ask you to call it rape too. But that's not an issue over there. There are no issues there. There're no pressing concerns. And everyone is so unbelievably grateful for the fine work you did over there. You're just a fucking little kid, with your crush on a pretty girl from school.)

"You know what I learned over there?" Plant said, speaking not really to Raul, not to himself, but to the void. "I learned about love. I learned that love means many things. Well, I learned that many things mean many things. And one of the things love means is the ability not to kill the person you're fucking because you're so frustrated by all the other things going on around you."

"I don't understand." Raul winced and tore the blade of grass apart and sprinkled the aftermath onto the dirt below. "What are you talking about?"

"I need to make myself clear. I'm not saying you should force anyone." No. But maybe, maybe, Plant continued, it's better to take what you want and get it over with. Was he talking aloud? The boy didn't seem to hear. "What the hell are you supposed to do? And me? It's not like I'm ever going back there. Jesus. I was told to avoid stress, you know. Told to avoid stress. Avoiding the perils of stress is really pretty easy when they've taken your fucking weapons from you, and all that matters is that they get handed to someone new with two legs and a God-loves-ya golden smile. That's what it was there. That is what we were. Over there. And over here everyone's very grateful and will tell you so. Just don't say what happened over there. Because it's about manners, you see."

"You mean Vietnam?"

"So . . . I did what I needed to do. Trust me. Sometimes you have to fuck them very, very brutally if you want to stay manly enough for your fucking superiors. You fuck until you feel your balls overflowing with testosterone, and your heart is racing as though someone were holding a knife to your neck. Didn't they do that? And no. Not all the guys at the top were like this. Just the ones who come over to tell you maybe you're not fighting hard enough. Your friends depend on you. You depend on yourself. Don't you?"

"What . . ."

"Don't you want to be a man? Isn't that what gets you by? If everyone needs your strength, can you deprive them of it?"

Raul, baffled: "Do you want me to leave?"

"No, I want you to stay." And listen to me. Nobody listens to me. I don't shit myself, do I? I'm not an invalid. "See the wheelchair," he said, pointing somewhere behind him. "That is me. That's how I move around. You know what you need love for? You need to find it before you lose part of your body, so you can pretend to be whole again in the arms of your lovely, caring wife and she can scuttle you over like the world's most important cripple. Bring the wheelchair over. Hurry."

The boy opened up the wheelchair and pushed it along the porch and stopped near Plant. "And now?"

"Now," Plant said, "I want you to kick the fucking thing. It's okay. Just kick it."

"What for?"

But the soldier wasn't listening anymore. It made perfect sense—kick the wheelchair for a minute. Kick the thing and watch it roll. It's not going to hurt anybody, and you'll see what I mean. Just as suddenly, it made no sense at all; the point eluded him now. So he said, "Raul, let go of that. Come here."

Raul sat and stared.

"Listen. You want a girlfriend, you need to be able to give her something."

"Like what?"

"Something. Not material stuff. That only works some of the time. You need to make it win-win. Always make it win-win. If you don't, then she'll resent you in the end. Don't let yourself be someone else's big resentment problem. You know my . . . You know Gordon's mom. Now she resents me, and I can't do anything about it. I didn't make it win-win. I mean, I fought for her once to win her heart, and that was fine. I got her in the end, and I made her happy. Then I went off to fight those little fucking monkeys, because I believed it to be the right thing to do. The right thing, you know. Leave and go kill people, that was the right thing in my head, and it was the right thing, because how else do we keep those fucking little monkeys in check? How do you keep yourself in check? How can you keep a family if you can't hunt an animal? It's not even about the little people out there; it's here. It's the . . . aggression in me. Us. Aggressive children. Like you. You'd be a good soldier because you hold everything in. People mock you, and you want to show them you don't give up. Me too. And I come back without a leg, can't satisfy my lovely, caring wife in any way, and she starts to resent me. She's impatient, even when she's being patient. She hates me because she has to love me. See? Everyone around her tells her how glorious it might be to have a hero sitting on her porch. A man who goes beyond himself. But all I really do is sit around and tell stories and complain about politicians and piss myself wet every once in a while. Gordon is scared of me. So the situation isn't exactly win-win, is it?"

"No."

"What you have to do is work on yourself. Make yourself attractive through the things you do, the principles you hold dear, and the goals you've set for yourself. Then you can try to get a woman. You can't expect her to love you just because you love her back. That only happens when the woman is weak. And my fucking God, women are weak—they're as weak as we are. Don't kid yourself about that. Nobody's going to save you. But if you want a good one, look for someone you have to work toward. Work on yourself as much as possible while you're young, because habits get harder and harder to break. Fuck! Once you've sorted yourself out, the women will flock to you. Believe me. Do you believe me?"

Raul was staring at the ground. "No. Can you help me? Can you tell me how to get there?"

"Make mistakes. Make a lot of mistakes, and learn from them." Don't go into the wild. The wilderness of the city

or the ocean or the battlefield. Don't take a knife with you.
Don't be armed when you see the women in the village.
Because you see one of them trying to teach herself to enjoy
it as you fuck her (ha! yes, that happens; I saw it), your
knife to her throat, and you feel so much self-loathing that
you want to give her the knife and have her cut your own
throat. "Cut it! Come on. Rip my heart out. Go, go, go. You
can have your revenge." And you're about to do it. You're
about to hand her the knife. If she's so angry, why not just
let her kill you? But now you want to win. Now that you've
seen her fighting back and yourself in that desperation, you
only want her to despair more than you. It's not the war
that brings out the worst in you. It's anyplace where nobody
can know what you're up to. But he wasn't looking at Raul
anymore. It was something, someone else, a stranger—fat,
stupid, getting paler by the second. A shapeless thing. Not
again. Not this. Falling like a hammer on himself. He forgot
where he was, and everything around—the environment, the
fields or roads, this wretched place called home—forgot him.
The sun grew brighter; everything went silent, cold, illuminated. He could barely make out what the thing was saying.
"Mr. Vanderloo?"

Yeah, his name. The explosion of light, talking to him.
The sun. He morphed out of himself, dropped the role of
husband, father, mentor, soldier. The great message of life
had been presented to him in a language he couldn't read.
All at once the grandeur of the world seemed a joke, the
innocence of youth was a self-serving lie, and he knew the
shape before him sought no more but its own demonic
self-gratification, not advice. Not a bond. It cared nothing
for Plant Vanderloo, Hero. It was sheer and simple mockery

that had brought the stranger to him, walking to him on those little chubby legs. "Raul, what the hell?"

"What's wrong?"

"What the hell?" But the sirens were wailing again, the fire of machine guns, the earth turned to mud and blood, the jungle . . . Get a grip on yourself. Get a grip.

"Go get my wife." He drummed his fingers on his temple and looked at the shapeless thing, almost ready to plead, squinting in the light. "Get my wife."

Raul hesitated, said, "She's at my house. With my mother."

"Oh, good fuck," Plant murmured. "I'm hallucinating. This isn't real and I . . . I know that. If you want to help. Something isn't here. You're not here at all."

"What?"

"You son of a bitch," Plant said. "With your girl problems. Girl problems. Grow up. Lose some weight. And stop fucking with people's heads. Do you understand? Stop fucking with people. Stop fucking with them."

"I'm sorry," the shape said, edging away. "I don't know what's happening."

"Well, neither do I." He was crying. "Neither do I. This happens sometimes, it . . . I know I'm hallucinating. I'm not crazy. It's a bunch of symptoms, and a doctor can help, yeah? You see? I don't have to take any kind of medication because this is my truth and I am right. You see that, don't you? This is me. An unfortunate fucking thing. I just . . . for God's sake, Raul, go get my wife." I'll kill him. I will kill him. I will. He'll die. He will die. "No, come here. Come here."

Tentatively, the shape loomed closer and knelt beside him. He will die.

"You want to know what I'd do, if I were your dad?"

"I don't really know my—"

"If I were your dad," Plant said, wrapping his fingers around the shape's neck and squeezing, "I'd be embarrassed." He pressed deeper and deeper, feeling the thing's throat gurgling. "So damned embarrassed. I'd be ashamed. I'm already ashamed. It's little fucks like you that make things happen to the rest of them. Little fucks like us, we're in this together. We're the reason things go wrong, and I am fucking ashamed of you."

The shape resisted. Its fingers were clenched around his shoulders, and it tried to push him away, made repulsive noises, tried to swallow, to breathe.

Plant knew what he was killing. The void pretending to be someone. The void wearing a mask. There had been nobody there to begin with. His fingers were digging into the boy's flesh, clawing and prodding and throbbing with the ecstasy he'd always suppressed. Where's the knife? Where's my knife? I'll cut your fucking throat open, you see. You and your little games. A big blade of grass and nothing more and I will crush you until the world is rid of people like us.

Screaming all around. Someone clutched at his back, slapped him in the face.

Plant tightened his grip, and the colors of the boy's face deepened, a beautiful red, those fat lips.

And the voice of his son rang through the neighborhood, Gordon's deep, vacuous voice for once charged with real emotion: "Dad? What's happening? Dad?"

"Jesus Christ," Plant said, staring at Raul's empty face. Then he looked up and saw his son, that other shape approaching them, throwing his glasses off and grabbing Plant's arm.

"What are you doing?"

"The boy," Plant said, looking down. "Raul."

"What did you do?" Gordon Vanderloo screamed.

"Plant?" A woman's voice.

"Mom." A boy's voice. "What's happening?"

Plant felt himself slapped across the face but barely, numbly: he was aware of things—of events unfolding, of sanity unraveling—but couldn't ride along: his wife kneeling beside Raul, holding his head up, stroking his hair, Gordon simply staring on in perplexed (or admiring?) horror at his father who within seconds would understand what he'd done or hadn't and resume.

Pluck at the grass some more.

INGREDIENTS

Richard Lemmer

The nurse nearly falls flat on her arse. She's half jogging
down the corridor, misses the yellow cone that says, Warning, and slides like she just stepped onto an ice rink. She
reaches out and grabs a window frame to stop herself from
falling. A lucky nonbreak.

The confused and heartbroken man, he watches as the
nurse jogs past and out of sight. Out in the hospital corridor,
he sits down on a plastic bench and holds Morris's left hand
in his right hand.

"Why . . . why didn't you tell me about this before? Did
this happen when you got the scars?" Finally, he sighs, rubs
his stubbly chin, and says, "How did this happen?"

His eyes look wet. Not because he's upset. Because he
never blinks when he is being serious. It's a conscious choice.
When you love someone, you think you know all their dirty
secrets—the fluoride content of their water, the cyanide content of their apple pips, the fat content of their Happy Meals.
You think you know all their marks and cracks—their hemo-
philia, their crooked teeth, their allergies.

He grips the left hand. He really wanted kids, his kids.
He wanted to shower them with ethically sourced cotton
jumpers, blues for girls and pinks for boys, fighting gender
stereotypes one item of clothing at a time. Feed them baby

food made from organic, locally grown spuds and carrots. Treat them with fair trade, traditionally crafted toys from the developing world.

Now all he wants is to hear a story that's been buried for a long time.

In the silence of the closed store, a bored and uniformed checkout girl walks to the foods of the world aisle carrying a still-cold pallet of chicken satay sticks. Packs upon packs of chicken satay sticks.

They were a big seller before the Eurocup final. Prawns, farmed for pennies by semi-naked men in Bangladeshi swamps, sold well. From the deforested Amazon basin, burgers sold like hotcakes. Lager, transported by truckers across Europe's endless motorways, sold well—but it always does.

From behind the pallet, the girl's face blocked by pack upon pack of chicken sticks, she says in a slow, deep northern accent, "I thought he was going to hit me."

Most people, buying and buying and buying, they're oblivious to all the bodies scattered across the globe, the bodies that slave away so one happy customer can host a summer barbecue. All the effort, all the produce—spoiled by rain. A storm made a thousand feet above the Atlantic.

Some people, busy buying and buying, they're oblivious to the bodies that serve them at the checkout.

"But I kept saying, 'I'm sorry, sir, no receipt, no money back. It's store policy.' But will shit for brains listen? No, just on and on about this, that, and the other, and get this—customer rights! Arsehole," she says as she disappears down the cooked meats aisle.

The four girls restocking the foods of the world aisle laugh. They all know where Jen is coming from.

"Sometimes don't you wish you could spit on their three-for-two onion rings?" Jen says when she comes back to lean against a shelf of pasta products.

From the healthy lifestyle aisle on the other side of the foods of the world aisle, someone says, "Funny you should say that." The voice, coming through pack upon pack of sugars from far, far away, says, "Hold on one sec."

Sugar is a necessity that sells well constantly. Sugar from Fiji and Mauritius and Swaziland, where the plantation workers earn next to nothing while the king, owner of the Royal Swaziland Sugar Corporation, can afford a BMW for each of his ten wives.

A pack of Swaziland sugar, it says, "I've got a story for you girls."

The pack of sugar, the voice, Anita explains The Game. Anita's sister, Margarita, works in the Safeway down in Staines where the checkout girls play a game passed on by a friend of a friend called Stock Movement. Anyone competing has to put in a tenner. There is only one winner, who gets all the money.

You have to spend the day, racking up points by the hour, with your chosen object buried inside yourself. You have to bury it inside yourself in the way only a woman can. If you throw in the towel, you have to put your object back—where it belongs on the shelf.

"Unbelievable," Jen says.

"I simply don't believe that," says someone behind a cage full of pasta products.

"Crap, crap, crap, and more crap," says a blonde as she walks away from the group.

And then, to everyone's surprise, a bored and uniformed body stacking Italian spaghetti says, "You know . . . I could really do with fifty pounds . . ."

Then the floor supervisor appears and everyone shuts up.

The body stacking spaghetti, it belongs to this stupid, stupid girl who insists that everyone call her Morris. Most people ask why she has a boy's name. Colin, her mum's boyfriend, the idiot, he thinks it's some weird ultrafan thing for Morrissey when really it's a tribute to William Morris, the nineteenth-century radical thinker. And it's because her real name is Carolyn. But Carolyn deserves a cool name, because she's so edgy she thinks both Lennon and Lenin were sellouts.

This bedroom revolutionary, this suburban Gandhi with black lipstick, is always preaching, "Did you know 'fair trade' coffee pays the Chagga people of Kilimanjaro only about twenty pence extra for their day of hard work?"

This checkout iconoclast, destroying the corporate system one scrawl on the staff toilet wall at a time.

A week after the story, Morris is working at the customer service counter. Explaining to a middle-aged woman that the three-for-two offer in the fruit section applies only to strawberries, not raspberries. Strawberries, picked by minimum wage migrant workers in giant greenhouses scattered across England, they're always a popular buy in the summer.

Over the store Tannoy system, Morris calls out, "Supervisor to customer service, supervisor to customer service."

Standing behind the confused middle-aged woman is Margarita. The middle-aged woman wanders off with a supervisor, muttering something about shopping elsewhere.

Margarita, a peroxide blonde with earrings as big as donuts, she's come in to give some money to Anita but can't find her. Morris says she shouldn't, but she'll look after the money.

As Margarita lets the rolled-up notes fall from her hand, our bedroom revolutionary asks about Stock Movement.

Margarita smiles and says, "You girls thinking of playing?"

Morris says, "It's not real, right? It can't be real. It's just a wind-up on Anita. An older sister playing a joke on a younger sister."

"It's real. Last game, I won," Margarita says, pushing her hair away from her earrings. "Four hours with a mini chicken satay stick."

"No way," Morris says.

"Yes way." Margarita heard about The Game from a friend of a friend. Different stores call The Game different things.

Insider Trading. Stocking Up.

Packing.

Margarita, leaning on the counter, licking her pink lips, says most stores have something like The Game. In certain department stores, male members of staff dare each other to leave their seed on the clothes in the stockroom. In certain chain restaurants, the chefs literally chew your food for you before a waiter brings it to your unsuspecting table. In certain hairdressing salons, the hair products don't contain much hair product.

Stain Addition. Al Dente.

Root Booster.

"No way, no way." Morris, bedroom revolutionary, stares at the milling customers, with their stained clothes, their bulging bellies, their shiny hair.

The in-store radio playing over the Tannoy system tells customers to check out the great summer deal on raspberries.

Our suburban Gandhi thinks about making her own clothes, growing her own food, cutting her own hair.

"Not all but most stores have something like it. Our game is fairly simple. You've heard the setup. Ten points an hour. You all decide on your items beforehand—so everyone agrees they've got equal items," Margarita says, and she spins a pound coin on the customer service counter.

"And you have to walk around all day?" Morris says.

"Not all day," Margarita explains, the movement of the spinning coin forming a globe. "You're on checkouts—you spend most of the day sitting down. Sometimes The Game finishes after an hour. Although, one month, this new girl, out to prove herself, she bet fifty pounds she could last a month with a coffee bean inside her."

A long, long way from a blazing hot African sun . . . "This girl lasts the whole month, or so she claims. She said it was no problem, just had trouble sleeping. She gets the nickname Princess Flick—as in flick the bean and 'The Princess and the Bean.'"

"Isn't it 'The Princess and the Pea'?" Morris says.

Margarita says, "Whatever."

The coin stops spinning and falls flat on the counter.

Our checkout iconoclast says, "You're winding us up. A coffee bean, sure, maybe . . . but a chicken satay stick?" She blows a puff of air in disbelief.

"What about drug dealers?" Margarita asks. "Mules, they're called, smugglers paid to keep little packets of drugs deep inside their own bodies. Or what about fisting? A five-fingered, five-knuckled fist, all sharp angles and bone, shoved tight inside . . ."

The in-store radio tells customers, "Don't hesitate to ask an assistant if you need a hand."

"Okay, okay," Morris says.

Margarita reminds Morris to give the money to Anita, says "Ciao," and walks off.

The next customer who needs customer service, he's making a complaint about the in-store brand root booster and doesn't understand why Morris should find this so funny.

A few hours later, Morris gets relieved from the customer service counter. She's on her lunch break, goes looking for Anita. Surrounded by the countless colors of brands and packaging, as if the store were selling colors siphoned from a rainbow. Down the aisles stacked with shampoos, microwave meals, and store brand clothing. Pritt Sticks, Lynx Bullets, and cocktail sausages. Fold-up toothbrushes, lipstick, and mascara. Pepperoni and green beans. Mini Mars bars, mini Snickers bars. Mini bottles of liquor, big enough for a single shot, small enough for . . .

Anita is restocking the damaged goods shelf. Packets of chocolate fingers that have been opened but will stay fresh for a few more days. Cocktail sausage packets that have been opened. Fold-up toothbrush packets that have been opened. Anita stands with a sticker gun repricing the faulty or damaged items. By the end of the night, they'll all be taken from the shelf—taken to a campus by students struggling to budget.

"Money from Rita," Morris says and gives Anita the rolled-up notes.

"Oh, brilliant," Anita says, then playfully stickers Morris's left hand with the sticker gun.

Peeling the sticker from her hand, the adhesive creating a tiny wave of skin, Morris says, "The Game is real by the way. Rita won the last game, with a mini chicken satay stick."

Anita says, "Whoa, whoa, too much information about my own sister."

"Would you be game?" Morris asks, a sly smile across her face. Sure, winning some money would make it easier to get by on minimum wage. But a little revenge would be a prize in itself, payback for every customer who thinks the check-out staff are just extensions of the checkout. Giving a secret middle finger to every clock-watching supervisor.

This self-actualized eco-warrior, this teenage Marx with emo hair, always preaching, "Did you know prawn farmers in Dumuria and Khulna get as little as £250 for one hundred kilograms of prawn a year?"

"I'm game . . . as long as you play with this," Anita says, holding up a caved-in Pringles tube.

Our bedroom revolutionary, she starts to say, "I'm not a shopping basket," when a customer walks over holding a cardboard box with a picture of a flat-screen television on the side, and he asks where customer service is. Anita points him in the wrong direction.

Before the Eurocup final, flat-screen televisions sold well. Colin, Morris's soon-to-be stepdad, had offered to buy her one. "Do you know what coltan is, Colin?" she asked. "Did you know our televisions are made with minerals from a war zone? Do war crimes and the Democratic Republic of Congo mean anything to you?"

The customer walks off without saying thank you. Morris and Anita look at each other.

Arsehole.

Now, sitting in a hospital corridor, staring at the door of the doctor's office, this confused and heartbroken man asks again, "How did this happen?"

He doesn't know that the first time The Game was played, everything was fine. No problems. Northern Jen won with a fold-up toothbrush. Still smelling of prawns, she slotted it back into its packet, taped up the hole, and displayed it on the damaged goods shelf with an 80 percent off tag. The fold-up toothbrush, the winning item, was gone by the end of the day.

A ten-pence bargain, taken to a campus by a scruffy student struggling to budget.

Now, this confused and heartbroken man, he just sits there in ignorance.

The doctor comes out of his office, asks, "Do you guys need some more time?"

"Yes." He starts to stroke the ring on the left hand he's holding. "Please, let's go back in, and we can talk this through with the doctor. You can explain, and he can give us the best advice, okay?"

He says, "Okay, Carolyn?"

His eyes look wet. Not because he's upset. Because he never blinks when he is being serious. It's a conscious choice. When you love someone, you think you know all their dirty secrets.

He keeps stroking the ring.

The story, unsaid, it forms a lifetime of distance between us.

It takes two weeks for Morris, our suburban Gandhi, to convince the girls to play The Game again. Just one more time. To liven things up. One last time to teach the customers a lesson they'll never learn. It's only Jen, Anita, and Morris who play. Each pitch in twenty pounds. Jen chooses a Chupa Chups lollipop. Anita picks a cocktail sausage, and it's agreed she gets only eight points an hour because her item is the easiest. Morris, our practical rebel, goes with a previous winner.

Standing in the girls' toilets, holding a mini chicken satay stick from the delicatessen, Morris thinks about how she'd spend the sixty pounds. New jewelry for her mum's wedding is an option. Save some for travel to the climate camp in June. Maybe be a humble winner and buy the girls lunch one day. Maybe treat her dad to dinner or something or anything, if he'd be willing.

Fuck Colin.

Each girl steps inside a cubicle, and blonde Zoe, waiting outside, says, "Don't be too long."

Our eco-warrior doesn't hang about. She drops her uniform trousers and her white underwear and without looking down begins to push the four inches of chicken stick deep inside.

It's not easy. It takes some time to get the necessary natural lubrication.

One of her younger toilet wall scrawls, it says, Fight the Power.

"I can't believe I was talked into this again," Jen says through the cubicle wall.

From the other side of the cubicle, Anita says, "Hey, Morris, did you check to make sure your chicken's organic? Is it chemical free?"

Jen giggles, says, "Is it free range?"

Our bedroom revolutionary, she says, "Not anymore."

This college hippie, this middle-class activist, always preaching, "Did you know most battery hens have their beaks cut off with hot irons, so they don't peck themselves to death while they're confined to a tiny cage for the rest of their lives?"

After a few minutes, the three cubicle doors open, and the three bored and uniformed bodies waddle out.

"I'm not going to last an hour," Anita says, rearranging the crotch of her uniform trousers.

She doesn't.

About half an hour into The Game, Anita waddles past Morris on checkout 15. "I'm going to the loo." She says it in a way that says, "This is the last time I play this stupid, stupid game."

Jen, on checkout 8, she's breathing pretty heavy but hanging on.

Our checkout iconoclast, our teenage Marx, she's felt better. She can't get comfortable, no matter how much she shuffles her arse cheeks. The wooden stick is poking out by about an inch and keeps tickling her thigh.

If nothing else, having four inches of chicken satay stick inside you is distracting.

For over an hour, customers keep saying, "You didn't scan that properly."

"You forgot to apply the three-for-two discount."

"You look a little flushed."

The shiny-haired customer who comments on Morris's rosy cheeks and squinting eyes, she's buying fresh oregano from Israel, from the West Bank, from land stolen by walls and troops and bulldozers.

One hour and ten minutes after The Game started, Supervisor Mike asks Morris if she wants to swap lunch with Zoe. This would put her five minutes away from lunch.

Our practical rebel says, "Yeah, great."

Over the store Tannoy system, a voice says, "Cleaner to the breakfast cereal aisle. That's a cleaner to the breakfast cereal aisle."

The next customer with a bulging belly is buying multipacks of chocolate—packets with mini bars of Mars and Snickers and Twix. Chocolate that started life as beans guarded by militias, picked by children, chocolate slaves, thousands of miles away on the Ivory Coast.

The in-store radio sounding over the Tannoy system tells customers, "Treat your kids with Safeway's three-for-two offers on sweets."

As the chocolate customer bags up, Zoe comes over to relieve Morris. Zoe asks how it's going.

Our college hippie, our middle-class activist, she says it's going hot and sticky and itchy. She limps and waddles down the breakfast cereal aisle, heading toward the staff entrance at the back of the store. Our eco-warrior, our bedroom revolutionary, stares at her groin and belly, the linoleum floor out of focus. The floor, so shiny it looks wet. Shiny and wet and slippery. The only way to tell that it is wet is by the yellow plastic cone just out of Morris's sight.

The customers look away from their future breakfast cereal as they hear Morris's shoes squeak along the floor, her backside thud against the linoleum.

The milling customers, with their stained clothes, their bulging bellies, their shiny hair, none of them are aware they've witnessed an impaling.

The poor girl who's just embarrassed herself in front of all these people is struggling to stand up. She's taking deep, deep, deep breaths. Like she's going into labor. She tries to straighten her legs, her back, but it looks like she's about to burst into tears.

An old customer shopping with his wife asks the girl if she's okay.

The poor girl limps off without saying a word—letting out nothing but deep, deep, deep breaths.

Our teenage Marx, our suburban Gandhi, she just wants to get to the nearest toilet as quickly as possible. Men's, ladies', or disabled—as long as it has running water and a lockable cubicle.

A customer says, "Excuse me."

But Morris plays deaf. Limping on, trying to waddle faster and faster.

The thousand miles to the girls' staff toilets are nothing but agony. Cereal packets, Pritt Sticks, cooked meats, foods of the world, Supervisor Keith saying, "What's up?" are all a blur. Morris begins to focus when she realizes one of the toilets is empty. Limping to the cubicle, locking the door. Dropping her uniform trousers, dropping her stained underwear.

The underwear is stained red, the same red as on a Saint George's flag. Saint George's—made in Turkey. The store's Saint George's flags—made in Portugal. The Saint George's red mess dripping down her thigh—made eighteen inches above her kneecaps, a few inches below her belly button.

Our middle-class activist, our human satay stick, she feels just a centimeter of wood between her legs and flinches.

On the toilet wall, one of her younger scrawls, it says, Fuck the System!

This is not what she had in mind.

The chicken stick, there's only one way to remove it. With most of her fingers inside, it's going to take a firm yank.

So this is what she does with the fingers of her left hand. She doesn't look. She lets out a small moan as her knuckles become slimy. For ten seconds her whole body is nothing but her left hand and everything between her legs.

Then something wet and warm comes loose from inside, and she hopes to God it's just poultry and wood. It makes a wet pop as it's pulled out. Then the chicken stick gets thrown in the toilet. The left hand looks like it's punched a whole punnet of special deal raspberries.

Our checkout iconoclast. Our practical rebel.

Our bloody idiot, staring at the left hand, getting tunnel vision, feeling cold and weightless, then falling to the concrete floor.

When the girls found her, they nearly broke the cubicle door down. But Morris came round in time.

In the staff sick room, Supervisor Karen said, "It's okay, darling. Us girls get it bad some months."

They sent Morris home, but she went to the hospital. Because she was a hemophiliac, the blood wouldn't stop. The doctors did scans and gave her tablets, constantly asking where the round wound half an inch deep in her vaginal wall came from. Spending days and nights on a ward. Our check-out iconoclast, our bloody idiot, pleading ignorance, like it was some unholy stigmata. Even when the wound became infected. Even when operations were required. Even when the doctors said bearing children would be unlikely, considering the complications.

Colin paid £500 for surprise tickets to an environmental conference in Seattle, because it's a small price to pay when your stepdaughter may never have children.

Margarita came clean. The Game was a lie. A wind-up. An older sister playing a joke on a younger sister. She was sorry from the bottom of her heart.

Now, outside the doctor's office, this confused and heartbroken man sitting on the plastic bench in the hospital corridor, he asks again, "Carolyn, are you okay?"

Our teenage Marx with emo hair, our suburban Gandhi with black lipstick, Morris, she died a lifetime ago, but I'll carry her scars forever. Studying at university, working at Oxfam, marrying the man I love, Morris was left behind, but not her body.

Going to the hospital, pretending to seek fertility advice. Then blurting it out while the doctor dissected the ovulation cycle—this is pointless. There won't be any children coming from this body—the worst-case scenario stated as fact. An accident a long, long time ago is all I can say.

Now, from the cold plastic bench, the confused and heartbroken man, my husband, he asks again, "Carolyn, are you okay?"

He's still holding the left hand, and I'm still picturing it covered in raspberry juice. Remembering three-for-two offers. Minimum wage migrant workers. Our bloody idiot. The story, still running over and over, watching my younger self. Me and not me. Scared the truth will put me back on the shelf, back on the market of loneliness.

He stands up, hugs me, kisses me on the lips. He holds me.

Maybe my sister can be a surrogate mother. Maybe, I think, we can see where adoption takes us. What's worse than not knowing how a story starts or who the storyteller is? It's not knowing what happens in the final chapter or who the storyteller will become by the end.

"I love you," I say.

"I love you too," he says.

Blues for girls or pinks for boys, either way, Morris is never going on the list of baby names.

THE LINE FORMS ON THE RIGHT

Amanda Gowin

Where he was coming from didn't matter, and where he was going was only home, so it was the in between that ended up important—in between two buildings. He shuffled, hands willfully deep in pockets, looking for nothing when he saw it. A glance to his right and there it was. A pink pump, a Pepto-Bismol slipper floating in the air beyond all context. He stopped short, rocking back on one heel in a pause that hadn't quite made up its mind to be a pause.

But there was more to the shoe than that. There was another shoe. His eyes adjusted, and instead of hanging in midair the shoes seemed to grow a girl, much the same way the grin grew a Cheshire cat. She was on one foot like a flamingo, all in black, a shock of bleachy, tangly hair flipping back as she slid her foot into the shoe and plunked it to the alley stones with satisfaction next to the other. She examined her feet, then clicked purposefully away, with the authoritative step of all high heels.

That sound echoed back. Think quick—yes, no—the wet stones stretched between them, drawing out her broken reflection almost to his own feet even as she retreated, and he thought, *Yes.* Scanning the street, finding it dead, he ducked into the alley like a novice predator to follow her round ass wherever it may lead.

A disappointing door just a few feet farther, it turned out—one of those side entrances to a dive with the standard glaring bulb that rendered the sign unreadable.

The door fell shut behind her with an obligatory echo off the buildings as it struck home. A few quick steps and he held the handle she had. Taking a deep breath to block out any logic, he yanked and entered.

Standard dive, standard everything—except the girl. A cursory search found her on a red swiveling stool at the bar. She was tiny and pale and pushing back that mass of hideously wonderful hair, an unlit cigarette between her lips. He saw her in alternating profiles as she looked around.

He removed his jacket slowly to buy a little time, making sure she wasn't looking for anyone, wasn't meeting anyone, then he slid onto the stool next to her. "Nice shoes."

Turning, eyebrows raised, she plucked the cigarette from her mouth. "Thanks. I stole them off a corpse in the alley." No grin followed but he laughed anyway, and she shook her head. "I blame my voice. I was cursed with a high register, so I can say anything I want with no more malice than Minnie Mouse or Mia Farrow. That was a lot of *m*'s, wasn't it?" Her hands followed a quick and thorough path from her neck on down. Some time before reaching her thighs she produced a book of matches. The cigarette caught, and she tossed away the burnt match with no interest in where it landed.

Oh, she was entrancing. Too much eyeliner on almond eyes. Hazel? Was that hazel? And besides the hair and bright shoes, she wore gloves. Like the pale leather kind ladies wore to drive during the 1930s. What was a hand job like with a leather glove? "But think of all the horrible things you get to say. You have a built-in disclaimer."

Listening, but she wasn't still, not for a second. Her eyes roved—over him, past him; she took in every corner without missing a beat in the patter. "What if I don't want it? What if I just once want to tell someone I'm going to kill them and have them believe me?"

Their eyes locked, as he didn't know how to patter back to this, and her grin broke loose.

He matched it. "Actions speak louder than words."

She laughed. "What is this place, anyway? Some kind of Elk or Moose or other antlered establishment? It's like we wandered onto a movie set or something," she whispered conspiratorially. "It's all a bit too exact. The bartender is the standard Bartender Washing Glasses. Back in the corner are Billiard Players 1 and 2. In the second booth are—who? Alcoholic and Outspoken Barfly?"

"I think they would be listed in the credits as Male Patron and Female Patron."

"Aren't you kind?" She spun back to him. "But really. Fill me in. Is that Uncle Larry and Aunt Sheila? You got quarters on the table for the next game?"

He shrugged. "No idea. I followed you in here."

Finally she was still. Her pupils seemed to narrow to points for a split second, then relaxed again, and she put her pointy little chin on her palm. "Isn't that interesting." It was almost a purr, not much like her voice before. "And I was just ducking out of the dark."

Her searching gaze fell on him now—his gray T-shirt, jeans, black work boots like all skinheads and serial killers wear, mussed brownish hair, and nowhere to hide anything.

She seemed to slide him finally into a nonthreatening or at least manageably threatening category and ran a gloved finger across her lower lip before turning to yell, "Bartender Washing Glasses! Two Jack and Cokes!"

They were collectively five drinks in before she stopped looking around every seventh second and he stopped calculating her inebriation level and the distance down the hall to the secluded bathroom—and that was the moment of realization. There was Something Else happening, and ulterior motives slid audibly onto back burners as a look passed between them. He ordered tequila shots, and they held them up in a toast.

"To stolen time," he said.

Throwing hers back, she mumbled, "And that's exactly what it is. What time is it, anyway? And are there any limes?" She spun her stool. "Dave, got any limes?"

Of course there was an old cloudy clock with bent hands. It read just before midnight.

The on-a-first-name-basis-since-she'd-shown-him-how-to-make-an-origami-baby-Jesus-from-a-bar-napkin-and-he'd-laughed-hard-and-comped-them-a-round bartender smacked two limes and a medium-sized dull knife down in front of her and retreated demurely.

Smile returning, she spun back around, knife in hand. "Do you see that? I'm the kind of person strangers feel comfortable giving a knife—without a second thought." She split a lime with gusto, and one half rolled off the bar.

"You got somewhere to be?"

"Don't you? Of course you do. That's what I thought. So let's have another shot and forget it again for now."

They did, or tried, and sucked limes, and howled with puckered cheeks.

"Is there music here? Player piano, organ grinder, anything?" he asked.

Cocking her head to the left, she answered, "Behind you." A recon glance—so much became reconnaissance when two people got drunk together, he thought; the accelerated level of intimacy made everything else feel outside of them—revealed a jukebox. "I believe that may be constructed entirely of dust. Should Dave be consulted? We wouldn't want to disturb the natives, and they've been comfortably in silence the past hour."

Dave was consulted—then she clicked over to the jukebox in her pink heels. Wiping the dirty glass with the side of one glove, she pressed two numbers with little hesitation and was back on her stool by the time refills appeared.

"You don't walk drunk."

"And you don't piss much for a guy."

"I'm afraid if I turn around you'll disappear."

"I might."

"I know."

David Allan Coe came to life in the air, and he grinned and shook his head.

"I'm ingratiating us with the natives. I'm putting them off guard so they're too confused to attack during Madonna." She lifted her hair off her neck and let it drop, watching him take two cigarettes from her pack. He waited to see if she would lean into it, and she did, putting her mouth delicately around the filter without breaking eye contact. "You are being very dirty."

"I could say the same of you."

Then her hands were on his collarbones, across his
shoulders, down his waist, all business and thoroughness,
and she came up with a lighter from his back pocket in
under ten seconds, smirking at his startled face as she lit her
cigarette.

"You're as tender as an officer with probable cause."

This made her laugh again, and he almost didn't notice
her glance at the clock as she threw back her drink.

"Do you have to go?"

"I don't have to do anything," she snapped. The fingers
of her right hand drummed on the bar, and his eyebrows
knitted. "What?"

"Your voice lost its Minnie Mouse."

"And you lost your roll of duct tape. What's your point?"
Her face began to fold, just slightly, at the corners of her
mouth and eyes. "Look, in here it's the movies. We both
know it's not real." She jerked a thumb toward the door.
"Out there it's Minnie Mouse and the need for restraints
and corpses and DNA and reality. In less than two hours
the lights on set are going down, and we both have to
go back." She searched his face and nodded, satisfied he
understood.

"DNA," he whispered, thinking of the pockets he was
emptying when he found this alley in the first place. "Do you
love him?"

"Now that sounds scripted. Maybe sometimes. We work
together—it works somehow. I'm a monster and so is he.
My choice of company is quite limited—it's sort of like being
from a very specific religious sect. A Mormon wants to be
with another Mormon."

"Or many other Mormons."

She smiled and took a long drag off her cigarette. "Some-times when the edges are fuzzy it seems like love. If I were outside looking in, I could believe it."

He folded his arms on the bar and laid his head on them, looking up at her. "A place where I used to live—it had these long, tall windows facing the street. Across from it was an antique store, and its front window was a Christmas scene all year long. It was made up like a living room—tree with lights and little glass ornaments, cardboard fireplace, arm-chairs, and hurricane lamps, even these little wagons under the tree with bows on them. My apartment smelled bad, and it was tiny, but I had a hard time leaving. When I'd wake up in the middle of the night and pass that window, I would see it from the corner of my eye and stop, and it was Christ-mas—warm, fuzzy Christmas like Christmas never really is—just for a minute. Beautiful and fake but almost worth putting up with the other shit."

"That would be it exactly." Her face was blank and gor-geous, shock wiping it clean of emotion. She sighed. "I pop out for a bite and end up drunk and half in love in the bar where they filmed *El Dorado* and *Hang 'Em High*."

"Borderline" drew to a close, strange and soundtracky as it had been, and she said, delaying the silence that threat-ened to fall, "Quick, play me a song. You pick." Snatching a ballpoint pen from near the register, she scribbled furiously on a napkin.

He made a cursory sweep of the selections for something to change the tone, something to make her smile again.

Because everything they were saying was true and not true. He pushed a button, the number nearly worn off, and upon returning slid his hand behind her head into all that hair and kissed her, rather desperate to make it all not true, to keep the end from being inevitable, Bobby Darin assisting in the background, upbeat about slashing, romance in his voice.

Their mouths were wet and fit perfectly.

"Can't you taste the bodies between us?" she whispered, and he inhaled her words.

"Come with me anyway."

"What does that mean? What movie are you in? This is a horror movie, not *Alice in Wonderland*. Or maybe it is. It's all a dream, a dream of a chase. He won't let me leave. I'll never marry anyone else." She wadded the napkin in her hand, working it into a smaller and smaller ball.

"Married? You're married?" He realized he was drunk, and things were a bit out of control, and his jacket was long lost, and Dave was eyeing them, as well as Male Patron and Female Patron, because they were becoming loud.

"I'll never be married at all," she hissed, then snatched the knife, stabbing it through the third finger on her left hand. It stood straight up out of the wooden bar, dripping lime juice on the glove's empty leather finger.

Silence—thorough and anticlimactic silence.

Bobby ended with a flourish, and Dave came over. He put one hand over hers and pulled the knife out with the other. "You two start being stupid, and I'm cutting you off." He pointed warningly with it and retreated in a huff.

Her jaw dropped. "Am I seriously that cute?"

"So that explains the gloves. Can they sew it back on?"

"He keeps it in his pocket." She slid her hands out of the sticky gloves—the space between her fingers didn't look particularly unnatural, so he didn't stare. Her fingernails were chipped and a shade close to her shoes. "I feel like I need to pick something up on the way home—should I? Like flowers or some other kind of guilty offering? We can't drag this out much longer."

"I'm starting to believe you pulled those shoes off a corpse."

"And I always believed the duct tape in your jacket was recreational."

"You can't end it like this."

"You can't end it like this. Why couldn't we just be drunk and pretend to be normal and falling in love?" She tucked her cigarettes into her pocket, getting wearily to her feet.

His hand locked around her wrist too tightly.

She looked at it. "Really? Do you want to take it all the way back to the beginning? First intentions and everything?"

"If it's the only way."

Her eyebrows lifted; a smile twitched at the corners of her lips. "Then give me a twenty-foot head start."

"Ten." He yanked her close to try and kiss her again.

Resisting, she grinned as she pulled back and disappeared out the door in a flash of pink heels and blonde hair.

His breath was uneven, but he was coming back to himself, saw his jacket at the other end of the bar. He would drain his drink—that would give her a fair chance.

On the bar was the wadded-up napkin, stained with ink and lime.

Uncrinkling it, their movie folded back around him:

"Mack the Knife" and it's meant to be. We can get married tomorrow. The odds are against us.
Celia loves you, Mr. X.

"Oh, shit."

Maybe it wasn't lost. Maybe, maybe, maybe. He shoved the napkin into his pocket, grabbed his jacket, tossed some bills on the bar, and bolted for the door.

Two steps out and he opened his mouth to call for her by name so she would know.

He saw stars—the painful kind first, and as he went over backward the real kind, a spattering visible in the sliver of sky between buildings.

Duct tape was a painful binding material. In retrospect maybe if he had known this he would have been less cliché and more creative during conquests.

These were his first thoughts as he came awake, twisting his hands behind him, but voices broke in to interrupt.

"I think he's a lovely present. I do. It's just he's so awfully banged up."

"I got excited. If I'd known you wouldn't like him, I wouldn't have gone to all the trouble of getting him into the cab."

"But I do. You're so hard to thank."

"And you're hard to please."

The female voice was hers, but it was back to the high register, the innocent doe.

He opened one eye. "Oh, Miss Lorelei Lee, why don't you use your regular voice?"

"Shut up! I won. You wanted to play; we played." She rose from the high-back chair and crossed to him, face hard but eyes unsure.

"I like you better pissed if you use your real voice. But one thing—this isn't my duct tape."

Fighting a smile, she answered softly, "I thought it would be a nice touch. Normally I use plain old handcuffs."

"That sounds more fun."

He got a full-on grin from her this time and took the chance to get his bearings. He was taped to an office chair, and she must've used most of a roll—amateur but effective. This was a nice place, very nice. Bourgeois, modern, that glass and sterile look. The only thing that didn't belong was her. She looked wild on the white carpet, with her pink shoes and torn black panty hose, hair ratted up in a knot on the back of her head.

"I didn't want to play," he said. "I wanted us to fall in love and change everything—maybe not all at once but leave behind the duct tape and the handcuffs. Well, maybe not the handcuffs . . ."

"Bullshit! If I hadn't clocked you outside the bar, I'd be the one in tape right now." She snatched a very pretty pistol from the table and pointed it at him with disturbing ease.

"You're gonna ruin the carpet," he crooned.

"She most certainly is not. Put that down, you little bitch. What is he talking about?" The competition appeared, the finger-stealing asshole, and he was wearing of all things a black turtleneck and a little ponytail.

"Don't call her a bitch. Oh, Jesus, him? Are you serious? This Sprockets son of a bitch?"

Her laugh startled them, and she swung the gun back and forth, pointed it finally toward the carpet.

"What is he talking about?" The black turtleneck pony-tail man stepped between them. He put his palms together. "And seriously, put it down, little girl. We're taking him downstairs and I'm calling Richard and Shelly and we're going to celebrate."

"Don't call me little girl, Leland. I am not in the mood."

"She's not in the mood, Leland."

"And you shut your piehole. You're not getting out of this." The gun found him again.

"Did you just say *piehole*?" He looked at her pleadingly, then at Leland, who seemed more concerned with the decor than adultery, and back to her. "You think you're a monster? What kind of monster could you be when you turn murder into a dinner party? How hard is that to give up? Where's the knife? That little peashooter doesn't even have any bullets, does it? Fucking white carpet?" Yanking and twisting, he tipped the chair and thumped on his side on the floor, staring at his own face in the shine on Leland's loafers. "What's he got that you can't leave? A huge cock? Money? He won't let you leave, what a crock of shit. Shoot me then."

"A huge— oh, my God." Leland giggled and backed up. "Sweetie, he's yours. He likes you; I get it now. And he thought— oh, that's priceless." He fell into a leather recliner, put a hand over his face, and shook with laughter.

She stepped toward him, the heels robbed of their power by the soft floor, both hands still tight around the gun. "They're my family." She shrugged and knelt at his head. Her eyes were very green. "A family of monsters."

"So leave. I love you. I mean, I could love you, I think. It's only been a few hours. Couldn't we just get some coffee first?"

"I'd be in that chair if you weren't." Her voice was cold. "Love me? I bet you would." She placed the barrel against his temple.

"Celia," he said, "come with me. My name is Scott. I never told you before."

Celia was pale. "I thought only frat boys were named Scott."

"I wouldn't have done it to you. I couldn't have. I won't."

"Aren't you scared?"

"Of you, yes. But not the gun."

Leland groaned. "This is very sweet but—"

Celia pulled the trigger without hesitation, and his head poured blood all over the white carpet.

"I would love a cup of coffee."

"Cut me loose, and I'll show you where we can dump the body."

Celia used the knife from his jacket, the knife that still smelled of limes, to slice away the layers of tape.

While rolling her brother's body in a rug, Scott came across a gnarled little blue finger. Down on one knee as he was, he presented it to Celia with anticipation.

A VODKA KIND OF GIRL

Matt Egan

Ruby stuck a small plastic sign inside her car window saying, "You can never be too thin or too rich," and a year later they stuck her in the ground inside a wooden box.

The garage she bought the sign from is the same garage I stop at on the drive to the church. Paying for my petrol and extra-thick banana milkshake, I notice that sign on sale behind the service counter.

People saw that sign in Ruby's car and said it was so Ruby.

As though she came up with the mantra, lived by it.

"Did you know the average person burns around six hundred calories a day?" she told me once upon a cigarette break at work. "And that's just from being alive."

She kept a little white book in the bottom of her bag, and she'd search through its index, flick to a page, and find out the calorific expenditure for almost any activity.

"Walking, you get rid of two hundred eighty an hour, depending on the pace. Running, something like seven hundred. And you know something weird? You burn more calories eating than you do sleeping." Holding her cigarette to her lips and inhaling the thing into her lungs, she thumbed through the little book's pages with her free hand. "Listen to this. They reckon that ten minutes of sex uses between fifty and one hundred calories." She dropped her cigarette and mashed it into the ground with the tip of her shoe. "Depending on the pace."

Jabbing her finger into her stomach, Ruby used to say how she needed to do more sit-ups and cover more ground on her early morning jogs. She pinched some skin between her index finger and thumb and denied it was all in her head. The busiest pub in town was The Crown, and if you walked through its doors some time after midnight on a Friday, and if you were a young bloke whose wallet had enough spare change in it to get a double vodka Coke for the slim blonde leaning against the jukebox to stop her from keeling over, the chances were good that she'd lead you by the wrist into the men's toilets, kneel on the hard orange tiles, and demonstrate the art of impromptu fellatio.

Her party trick, she'd stretch her mouth wide open and cram her hand into it, push those fingers in as far as they would go until her knuckles disappeared. "No gag reflex," she'd say.

Waiting for service at the bar, you heard one guy tell his mate, "Buy Ruby a Smirnoff Ice, and the next thing you know her knickers'll be hanging round her ankles."

"Wait a minute," his mate said, tilting his head back and looking through narrowed eyes. "That bitch actually wears underwear?"

Most weekends, these guys and their friends would take Ruby into the men's toilets or behind the row of trees at the far end of the pub's garden. They'd help her burn a few hundred more calories. Depending on the pace.

"It's just use and abuse," Ruby used to say.

Standing in the churchyard with the rows of people gaz-
ing into Ruby's hole, I glance around and I can't see any of
their faces.

From the side, the walls of the muddy pit they lower her
into look like huge slabs of chocolate sponge cake, moistened
by an early morning drizzle. Her parents stand at the edge
of the hole, looking into it. They hold hands, his right hand
in her left, their fingers interlocked so tight the blood gets
trapped, turning their fingertips dark red.

When they heard the news, people at work said they
couldn't believe Ruby was gone. She was so young. There
was nothing in her appearance to suggest any kind of
illness. A family friend phoned in with the coroner's verdict:
acyanotic congenital heart disease. There was no way
anyone could have spotted it. Ruby's heart was defective
since birth.

Maybe that explained the frigid pallor of her skin and
the fainting and the tiredness.

It was only a matter of time, they said. A tragedy waiting
to happen.

But they didn't know.

They didn't know that the human body contains such
invisible, essential things as electrolytes, things so infini-
tesimal you wouldn't even know they're there. Vital salts
called potassium, sodium, calcium, and other names you
remember from chemistry in secondary school. These things
conduct your body's electricity and make sure your internal
organs work the way they're supposed to work. They keep
your heart and liver and kidneys and nervous system from
packing in. How the oil, coolant, and petrol in a car keep the
engine ticking and the wheels spinning.

All these electrolytes flowing through your arteries, pumping through your heart and liver and kidneys, an invisible relay team carrying electrical impulses around your insides. Squeeze enough water out of your body, and these salts get stranded. Flapping about in one place, they can't conduct that vital electricity to the inner bits of you that keep you alive.

Say if you don't drink enough water and dehydration kicks in.

Say if you can't stop throwing up the contents of your stomach.

I knew about such things, but when people asked me about Ruby, I'd say, "No word of a lie, congenital heart failure."

Who'd have thought?

Ruby and me stood at one end of the bar, polishing cutlery and wrapping pairs of knives and forks in scarlet napkins. Last orders had been called half an hour ago, and the place was empty.

"There's something I need to ask you, if that's all right," I said.

Buffing a steak knife with a kitchen towel, she glanced at me. Her eyes had the color of a newspaper left out in the sun too long. "If you want to talk about what I think you want to talk about, then no, not particularly." She dropped the knife into a tray of cutlery and started rubbing another one.

I twisted a napkin with my hands and leaned onto the wooden counter. "Listen, I'm not trying to psychoanalyze you or anything. I just— I mean, have you ever talked to anyone about it?"

"What's the point?"

"Your mum and dad, maybe?"

"What's the point?"

"Don't they know what you get up to?"

Ruby balled the towel up. "Why'd you put it like that?"

"What?"

"Asking if they know what I'm getting up to. Fuck me, it's not like I'm killing babies and harvesting their organs to make a bit of money on the side."

"I know."

"It's not like I'm hurting anyone else."

I blocked the words I wanted to say behind a wall of clenched teeth. I played with the napkin. "I know."

Unfolding the towel on top of the counter, smoothing it out with both hands, she said, "I know you're trying to help."

I lifted my elbows off the counter and straightened up. "I just thought there might be something I could do. You'd tell me if there was, wouldn't you?"

"Yeah."

"Because I'm just trying to say, if you feel like it, I'm—"

"You can't do anything." She smiled, but there was something the matter with her eyes.

They hold the wake at Ruby's house. People huddle in the spacious living room—their footprints zigzagged in little trails across the soft red carpet.

Arranged on a large wooden table in one corner of the room, framed pictures of Ruby: Ruby as a baby, sleeping in her cot; Ruby as a toddler, building castles on some beach; Ruby posing for a school photo; Ruby standing in front of a Christmas tree, holding a glass of red wine.

Eighteen years condensed into a few photographs.

Quiet music drifts out of oval speakers on the walls and blends with hushed conversations. People hover over white china plates patterned with sausage rolls, rice crackers, and tortilla chips from the buffet spread in the hallway.

Standing next to the fireplace, a woman I've never seen before turns to the bloke she's with and says, "I dunno. This doesn't taste like light mayo to me."

I don't recognize any of the people in the front room, so I go to the kitchen to get a drink.

Bottles of wine stand on the kitchen table next to a few bottles of spirits and cans of soft drinks. I drop a handful of ice into a tumbler and pour a large whiskey and Coke. Ruby's little white book would tell me it's worth about eighty calories.

"That was her favorite drink too," someone behind me says.

Turning around, I see it's Ruby's brother, Chris. I had met him only once before when I gave Ruby a lift home from work. "Actually I think she was more of a vodka kind of girl," I tell him, smiling in the sympathetic way you smile at anyone who's just buried his only sister. "What are you drinking?"

He nods at the glass I'm holding. "Make me one of those."

I turn around and make his drink. I can feel him looking at the back of my head, and I'm too afraid to turn around. I hand him the glass.

After draining it in one quick gulp, he places it on the kitchen worktop. He stares at the empty glass, at the ice cubes, for what seems like a long time before he looks at me. "Did you know about Ruby?"

I take a sip of my drink. "What do you mean?"

"Did you, you know, know about Ruby? I think you know what I'm talking about."

And I could say: yes, I knew about Ruby running off to the toilet after wolfing down a plateful of cheeseburgers and chips followed by a big slice of cheesecake slathered with pouring cream, all washed down with two pints of diet cola.

And: yes, I noticed the sickly tangy smell on her fingers and breath.

And: the blue cheese stench clouding up the toilet after she'd used it.

And: the pink raw calluses on the knuckles of her right hand, how her top teeth scraped and grazed the skin there. And those teeth stained and spoiled by splashes of stomach acid, hydrochloric acid strong enough to burn the skin off the palm of your hand.

Her chipmunk cheeks all puffed up, the glands in her neck swollen and sore.

The fluffy flecks of half-digested food that ricocheted against the side of the toilet basin and clung to her brittle hair and shirt collar.

Her eyes, bloodshot and cracked with red lines.

Chris is still looking at me, waiting for an answer.

I swallow a mouthful of my drink and try hard to make it look like that's the only reason I'm swallowing. "What difference would it make now?"

He keeps staring at me, and the second hand on the wall clock behind him tick-tocks full circle before he looks away, takes an unopened bottle of red wine and a wineglass from the table, and walks out of the kitchen.

I scoop some more ice into my glass and half fill it with whiskey, forgoing the Coke, my hand trembling on the glass. Turning to leave the room, I notice a gold Zippo lighter tucked into the gap between the microwave and wall, the letter *R* inscribed on one side. I pick it up, leave the kitchen, and head out the front door.

Parked in the driveway, Ruby's car. I move over to it and light a cigarette with the gold lighter, snapping the lid shut with a flick of my wrist. Someone's cleaned the car inside and out, but when I lean in to look at my reflection in the back passenger window, there are still three small white gummy marks where something else used to be.

GASOLINE

Fred Venturini

I was leafing through some random book with my scars
facing the shelves where reference met foreign languages.
I liked the bookstore more than books; it was the kind of
place where other people tried to be invisible out of courtesy.

My scar hiding wasn't intentional. In restaurants, I'd
always get a booth and sit scars in, pointing them away
from the waitress and the rest of the patrons. While sitting
on a bus, at a desk, on a bench, or even my sofa at home, I
would prop my scarred side in my hand, looking contem-
plative while hiding them. My scars never itched—they
were in fact numb—but I'd find myself lightly scratching
them in public places, my busy hand shielding the confluence of jagged pink lines from the eyes of strangers. I
never walked out of my apartment planning these little
strategies, but I found myself doing them anyway. They
weren't habits, just well-practiced methods from my
younger days when I learned, through trial and error, how
to hide them.

"Larry?" a voice said, jarring me from the book I was
holding but not yet browsing. "Larry Benton?" The guy
was balding and heavyset and wore a white dress shirt with
yellowed armpits, his face shining with sweat. "I guess you
don't remember me."

"I'm sorry," I said, shaking my head, smiling as if I should remember.

He tried to get a gander at the scars, see what the years had done to them. But at least he was somewhat polite about it. Children, if they saw, were far worse. They called me all sorts of things, smiling, thinking it was cool that Franken- stein or Freddy Krueger was standing right in front of them.

"We knew each other when we were younger," he said, not offended that I didn't remember, probably chalking up my spotty memory to childhood trauma. "How have you been?"

"Good as can be," I said.

"It's weird, but I thought about you a lot in my line of work," he continued. "Especially recently."

"What is it that you do?" More kindling for small talk I didn't want, but I was curious.

"I'm not sure if it's something you're comfortable talking about, but I worked for BOP—that's Bureau of Prisons—up by Marion, and, well—"

"Eric," I said. Hadn't uttered the name in twenty years. "I'm sure you heard then."

"No." I expected him to tell me that Eric was in prison yet again. Maybe this time for good.

"He hanged himself in his cell last month," he said as if he were reporting something as mundane as the weather. "It was on my watch, of all the coincidences. He didn't even leave a note."

I shrugged. Probably wasn't the trumpets and fireworks he was expecting.

"I know it's weird to bring it up, but every day I saw him, I would think of what happened. With you, you know?"

"I understand," I said.

"I probably shouldn't have bothered you."

"No, it's fine. But since we're talking about it, do you remember if he said anything? About what happened?"

His face tightened. If the guy had a time machine, he'd be rewinding himself right the hell out of the conversation, so at least we had something in common.

"I don't want to bother you anymore, but there were conversations. Probably ones I shouldn't be recounting word for word, if you don't mind. Leave it at this—Eric Harris died without a regret in the world."

We didn't even bother lying to each other, saying it was nice to see you. There was just silence, and I flickered my gaze at my unopened book. He walked away without telling me his name.

Lying in bed that night, the thought that got me to sleep was that Douglas Ames, who graduated two years ahead of me and once called me French Fried Larry from his post in the backseat of the bus, recognized me by my good side.

Eric was thirteen when he popped open the gas can in my garage and said, "Suck up the fumes, and you'll see Jesus his fucking self."

Gas yanks your soul right out of your body. Pump on the fumes enough, and you feel your mind twisting in two. Sounds painful, but it isn't. The feeling borders on delicious, especially when you're too young to know the chemicals are wringing important things right out of your brain.

The muddy floor of the pole barn was wet. Cold patches spread through the knees of my jeans as I knelt over the can, sucking my fill, and everything inside me was light and fizzy. I'm like a balloon, hovering until my soul-head hits the ceiling. The high dissipates and the dots fade, and then you're connected with the world again. Sort of.

Huffing gasoline was just one of the creative ways Eric found to pass the time in a small town. We lived in Vernon, a footnote village on the way to the metropolis of Patoka two miles south. Patoka had six hundred folks, a bank, an IGA supermarket where the meat was always bad, and people drove their riding lawn mowers around to visit the neighbors. Vernon boasted a population of one hundred, if the white letters on the green highway sign were to be believed. Vernon, where some houses had spare-tire fences and collapsing roofs. Patched-up trailers with cars on blocks, cars that will never run again, missing limbs, put in a yard to warn against invaders. One business, a little diner joint called Joyce's, and they closed at lunchtime—they only made money from early-rising farmers passing through, and I don't remember them serving anything but biscuits, gravy, and coffee. Sometimes the place closed early when the biscuits ran out.

If you lived in Vernon, you didn't have video games. The commute to baseball practice was too far, and mothers worked. You went outside and passed the time. Dug a hole. Played with a stick. Went turtle hunting in the shit-brown ditch water, then found a turtle and wondered what the hell you were going to do with it, so you painted a number or your initials on the shell and put him back.

If all of us were out, if Glenn, Patrick, and Jerry were out, we could have even teams. We'd play football or Indian ball, maybe even our favorite, basketball, but on a saggy rim in Jerry's backyard that didn't quite make ten feet and leaned to one side. We played hoops in strips of mud where dribbling and old sneakers had worn the grass away.

In the summers, we would hike down the railroad tracks and camp and pretend packs of coyotes would kill us if we didn't keep the fire high. We played night tag, slipping down hills with grass wet from the early morning, thinking it made us cool to stay up all night.

Glenn was the oldest and would smuggle out a couple beers every once in a while, and we'd drink and grimace and act like we liked it. Jerry, ever the jokester, would piss on the dead fire every morning and proclaim that the bacon was cooking as the blackened logs hissed, a joke that never got old. But the burned piss smell feels closer than the memory of him laughing.

Eric went camping with us, but just once, during our last normal summer. We were all sitting around the fire, Jerry, Patrick, Glenn, and myself. We weren't Boy Scouts, and Patrick started the fire with a thermos of gas he'd brought with him, then we burned whatever we could find. We'd roast wieners over creosote-soaked railroad ties, the heat splitting the hot dogs down the middle, and they tasted like old smoke. We'd cook marshmallows on bent hangers until they were black and bubbling. The treetops would disappear into the dark of night, their trunks lit by the fire—crickets and loons yipping and chirping around us. Sometimes a coyote would yodel, all too close. We'd throw on another log or railroad tie, open another beer, and try not to be the first one to act scared. Glenn would tell us about the world. He was an ancient thirteen and a half and had a girlfriend, and he told us stories about where, exactly, the hole to the vagina was located (not up front but underneath, near the asshole). He went through the proper position of the hands during a kiss, which is to say, in all the soft places young hands weren't supposed to be but wanted to. He chugged a beer when I couldn't even choke down two sips in a row without gagging.

"Boys, kissing a girl's like sucking whipped cream straight from the plastic spike, all wet and sticky." He sat on a dead stump, a heavy throne only he could heft up the hill and into our campsite. His elbows dug into his knees; as he leaned over, the can of Natural Light in his hand dangerously tilted to the side.

"Kissing a girl ain't no big deal," Eric said. "Done it a bunch."

"With your skinny-ass sister," Glenn said and laughed, then drank his beer.

Eric sat on his stump, staring at his shoes, never once looking at our eyes the rest of the night. I guess he was my friend at the time. He taught me how to huff gas, how to start a fire with a magnifying glass, and how to skip rocks on shallow creek water.

Eric brought a spray paint can out of his knapsack and started shaking it while we talked. We all looked at him funny. The balls inside the can sounded like a snake rattle, and he threw the can in the fire.

No one moved. We waited for Glenn to speak on this particular action.

"You a retard or something?" he said. "You want to get burned up?"

Still, no one moved. Jerry, a skinny kid who looked like Howdy Doody, just sat there roasting marshmallows over the hissing can, which was blowing quite a stream of flame out the top where the spray knob had melted.

"Is that going to blow?" Patrick asked. It was one of his more intelligent questions; he was always kind of slow.

Then the pop rattled my ears. The explosion knocked
me off my lawn chair; I swear the can whizzed by my head.
I remember Eric laughing at me, at how scared I was. The
smell of everyone's singed hair was heavy, then swept away
by a night breeze, my skin intact for now. Eric and gasoline,
Eric and fire—I should have known then.

He laughed at our fear until Glenn pushed him down,
the dust puffing up in whooshes around the impact of his
landing. "Fucking retard," Glenn said, then drew back like he
was going to punch him. Eric flinched, and Glenn dropped
his hand, as if he weren't worth it.

Eric was the only kid in Vernon who never made it all the
way into our group. We were already into sports, starting to
prefer them instead of looking for turtles. He made uneven
teams and sucked at sports anyway. He went from turtles
to looking for kittens on his own. He found a wild litter of
kittens, and he kept them in an empty hay barn where he
would hang one up by its tail and throw knives at it. One day
he invited me to come over and check out his new game, and
I did. He lanced a kitten with his first throw, as if he'd practiced long hours to show me how good he'd gotten.

Felt wrong to see a dead kitten swaying from the end of a
rope, no longer squirming or mewing, and I wanted to leave.
I wanted to throw the football around.

"Got six more runnin' around here, if you want to stay,"
he said.

I left anyway.

We kept camping out without inviting Eric, and I guess
he had enough of that. He invited me to his own campout,
right outside his trailer, a dirty white single-wide bitten by

rust that had holes in the floor and leaky faucets. Made my little house look like a mansion, so it felt good sometimes to go inside and see how he lived, to see that I was somehow better than he was.

"My mom's gone," he said, standing on my porch. He'd come over just to invite me and waited for the answer like a shy girl, his skinny hands in the pockets of his familiar, hole-filled jeans. "It'll be better than going out to the tracks. I promise."

I was bored, the other guys weren't camping that night, and he looked sad, so I said yes, but I told him, no kittens. He said he had a can of gas instead.

I didn't get out to his tent until after the chores were finished and it was dark. A one-pole tent was set up next to his trailer. No fire, no lantern. The grass was wet, looking white and silvery under the distant sodium twinkle of the street lights. I wondered if he was even inside, but I heard some muffled noises coming from the tent.

Can't really knock on a tent, so I just pulled the flap open. Eric was on top of his older sister. I couldn't tell if they had clothes on, but I saw her bare shoulders, and his face was buried in her chest. I smelled gasoline mixed with salt and sweat. She didn't struggle or scream. Her eyes, catlike and open too wide, gleamed in the dark. Figured they were huffed out and didn't even know I was there.

"Want some?" he said, knowing I was there, frozen at the tent door. I don't know if he meant the gas or to take a turn on his skinny, ugly sister, but I was passing either way.

After that, I stayed away from Eric. My other friends agreed. We camped and talked about him, comparing notes, and Glenn made the proclamation that Eric was "fucked up," that he got high on gas and grabbed his sister's ass when they played in the yard. I told him he grabbed more than his sister's ass and threw in the story about the kittens, and he was officially banished from our campouts and activities.

Glenn beat the snot out of Eric a few days later. We were out at the rock pile, where the local townships kept their road chips in huge heaps as high as the power poles. We would play king of the mountain or tag or just plain climb and fall until our sweat mixed with gravel dust to make gray war paint.

Eric tried to join us near the beginning of August, a scorching day when the rock was hot enough to feel through your sneakers. The top of the pile was flat that summer, making a platform of sorts, perfect for our king of the mountain games. We'd sent Patrick rolling to the bottom at least six times, but he kept scampering back at us. Jerry turned on me in the middle of it; "All's fair in a royal rumble," he'd said, and I rolled down so fast that I came to a stop in the high, cool grass of the ditch, laughing and itching.

Eric pulled up on his bicycle, and we stopped and watched in sick wonder as he walked to the base of the pile and started to climb.

"Stay off the pile," Glenn said from the top. "Go fuck your sister or play with your stupid kittens. Do you fuck 'em before you kill 'em?"

Eric's eyes met mine. I was perched against the side of the pile, leaning on my elbows so I didn't slide down near him, and I just kind of shrugged at him. I continued on to the top, where we all stood together, looking down at Eric.

He tried to climb up; Glenn made him eat gravel. They scuffled but Glenn overpowered him, a for-real game of king of the mountain. He threw Eric down onto the loose stones, then rubbed his face back and forth by the hair until Eric's face was skinned up like someone made him kiss a cheese grater.

"How important are those sister-fucking balls of yours?" Glenn asked, then kicked him right in the junk. Eric's breath came out in a squeaking gasp as Glenn cocked his leg slowly and punted Eric's groin one more time for good measure.

Eric rolled away from the beating, lying at the bottom, quivering, until he had enough gumption to hobble home.

He didn't wait long to retaliate.

The next day, I went to Glenn's house to hopefully start up a game of football. It was early afternoon, before the sun was fully over the broken houses in eastern Vernon. The grass all over town was brown and dormant and itched when you fell in it, sticking to sweating skin in dead little bits until you took a bath.

I never saw Glenn cry before—he was older. Tougher. His beagle, Frankie, was curled up near Glenn's old shed. The eave of the shed made a slice of shade that Frankie found, and he had his bloody snout tucked against his body.

The blood was coming from Frankie's eye sockets. Glenn stroked his fur, comforting him. I could see Frankie's rib cage pulsing, breathing fast. He was shivering and whimpering.

"What happened?" I said, kneeling next to them.

"Eric. Right?" In a town so small, it couldn't have been anyone but Eric who took out Frankie's eyes, and it looked like a knife did it. Sloppy work.

"What do we do?" he asked me. "Can he get all better?"

I shrugged.

He grabbed my shirt and screamed, "You're the smart one. You know what to do, so what the fuck do we do?"

I asked him if he still had his .22 rifle, because Frankie
either needed to be put down or he'd live blind, and we
agreed that living blind was no way to live for a dog.

He shot him right under the eave of that shed,
point-blank with his eyes closed. I helped Glenn carry
Frankie's body out to our campout place. The dog never
camped with us, but it was our favorite place, and we could
visit him often. We dug a hole with little garden shovels and
our hands until our fingernails were gritty with earth. Glenn
dug slow, crying into the hole, Frankie's body limp by the
growing pile of dirt. Eric wasn't safe on the streets anymore.
Even when school started, Glenn hunted him. The school
was in Patoka, and kindergarten tots through high school
seniors were all under the same roof, making for about two
hundred students total. The sidewalks always had tobacco
splotches on the concrete. Inside, brown rings were on the
white panels of the drop ceiling in every classroom, and they
were left that way, so when it rained teachers knew where to
put the buckets.

Glenn caught Eric on the first day of school and dragged
him into the boiler room, then flailed at his face until it was
bloody. He spit on him. Not a week later, he put him in a
figure four leg lock, the corny old wrestling move that looked
fake on television, and cranked Eric's knee so hard, he
limped all day in the hallways, cupping his throttled crotch. I
do believe Eric's crotch got kicked more than the soccer balls
at recess early that school year.

Eric was too skinny and weak to fight back when Glenn
cornered him. He didn't run. During our campouts we'd
marvel at just how much punishment Eric could take,
almost like he enjoyed it. We figured that he was taking it

out on his sister's pussy or on more animals. We laughed and choked down our bitter beers that tasted a little better every time we camped.

In September that very same year, I remember standing in the crook of my tree, climbing for climbing's sake. I remember wishing I could kiss a girl soon so that Glenn wasn't the only one, when I heard noises from my pole barn, reminding me that Eric had a key to the padlock. During our brief friendship, my pole barn had been a bit of a clubhouse, where we locked ourselves inside and huffed gasoline or made shitty birdhouses out of scrap wood. But now, Eric wasn't my friend; he was an intruder.

I noticed the lock limp against the bracket and knew it was him inside. I eased the door open and saw Eric kneeling by my mom's riding mower, sucking on a piece of garden hose. The delivery end of the hose was spitting into a plastic mixing bowl he'd brought from home. I didn't know anything about siphoning back then, but I guess he couldn't get gas anywhere else.

Eric had glassy eyes but not from the huff. Maybe sadness. He held a girl's doll, one with ratty, hay-colored hair and no clothes.

"Watch," he said, and I watched. I couldn't beat him up anyway. He was thirteen, tall and lean, and I was almost eleven. He dipped the doll's head in the gas-filled bowl. He lit a match. The doll became a two-foot torch, and Eric showed off, making glowing circles in the air as he swung her around, proud, but he couldn't control the flame that was melting her face off in pink drops. He threw the burning doll at the pole barn wall and shook his hand, like it burned him.

A single ember of her burning hair fluttered through the air, rocking slowly down like a single snowflake, landing in the gasoline, setting off a geyser of flame.

Eric kicked the bowl to keep the rising pillar of flame away from him, and I didn't duck. I just stood there, the smart one, paralyzed by the swelling, twirling ball of fire that twisted in midair, hypnotized like we all were by the spray paint can in the fire. The gas ball hit me right in the shoulder, eating the fuel of my shirt and swelling. The flames smarted with their hot tips and rooted into my right arm, shearing the flesh away with their sharp bite.

I heard Eric screaming to stop, drop, and roll. I did. I rolled until my head hit the lawn mower, and I got up, my leg still on fire, and I beat it out with my bare hands, slapping my jeans until the fire was gone.

I looked around, the smoke from my own skin making me squint. Eric was gone, and I heard the clopping of his frantic steps against the gravel outside as he ran away. I stood there, stupid me, smoking, hairless, charred, and dying, falling to my knees.

People sometimes ask me if it hurts to be on fire. The answer is no. It only hurts after you put yourself out. That pain is measured by how much nerve damage you've done. Third-degree burns, like the ones on my arm, burn to the bone. No nerves left to register any pain. But second degree? Like the ones on my neck, lip, chest, arm, elbow, and torso? Like the ones on my leg? The nerve endings are exposed. The pain explodes and dots form in your vision, but this isn't like huffing gas. You don't see Jesus.

I didn't know what to do after I put myself out, but going inside and calling my aunt and uncle seemed like a good idea; Mom was at work. They took me to the hospital, my fat uncle refusing to speed, my aunt hysterically telling him that no cop would actually keep us stopped. Clear fluid was dripping from my face and chest—burns don't bleed; they leak. I couldn't help myself and looked into the rearview mirror and saw pink and black, orange and brown, my raw skin spread back in little curls.

The doctors stuck multiple IVs inside me and cut off my clothes. The sneakers, shirt, watch, and pants all melted to my skin, torn away like Band-Aids. Sterile lights in my eyes, the shadows of grown-ups huddled over me, working me over like a pit crew. They used tweezers and other cold instruments to tear off the dead, charred pieces of skin, to remove the blisters, to make my wounds as raw and clean as possible. They jammed fingers in my ass and asked if I could feel it.

I told anyone who would listen that Eric stabs kittens, fucks his sister, huffs gas, and burned me on purpose. I told them he threw the gas on first, then tossed a lit match at me and said, "That will teach you."

I was in the hospital for three months, with every visitor, every nurse, and every doctor reminding me that the burns were not my fault.

When I went home, my friends came to see me. I heard that Eric tried to go to school, but Glenn would hunt him every day and put a vicious beating on him—only now, teachers would look the other way. Glenn told me that men with suits and clipboards visited Eric's house one day, and then Eric wasn't in school anymore. He told me that I was still a poindexter, my brain wasn't burned, and chicks dig scars, but I was growing up fast by then. I knew better.

I worked at a greasy spoon called Gary's Diner my senior
year when I was seventeen. It was a dirty place to eat and
work, but they were hiring, and it was twelve miles away in
Centralia, where they had a Walmart and two banks. The
diner smelled like the rich kids in grade school when they'd
get out of their parents' cars in the mornings with their
McDonald's sack lunches and fancy Trapper Keepers.

I worked with Glenn, who would rather work at Gary's
with me than try to find a better job, since the community
college was too tough for him to handle. In the Eric-less
years that followed, the scars faded and became a part of
me, and I started training myself to not see them. Glenn
would talk about girls as if I looked normal. And I did for
the most part. I had my ears and nose and one perfect side,
but the right part of my jaw had crooked lines from surgeries
and pocked skin from grafting, a permanent road rash of
sorts, all twisted together, hard in some places, swelling with
infected hairs since the days that puberty hit.

I was washing dishes in the back when Glenn came from
his post in the grill area. He looked suspicious and angry,
like he was swallowing pride.

"What?" I said.

"Just stay here," he said, and I knew. I tried to get past
him, and he wouldn't let me, but I looked over Glenn's
shoulder and saw Eric at the service counter. The manager
was kicking him out—don't know if he did anything to get
kicked out or if Glenn was simply grown up now and trying
to make sure there wasn't a scene by telling the manager
that Eric had to go or shit was going to hit the fan.

Eric was tall, filthy, unshaved, and looked like an ex-con,
which he was. Battery, theft, drugs—he'd become a repeat

customer for the state's version of hot meals and accommodations and all this at the age of twenty. I knew because people told me about his arrests, about the current events of Eric's existence. As if they were doing me some sort of favor. As if they were cheering me up.

Eric caught my eyes, and he was shocked. He wasn't seeking me. He just wanted a hamburger, and here we were. "He knows I didn't mean it," he screamed, words we'd both heard in our heads in the years since. "We both know what happened." Not anger but hurt. He couldn't struggle against the lie, but he, of all people, had the truth on his side. He pointed and walked past the counter, coming for me.

Glenn left me unguarded and sprinted toward Eric. Eric was much bigger and taller than Glenn, who stayed short and stout even at twenty, yet Eric still ran when he recognized him. I looked out the drive-through window, gawking, frozen again. Glenn chased him when I should have, but Eric had huge animal strides.

Seeing Eric again, feeling myself not moving, made everything inside me come open, fresh. I knew what he was when he was thirteen and always knew what he would become. We all did. But he had seen something kindred in me, and he'd wanted us to huff and stab together, to share his sister in that hot tent. I thought I severed him with that lie, but I was part of his history now, sewn into the fabric of his life. He could blame me for everything he was, and I couldn't tell him different.

Glenn couldn't keep up. He leaned over near the intersection, hands on knees, getting his breath. Drivers slowed down, staring, but they kept moving all the same. I lost sight of Eric when he turned the corner by the auto parts store, and I never saw him again.

Glenn walked back inside. "Sorry, man. He must be used to running from the cops. If I got him this time, I was going to curb stomp that fucker once and for all."

I patted him on the shoulder. "Not worth it," I said. Then I went back to my dishes.

Would Glenn have blamed me if he knew? Once, we sat on that rock pile, only with my car parked near the rocks, a five-hundred-dollar Corsica bought with money earned from washing cars. I'd just turned sixteen, and we were celebrating. The sun was down, and we were the same height as the street lights, a living piece of the town's constellation. In the dark, though, it could be sort of beautiful. From there, we could see the kind of town I live in now, the kind that puts out a huge dull bulb on the horizon—kids suffocating in the black of country nights can look and know it's out there somewhere. That light, the confluence of traffic signals, of gas stations open all night, of stores that leave their big signs on even when they're closed.

We drank a few beers, the crushed cans clinking down the side of the pile as we emptied the cooler. Glenn didn't ask anything; he just told me. "Larry, bad things happen to people, and then you wonder why and wish it were different. Don't ever wish it were different. That's the wrong way to go about the whole thing."

He could've been talking about anything or wanted me to talk about it, just one time, because I never did after I got home from the hospital.

I asked him if he remembered the time he mapped out where a girl's vagina was actually located and how Jerry

pissed in the morning fire and said he was cooking bacon.
We laughed, and I drove him home only a block down the
street. His mother left the outside light on. Glenn stood
on the dimly lit porch and slapped at his jeans, sending up
puffs of rock dust that mixed with the fluttering moths, the
yellow light and his smile, and that's how I remember him.

After the Eric chase was over, after the diner closed, the
waitresses, Julie and Janice, asked about what happened,
why the ruckus, why the chase.

Glenn stayed quiet.

I told those girls how Eric lit me on fire on purpose,
with malicious intent. The story was alive—I couldn't
stop it from coming out in one whole piece, like it was all
greased up.

They hung on every word, then told me I looked really
good, that they didn't even notice the scars.

Glenn listened, quiet, a look etched on his face like he
didn't want me to break the silence he'd leaned against so
long. We stood in a circle in the unlit parking lot, with me
the center of attention. The girls fawned, and I felt them
attracted to me because I told them such a painful story.
Julie especially, the brunette waitress a year younger than
me who had the clearest blue eyes I'd ever seen, eyes that
never looked away from mine while we talked.

Julie and I left together that night. We made out on
Jolliff Bridge Road, concealed by corn and the night; her
mouth was wet and warm, her hands clumsy. In the coming
weeks, we went to see movies, went to dinner. I met her
parents, and I could tell they were proud of her for dating
someone damaged. Her dad asked about college, said he'd
heard I was a real brain and might be valedictorian. Julie

squeezed my hand while he talked, proud. She loved to hold hands in public, loved reading, and loved books.

We'd been dating for six weeks when Glenn asked me over a grill full of cooking burgers if I'd finally done it, if I'd finally joined the club.

I had in the basement of her parents' house. Julie made it a point to kiss my scars. With her hand against my bad side, she whispered that she loved all of me, and I heard her jeans unbutton, her bra unclasp, clicking noises in the dark. I heard every tooth of her zipper part, and she asked me if I wanted her. We made love, and it wasn't what I thought it would be, but I told her I loved her all the same because I did.

I told Glenn yes, I'd joined the club.

"Sounds like your life is really turning into something," he said, as if to say his wasn't, but he still smiled.

Because of me, a little piece of him felt smart; a little piece of him was dating a girl as beautiful as Julie. I knew it, but I knew a little piece of him was poisoned because I'd never told him. I never gave him the choice to be my friend.

I loved Julie. But I was the smart one and knew what had to be done. On our six-week anniversary, I bought her a sterling silver bookmark with her name engraved on it. We made out on that basement couch, and I asked her why she loved me. She said handsome first, as if to stress it. Smart. Sweet. Genuine. She could just tell I was a good guy.

She turned the question back on me. I told her I couldn't answer because I didn't love her—the second big lie of my lifetime, a fat, noble seed that never grew the way I thought it would. I tried to kiss her good-bye, just on the cheek, but she slapped me on my numb side. I still felt it, like dental instruments prodding a cheek swollen with drugs.

I left that night and didn't come back. I ran to a city
an hour away because that's as far as a Corsica can go on
half a tank, but it was a city with a big mall and diners that
could fit three Gary's Diners in them, and I might as well
have been on the moon.

After learning Eric was dead, I picked a new bookstore
hangout, this one less commercial, without the huge kids'
section and the racks of DVDs. Less people, more dust and
dampness, with books priced by hand, blue ink on tiny,
white tags.

The first day I was there, a little girl called me a monster. She hadn't learned the value of not saying. She knew
nothing of white lies, as opposed to those black lies that
feed confrontation and embarrassment.

The girl held her mother's hand, staring at me, and I
smiled to diffuse her. She had curly brown hair, an incom-
plete set of kiddy teeth, and big old blue eyes.

We were all silent, the girl, her mother, and I, looking
at each other for the longest moment. The girl's expression had Julie's name caught in my throat, going nowhere,
lodged like a razor blade. She asked her mother if I was
a monster. The mother muttered, "Sorry," then tugged
her right out of the aisle, then right out of the store, as if
she were a misbehaving puppy. I was sure my scars were
angled toward the corner of the store, but maybe my scars
wandered out of hiding and I didn't notice—not noticing
was that trusty insulation from the truth that makes me
all grown up. But children cut right down to the bone
of it, and maybe the little girl knew a monster when she
saw one.

I looked at my book, not reading a word, not registering a picture, but feeling eyes on me again, searching. An itch built up in the flesh of my face, a real itch, the kind that feels on the verge of eruption, like a mosquito bite on a sweating, socked ankle during a game of night tag.

So I scratched, and scabs broke away when my fingernails crunched through them. I was surprised at the feeling—surprised when little spots of blood began to drip onto the book I was holding.

But no one was in the store except for the clerk. He was oblivious, jotting something down behind the counter, so I turned the pages until the bleeding stopped.

DIETARY

Brandon Tietz

On Fridays the snide remarks are almost tolerable.

(9:37 a.m.) Dr. Varden: "Tell me something, Pritchard—if I actually muster the necessary courage to reach across your face for that cruller, exactly how much danger are my fingers in?"

(1:03 p.m.) Dr. Grint: "If you keep eating those Big Montanas like you do, you're going to turn into one."

(1:55 p.m.) Nurse Fowler: "Oh, great, call the patent office. I've always wanted a three-hundred-dollar phone system that smells like curly fries."

This is exactly twenty-one days after the invitation came in the mail.

Eighteen days following the initial order that required a Spanish-to-English translation, a peso-to-dollar currency calculator—I'm beaming for the first time in years when the creepy landlord of my apartment building called. "Miss Miranda, that package came today," he drawls.

With relief cascading, I'm thinking, *Oh, Jesus, thank God, yes!* because there was no tracking number provided. No confirmation code or customer service line.

"Two Big Montanas, two large curly fries," I order, with debit card at the ready.

"It stinks re-e-e-eal funny, Miss Miranda," he says in a leery tone, sniffing. "Kinda like a bathroom."

"Actually, go ahead and tack on another Big Montana," I say, unable to control the impulse, and add with a friendly wink, "The husband might want seconds."

But the skinny waif of a girl in front of me is scrutinizing my face, my gut chub, and probably not buying it. Definitely should've gone drive-thru.

"It's all in Mexican," my landlord says. "Do you speak Mexican?"

"Yes, honey, I'll be home real soon," I say, slamming my phone shut.

(1:59 p.m.) Nurse Fowler: Well, the good news is I'll save money on the diet pools. I honestly thought you'd last four days on the Atkins deal up until Dr. Kessler ordered that French bakery into the waiting room, the fuckin' cheater.

The little RN groans. "Can't believe you let him bait you out with scones. The way I see it, you still owe me fifty bucks."

This is not a joke.

This is not my first attempt.

(2:01 p.m.) Nurse Fowler: "Just between us girls, though, I think it's good you're finally cutting out all this nonsense."

She's talking about that ridiculous popcorn diet.

Other minimalist regimes include yogurt, prunes, lettuce, and cheese cubes. Pick one food and commit. For the rest of your chunky, pathetic life.

"I now pronounce you Mr. and Mrs. Grapefruit."

These methods have a proven 97 percent rate of failure.

Nurse Fowler sweeps that black silk curtain behind an ear with her left hand, the one with the seven-karat skating rink on it, whispering sweetly, "Sometimes giving up is better than losing. Wouldn't you agree?"

The phone beeps, granting me a reprieve. "Breckenridge Medical Group—Miranda speaking."

To quote Thomas Edison: "I have not failed. I've just found 10,000 ways that won't work."

Jenny Craig, Slimfast, and Nutrisystem are merely three of them.

These methods have a proven 92 percent won't work rate. And later on at home, holding the smelly little box that cost a couple Franklins just to ship and handle—I know this won't be an issue again. I read the invitation's silver cursive on eggshell stationery for the umpteenth time:

Miss Miranda Pritchard,
As Homecoming Queen of your senior class, you are cordially invited back to your alma mater, Pleasant Hill High School, for the Royalty Court of the Decade ceremony, which will commence October 15. Dress accordingly.

Gown shopping changes over ten years. The colors shift from it's-my-first-time pink to don't-forget-me blue and please-envy-me-again green.

Just between us girls, this is how that saying "what goes around, comes around" gets put into practice. It's how you add insult to injury.

Everyone is going to want to see how fat Miranda Bitch-ard got, standing at the fifty-yard line all sparkly and spilling over the sides of her satin wrap. They'll take time off work and purchase airfare just to see Karma come full circle, but they're in for a disappointment.

This wretched little box, the one that's getting piss and dirt smells all over my hands, took nearly three days to track down on the internet, and you can't just Google search "lose weight fast" or "best crash diet" to find it. You have to use terms like *dangerous* and *illegal* and *not approved by the FDA* to even get started. Key in "100% effective viral diet," and prepackaged flu should pop right up along with Asiatic cholera.

"You will literally shit the pounds away!"

A less extreme version of this has already been tried.

In addition to turning yourself into a walking fecal factory, the ex-lax diet fails 98 percent of the time.

"This has gotta be your smelliest rebellion yet," Nurse Fowler had said, fanning her spray-tanned face, her God-given, man-improved nose cringing. "If you still smoked, I'd tell you to waddle your ass back in there and light up."

My marriage to Marlboros lasted less than a week.

A 99 percent rate of failure, just in case you're wondering. And the wet garbage smell only gets worse when I actually open the box, saturating the bedroom and hallway in moist stink as it's transported to my tiny home office desk next to the computer. The little piece of paper, tie-dyed shit shades of beige, coffee, and pine, included.

My pudgy hot dog fingers type in *no masticar* and *trager con agua* to be translated. The stinky little slip of directions warns, *¡Tener sólo una!*

Guts begin to lurch, pins and needles bursting sickly inside me as those first waves of buyer's remorse set in. I breathe heavier and tremble—until I scan the last line.

100% eficaz.

And the snide remarks are at their worst again on Monday. (9:02 a.m.) Dr. Kessler: "Geez, Pritchard, how many breakfasts did you have?"

(9:05 a.m.) Dr. Bresden: "Can I assume all the long johns are in your tummy, or did you leave one for me this time?"

Contributing to the obesity epidemic gets you teased.

Fail at being thin and torment ensues. Good bedside manner is the last thing these guys are going to waste on a loser secretary.

(9:16 a.m.) Nurse Fowler: "I'm supposed to remind you that if the castor stem or the gas mechanism goes out on your chair again—it's not coming out of petty cash this time."

She's looking for my trademark sad bastard frown but isn't getting it. The present becomes considerably easier to deal with when you know the future. But don't tell Nurse Fowler that—you'd be wasting your jelly-scented breath.

"Why are you smiling like that?" she asks, Botoxed brow on the furrow. "Are they deep-frying the Munchkins in Zoloft now?"

The happy bluebird inside me sings, "Thank you for calling Breckenridge Medical Group—Miss Miranda Pritchard speaking!"

Nurse Fowler premieres an extended eye roll my way before stomping off.

She can't see it. None of them can. My dirty little secret.

Fourteen pounds and a dress size later, Nurse Fowler is telling anyone who will listen, "She's either getting laid or planning to bomb this place—no one is that cheerful." She stomps her Vera Wang pumps like a child—like a contestant afraid of losing her crown.

I'm daydreaming *elbow-elbow, wrist-wrist. Chin out, smile and wave.*

Wave to the crowd.

Hips cocked and locked, she's pleading, "Look—just promise me if you smell rotten eggs you won't automatically assume someone broke wind."

Casing my second Whopper, I hear those pillow-soft lips say, "Because it might be plastic explosives."

I'm thinking, *Shoulders back. Look left. Look right. Center.*

"That's ammonium sulfide, you twit," Dr. Allen sneers. "And three-to-one odds says she's back on the pills. Any takers?"

Apidexin, Fenphedra, and DecaSlim. Leptovox and Lipofuze.

They all fail 93 percent of the time.

The real trick to finding your success story out of the ten thousand possible disappointments is to remove your will-power and obedience from the equation. Find the method that allows you to be the most yourself and let time do the rest.

For as long as it takes. Another month.

Another twenty-four pounds and three dress sizes later, my bare ass is rolling in crinkly paper as eleven chocolate éclairs exact their revenge on my stomach, counting one . . . two . . . four liver spots on Dr. Spicer's shaft each time it withdraws from me.

He heaves, "God, you're so small."

My gaze darts from the russet spots to teddy bear wall-paper framing a brochure rack of heart disease, prostate cancer, and low blood sugar.

I'm reading autism . . . brain tumors . . . herpes as aluminum-colored tufts bump against my pelvis again and again, the cramps in my stomach forcing a groan out of me.

Dr. Spicer's eyes go dry and wide. "Are you coming?" The Looney Tunes necktie billows and rebounds off his stomach as he plunges me harder, the pasty chicken-skin cock throbbing. "You're coming, right?"

. . . muscular dystrophy . . . mental retardation . . . Smile and wave . . . wave to the crowd.

I grunt, "Uh, sure."

But he's already turning me into his personal Twinkie as the pumps slow down to one prolonged deep thrust, the excess man-cake batter sceping out along the edges.

Dripping.

He's panting, pressing that tie against his forehead, his cheeks—the smell of coffee breath stymied by Porky Pig and Wile E. Coyote as chunks of white slap tan and taupe linoleum. The doc allows the sodden fabric to slip between his fingers, assuming aloud, "You're on birth control, right?" as the white ropes bungee jump and hang from his cock.

Dropping.

I try not to frown as another wave of cramps sweep through, and my fingers break a couple of nails when they tunnel into the sides of the examination table. Groaning again. "It was good for me too." He smiles, penguin-walking over to the counter with the pants handcuffing his ankles, pulling a few paper towels out of the tin dispenser, and wiping his rod off.

"Seriously, though." He wads up the damp paper, pitching it as my vagina continues to salivate rabid. "You are on birth control, right?"

So like a man to shoot first and ask questions later.

I'm sighing, "Breckenridge Medical Group—please hold," when my headset beeps, and Dr. Spicer finally pulls out the pad of scripts, putting pen to paper as I search for anything within arm's reach to clean myself off with.

"I'm going to tack some Levonelle on here . . . just in case," he mutters.

And finally, I snap, "I'm already on fucking birth control. Now, can you hand me a goddamn paper towel?" This fall from grace has already begun.

Not quite at goal weight, but already I'm settling back into my former horrible self, little Miss Miranda Bitch-ard: supercunt. Just like those boys so long ago, the doctors all scratch their heads, wondering how the docile secretary became such an ice queen, using the water cooler as their think tank.

(11:04 a.m.) Dr. Langley: "My money's on meth."

(11:04 a.m.) Dr. Ulmer: "Got a grand on home colonics and speed."

(11:05 a.m.) Dr. Deville: "Well, whatever she's doing—it's sure as hell having some side effects."

The rumors are only heard in sound bites, but not one of the doctors ever stops to consider how my new bestie might be encouraging this behavior. We become whom we surround ourselves with.

(1:04 p.m.) Nurse Fowler: "Let's do lunch, hooker. We've got to do damage control before your gown fitting at the boutique."

My headset beeps and I say, "Breckenridge—hold on a sec."

As partner in crime, Nurse Heather Fowler removes various bottles and containers out of a Macy's shopping bag.

Popping my third Percocet of the day, I quickly do some mental math as to how long it's going to be before another script refill has to be banged out of Dr. Richards or Camden or Lacey.

Heather catches that faraway look in my eye, suggesting, "You might want to chill out on the Percs if you plan on staying conscious, babe."

So many months and dress sizes later, D-day is right around the corner, and the cramps are at their absolute worst. This game that started out innocently, yet dangerously, has now become a systematic routine of maintenance and self-preservation. The means—although unknown to Nurse Fowler—are ferociously supported to their ends via supplements, cosmetics, and her been-there-done-that advice. It seems we've developed an accord of her living vicariously through me, as my beauty and vitality holds steadfast because of her.

With mani-pedis. Exfoliation.

High pressure tanning and deluxe hair care.

Not even recrowned yet and already the royal treatment has begun.

Heather hands me a tube and three bottles out of the Macy's bag. "We've gotta control these breakouts unless you think the pizza face look is sexy." After slamming another couple bottles on my workspace, she adds, "That was my attempt at humor, by the way."

The little green tube reads: Proactiv.

Vitamins A, B6, and C get added to the collection.

As I watch Nurse Fowler unpack, my fingertips routinely drum the wooden countertop, chipping another nail. It ricochets into the distance of office space.

"That keeps happening because your calcium and zinc levels are too low," she explains, removing another couple pill bottles, another tube of skin care. Her pointer finger draws level with my nose as she declares, "Nothing but high pulp screwdrivers for you, young lady."

If you're a beauty queen on the comeback tour, never forget how your own personal nurse is just as important as having a fashion consultant, trainer, and nutritionist. You're only as good as your corner, and it's because of Heather that I haven't fallen apart already as she finger-feeds me another legion of pills and supplements. More lotions and moisturizers.

She orders me to, "Double up on the vitamin C until your gums stop bleeding," and those get popped along with another four Excedrin. Another thiamin and niacin.

"And here's some B7 to stop the hair loss and dry skin." Nurse Fowler places another couple tablets in my clammy palm before they're chased with Diet Coke. She slides a few little expensive tubes my way, steals my soda, and uncaps an Evian for me, affectionately ordering me to, "Rinse and spit, ho-bag," but the watery emission comes out looking like pink lemonade.

Heather's Korean carved fingernail taps each tube in turn, and she lists, "Disinfectant . . . shine and gloss . . . enamel repair . . ."

But I'm shaking my bratty pretty face at her, giving the ol' pouty frown that millions of dads everywhere fall prey to when there are toys to be picked up and shelved away.

"That shit makes my gums hurt." I take the poor-me approach, but I keep forgetting how Nurse Fowler sticks kids with hypos daily. This is nothing to her.

"Your little vomiting stint did a lot of damage to your teeth," the nurse lectures, pushing the first tube that much closer to me. "I mean, seriously . . . do you even know how acidic that shit is?" she asks in a how-the-hell-can-you-not-comprehend-this? sort of tone.

Bulimia fails 92 percent of the time, but that was found out the hard way ages ago.

When the headset beeps again, my sore and bloody mouth says, "Breckenridge—hold."

"But it really, really hurts." Adding pathetically as I sneak another Perc, "Like . . . really."

Nurse Fowler dons a conniving little smirk. "The mouth, Miranda, is like the vagina of the face." She picks up the first tube and unscrews the plastic nipple cap.

My lips instinctively curl tight against sore, bloody teeth. "Now that crown could be made of platinum and diamonds, but it won't really matter in the end," she tells me, squeezing a clear pearl-sized glob onto her forefinger. It draws so close that the bouquet of polish and disinfecting agents enter my nostrils without inhale.

"Because no matter how you dress it up, no one likes a chipped, bloody vagina."

And again, my face goes all pouty and sad. For real this time.

With the blob almost kissing my shuddering lower lip, super coach and BFF Nurse Heather Fowler demands, "Now smile, bitch," before plunging the stinging digit into my mouth with a brushing motion. The gum fires hurt just enough to mute the cramps.

Then Fowler gives a hopeless sigh, finger circuiting my gums, my teeth, saying for the millionth time, "Y'know, this

would be a lot easier if you'd tell me what's up with you."
But by my frown, she can already see this is a lost cause.

Always remember how clichéd the road to skinny and
beautiful can be.

Even if you reach your goal weight, technically, you can
still fail.

"Too much of a good thing," the saying goes.

We can apply it here as the local seamstress of Pleasant
Hill rushes me to the OR of her little shop, the chiffon black
silk sliding off my bony shoulders as I stagger five Percs
deep behind her, cramps raging nonetheless. The tailor
positions my skeletal form before the wood-framed tri-fold
mirror as Operation: Resize commences with needles being
removed from the nearby tomato cushion to staple the Italian
fabric taut.

My body sways with the current of the gown that she's
pinching, those skinny bitch fingers of mine gripping the
top of the mirror for stability.

She says, "Miss, you have to hold still, or I'm going to
stick you."

This fashion emergency came to pass an hour ago in the
hotel room when my dress size had finally dipped subzero.
All that vanity fitting and custom measurement—laid waste
as the gown started to flow over my breasts and ribs and
hips. Down to the floor.

It's my own fault, though. Nurse Fowler said this might
happen.

"If you don't gain some weight the damn thing's going
to slide off in the stadium parking lot," she warned me over
lunch, pushing a Double Quarter Pounder or Wendy's Baco-
nator my way.

This diet is 100 percent effective.

"Been missing a few meals, I take it," the shopkeep comments.

A yellow band of notched tape belts what's left of my waist. I struggle to read the numbers, but it's all too blurry and my gums are bleeding again. "You wouldn't happen to have any xylene, would you?" I mumble, little flecks of blood hitting the center mirror in front of me.

"Never heard of that designer," the seamstress tells me. "Or this Versayce you're wearing."

She meant Versace.

I meant oral disinfectant.

"Well, the dress is beautiful, anyway," she remarks, stepping back and examining her work. Not the pill-drunk, gaunt-faced woman wearing it. You can almost see her trying to imagine someone else in it by the way she's squinting.

I'm assured the gown will be ready before tomorrow night, then I put on my size 00 jeans and XXS blouse, both acquired from the junior's department as that's the only place where clothes still fit.

The demographics have been broken along with all the rules, and as I wander into a little local pub looking for nothing more than a few sleep-aiding drinks before heading to the hotel, there's some comfort in the fact that no matter what happens, this will all be over soon and I can get back to being myself: fat or thin or somewhere in the middle. And the middle sounds just fine at this point.

I'll wear my crown, smile, and wave. But I'll be waving good-bye.

When I wake up, the day is unknown, and the snide remarks are like nothing I've heard before.

"How are you feeling today, Miss Pritchard?" the little bearded man in a white lab coat asks. His entire face is frowning, and his glasses magnify beady, disappointed eyes.

"Feel free to answer," he presses, resting the metallic clipboard in his lap. "The question wasn't rhetorical."

My frail, punctured hands instinctively dart to my abdomen, feeling bandages and tubes under sterile white sheets. The cramps are gone, replaced by a new skin-level pain, but my fingers can't decipher the Braille of the dressings as they smooth down my stomach and pelvis.

"We took them out," the doctor reveals, not bothering to hide the undertones of disgust in his voice, then writes something on the clipboard. He looks at me with pity, like I'm a wounded monster (and perhaps that's true). "Tell me something, Miss Pritchard—is eighty-nine pounds thin enough, or would you like to speak with our staff dietician?"

This is not a joke. This is not my first attempt.

The insults have officially reached their polar opposite. From donut-hoarding heavyweight to walking-stick freak.

Eighty-nine pounds means I've lost another five during my stay here.

"Are we not answering questions today?"

I press and circle my temples, eyes closed tight, and I can hear strands of bleached blonde snapping like brittle wheat, my eyelids pressure-cooking hot tears. "I was . . . supposed to wear the crown . . . and then wave to them," I quaver, blinking wet salt.

He sighs, telling me, "You're not going to like this." Chair legs scuff as the doctor stands. Lips pursed and brick red, he shuffles through the contents of the clipboard. He pinches a photograph and frames it in my view. "Did you not know about this?"

I'm making the pouty prissy bitch face, shaking my head.

No, no, no, I don't wanna see that.

"It was deprived of the nutrients it needed to survive. That's why it looks dried out." The doctor keeps framing the photograph in view no matter which way my head turns.

My eyes burn each time they're closed.

"You must have known there was a problem," he tells my sallow face and thinning hair, the flaky skin and empty nail beds. "Honestly, do you know how close you were to dying when we admitted you?" he asks, picture framed as close as ever but so blurry through the stinging wet.

I'm replaying the timeline of symptoms, attempting to piece together what came from which, absently shaking my head because if you know the percentages like I do, the numbers don't add up.

"Fine then. We'll move on." The doctor swivels my head. He thinks I'm rejecting him and takes out a second photograph from his clipboard. "This is what we removed," he says, again framing things within my view.

From rice grain to shoestring, I can't help but think, Oh, my, how you've grown.

"Is this what you do when all else fails?" he speaks in rhetoric.

I have not failed. I've just found another way that doesn't work.

"Do you know where this came from?" He motions to the photo, tracing its rippled body with a finger.

"Mexico," I whisper.

"Dog feces, more specifically." His following speech falls into that too-much-information category. The doctor tells me about underground dogfights and how just like a human, the closing requiem for these animals is the release of their bowels: a final golden egg. These poor animals bequeath one last product to be jarred and shipped overseas for profit by the cartels.

"They make quite a bit of money with this sideline." He frowns. "But you probably knew that, huh?"

I shut my eyes.

Smile and wave . . .

. . . wave to the—

"I mean, really—of all the things you could do to lose weight, why a tapeworm?"

Because it worked in the early 1900s and it still works now. And it took the one thing out of the equation that makes most diets fail: the person. Me, Miss Miranda Pritchard.

The doc throws a pathetic grin, saying, "You don't even want to know how we found you."

Ignorance is bliss, but he's not really sparing me.

When a former homecoming queen publicly passes out from mixing too many painkillers with alcohol, not to mention the obvious malnourishment and starvation—this is what the local press refers to as a big scoop.

"You were covered in diarrhea and tapeworm larvae," he practically gloats. Teaching me my lesson. Imparting those small-town values he holds so dear. "Birthing a bunch of parasites in a bar full of truckers and construction workers isn't exactly what I'd call glamorous."

I'm looking at him like, Huh?

"Yes, these things do reproduce if you let them sit long enough." He pinches the corners of paperwork and photos as he thumbs through them.

I see it again . . . the first picture: wax-colored mummy skin. The figure is surrounded by blood spatter and gelatin, reaching out with its tiny frail extremities. Sitting in the steel pan, it reminds me of dried-out seafood.

"But my birth control . . . the pill," I whisper.

The doctor resumes his paperwork, checking monitor levels over my head on the machines.

"It has almost a zero percent rate of failure," I state.

The doc looks up once more but with a condescending smile this time. He knows that percentages don't mean much if you're not factoring in all the variables. "And where do you think those pills were going?" He smirks at the stupid, blonde monster. "You or the parasite?"

Silence is golden when there's no right answer.

The doc glances at the clipboard, flipping a couple pages. He views me for the first time without complete disdain. "Maybe it's a dumb question to ask someone who's clearly as misguided as yourself," he says, sounding sorry for me, "but why were you carrying around all those placebos in your purse?"

Keep your friends close and your enemies closer.

Nurse Heather Fowler is more of a bitch than I thought. Back at Breckenridge Medical, she says to the doctors, "What the hell did you expect? The pot was over ten grand, and I'm in debt up to my friggin' eyeballs."

The supermodel RN stomps her feet so hard she snaps a heel, storm-limping about the office, proclaiming, "It's not like I was trying to kill her or anything."

Vitamins B and E sugar pills. Proactiv generic foot lotion. Oral disinfectant glue.

(8:33 a.m.) Dr. Arliss: "What she does to herself is her business."

(8:33 a.m.) Dr. Rhinehold: "Cheating a friendly bet is one thing, but knowingly endangering someone's life is another. You can't pretend to help people, Fowler."

(8:34 a.m.) Dr. Evans: "We're all really sorry, Miranda. We honestly didn't know."

It's not because these guys are so concerned about my weight problems that they feel responsible for this latest extreme. Each doctor is wondering which of their contemporaries was the father, if not himself: our own medical Mamma Mia! And because they'll never know, the whole group naturally feels accountable.

Nurse Heather Fowler parades toward the front doors, a middle finger held high over her shoulder, announcing to God and the whole world, "Fuck this place! You can keep the pig!" She limps and stomps away.

I call, "Hey, Fowler!"

She stops cold and pivots to face me for the last time, no longer pretty or in control—a sad, simple woman melting mascara from her simmering eyes and posed awkwardly on that broken heel.

I do the worst thing a woman in my newfound position of power can:

Elbow-elbow, wrist-wrist. Chin out, smile and wave. I wave to the bitch.

INVISIBLE GRAFFITI

Adam Skorupskas

In the basement of a vacant house on Chalmers on the east side of Detroit, lying on the floor next to a Bible, a teddy bear, and a crack pipe, she slept coma peaceful with an empty syringe dangling from the inside of her thigh.

How she got in left me puzzled—when my flashlight spotted her, it was plain to see she had no arms. One stump was under her head; the other hung over her breast. She wore a yellow sundress, covered in tiny orange flowers and held up by spaghetti straps. Judging by her features, she had to be the offspring of a black and Asian pairing. Her nostrils trembled. The circle beam of my flashlight made it seem like she had a halo. Drying on the wall behind her was a mural of a zebra eating money off the ground, with holes in it that real rats crawled out of.

Words slammed together in that gray matter between my mind and mouth. I took out my pad and pen. The first note said, *Hi, my name is Sixto (pronounced Seezto) Lomax. Detroit city foreclosed home inspector. Please excuse my lack of speech. The bank forbids trespassers, so you must vacate the premises. Want to go to the hospital?*

The corrugated skin of her nub felt reptilian. She weighed about the same as an empty suitcase. With the flashlight in my mouth, I carried her up the creaky stairs and out the front door. Rain banging on the tin roof of the porch woke her. She squirmed out of my arms and landed with a dull thud. Her sight touched my ugly Mexican face. She rolled away. I held the notebook close to her face.

She read the words and relaxed. Her gaze paused at my neck, where a scar shaped like a caterpillar went from one side to the other. The paintbrush stroke of her eyebrow raised inquisitively. "That's what I was trying to do. And the hospital is the last place I want to go."

Convulsions seized her. She slumped over and vomited a transparent golden liquid, followed by dry heaves, then collapsed on her side and panted quietly. The capillaries on her cheeks burst, creating a mask of red freckles.

Catching her wind, she said, "Fuck, still here."

My busted-up voice box could offer no reply.

"You got a gun?" When she saw me nod, she continued, "Can you please shoot me in the head? I tried to kill myself last night, but you being handicapped yourself understand that sometimes we need a little assistance."

I scribbled, *Maybe it's just a really bad come down. You can get past it. Why don't you roll with me for the day?*

A lowrider turned the corner, blaring "Ill Street Blues" by Kool G Rap.

She closed her eyes and said, "You don't understand. I can't take it here one more second. Every moment I live is agony. Please kill me. Tell them it was self-defense."

The ink level of my pen steadily decreased. *I have some hamburgers and root beer in the car. What is your name?*

"I can only eat when I'm high. And you seem like a nice guy. The kind that gets attached. So you shouldn't talk or write to me . . . My name is Luchi."

I got weed.

She took in a long breath, then slowly let it out. Luchi got to her knees, then to her feet. Dense raindrops fell. Getting the blue umbrella from my car soaked my clothes. She sighed when it shielded her head. We stepped through the overgrown walkway with our sides touching. The grass grew as high as first-story windows. It was filled with dandelions whose heads got ripped off by strong winds and floated in the air like a snowstorm in reverse.

I opened her door and slid the seat back. The floor of my '86 Corolla was littered with so much garbage, she could barely find footing. I jumped off the curb over a deep puddle, didn't make it, and soaked my socks.

Before I got my door closed, Luchi opened the glove compartment and rummaged through its contents with her toes, which moved with the dexterity of a chimp. "You got paper?"

I held a freshly torn piece of notebook paper up. *First, can you promise me at least one day?*

She grabbed the sheet with her teeth and spit it on the floor. I got the dime sack from the center console and dropped it down. She slipped off her flip-flops and origamied a perfecto Bob Marley–style baseball spliff with her toes. Better than I could have ever done with my cumbersome fingers.

You ever think of doing that trick for money?

"I don't do shit for money."

I lit us up with an old Zippo that had "Fuck Communism" carved into the side, found in a house on Courville in East English Village.

So, how should we celebrate?

"Celebrate what?"

You're alive!

She kung-fu gripped the lighter with her pinky toe and ignited the smoke I gave her.

"'Cause there ain't no nothing to celebrate. This ain't another day. Just another moment in a long line of old bad moments, tied to some miserable beginning, too bad for anybody to really know."

The engine argued but eventually kicked into gear. I buckled her safety belt. She shivered a bit when its cool fabric touched her skin. The light turned green, green as her eyes. Smoke rings leaked from her lips.

At a stop sign I unwrapped a burger and held it close to her mouth. She took two monster bites, and half of it was gone.

She said, "I'm not a nice person. I'll rob you if I get a chance. I can't even trust myself."

The open notebook rested on my lap. *Don't worry. I'm broke. I have enough money to get drunk, and that's it.*

She smiled. "Ain't you got a girl waiting for you somewhere? You're not a bad-looking guy."

I shook my head, ran a late yellow. *I'm married to my work. The inspecting thing is just for health insurance. But in my spare time I do cartoons.*

Luchi laughed, and it sounded like an opera tune chopped and scratched on haunted turntables. "You in the funny papers?"

A red light caught us. Two elderly black dudes played billiards in the window of Circa Saloon. The jukebox only played the blues.

Maybe someday. Right now I can only get published in adult magazines.

Rivers of tears streamed down her face from laughing. "That's cool. Got to get in where you fit in. I used to be an artist, too." Her voice cracked on each word. "Pretty much spent the first ten years of my life making fine etchings on the sidewalk in front of my momma's house. And just about any animal graffiti you see is me too."

Writing and driving had me swerving. *Want to help me come up with a satirical jab at society?*

A giant burgundy bubble of smoke popped.

"I don't mean to be funny. It just come out that way." We passed through the 7 Mile and Conant intersection, a particularly ravenous part of town where the traffic lights weren't even on. The Sunoco gas station was a regular chalk outline gallery.

It's easy. Just take the most tragic moments of your life, and make them as grim as you possibly can. Eventually the tragedy goes past the point of bleakness and morphs into comedy.

A squirrel ran across a telephone wire, and a murder of crows flew in oval flight patterns.

Things can be done quicker than you think. Scientists recently proved our perception of the world is nothing but a mysterious projection. Time and space don't exist. Subatomic particles can charge each other regardless of distance. Soon there will be a machine that can look clearly into what we think is the past and future. Death might not even exist. What a time to be alive!

I held the joint to her lips.

"That's just a bunch of fancy words. Don't change the fact we in this dirty ass car on this dark rock spinning with no reason. You know the only thing that scares me about death is that it won't be the end."

Exactly. What if we go to another realm? Maybe it's better than this, but it could be a lot worse.

We ended up at University Liquor on Third and Forest. An outline of a turtle covered the back of the building.

It seemed like no one held a door open for her in a long time.

She danced through the food aisle, a shoulder shimmy past the ramen noodles, a spinning jig by the cartoon characters on the cereal boxes. She twirled over to the magazine rack and pointed her nose at the porn magazines. "Which one of these has your work in it? Open it up for me."

I grabbed the last *Gent* and opened it to the funny page. Luchi rested her chin on my shoulder. The comic, a single-panel drawing of a businessman crying for help, because the escalator stopped.

Luchi laughed so hard her body bent over. I hoped the security tape wasn't erased at the end of every shift, and that moment could exist outside the falseness of memory somewhere forever. She suggested we get a large amount of cheap white wine.

A love note sprang to mind. *You have really nice posture.*

"It helps not having arms to lean on."

In line, Luchi paused for a few pulses. She said, "Did you know my cells are brand-new from the day I was born? They suicide themselves. The ones that don't cause cancer. And that when you look at Detroit from an airplane window at night, it looks like cancer. That's what people are, you know? Just a disease. The only cure is when we can all give this up. That burning monk had the right idea."

The famous photograph of the monk sitting lotus style calmly burning alive hung behind the bulletproof glass, which guarded the hard stuff.

After the purchase of the two finest jugs of wine, my wallet was empty.

Looks like the next tank of gas is going to be retrieved from the siphon hose.

Luchi had me open the bottle as soon as we got in the car. We passed boys playing basketball on milk crate hoops, girls playing double Dutch in driveways, young dudes drinking from paper bags on corners, and old men flipping dominoes on porches. Luchi took long sips from the bottle in her lap, from a straw she had to hold firmly between her teeth. Between drinks she'd chew it. "Night Moves" came on the radio.

Want to come back to my place?

"Where is that?"

I wrote, *Anywhere I want.*

"So you a homeless home inspector?"

The bank owns 30,000 houses. I can get us in any one. But lately I've been staying in my mansion off the coast. Over on Lake Shore Road. The Points. You ever been there? I got a nice view of Canada from the bedroom window. Even has a dock. But I don't have a boat.

Luchi said, "Sure, I'm down."

I took Michigan, then hopped on Jefferson and almost got hit by the Baker bus. It always seemed like a hallucination, how the broken-down houses turned into estates with finely manicured landscaping.

I parked behind Saint Paul's Church. We sat on the black hood of the car and drank. We brainstormed. Luchi took long swigs and laughed at everything.

She said, "I once saw these people fishing for bums from their balcony. They used beer cans as bait. This poor guy got himself all tangled in the string."

I lost track of things. With all the sketching, my paper was almost gone. My pen was nearly out of ink. I had to lick the end to get anything to come out of it.

The wind from the lake howled at us. We moved toward it. The clouds passed. Stars made a rare appearance. We walked to the rocky edge. The lights of the Windsor skyline beckoned. I wanted to say, I could take you across this lake into Canada. Sneak you in the trunk. They have great weed. We could get under-the-table work. We could leave our old problems behind.

We came up with a four-panel deal. The first showed a smiling man facing a firing squad. The second panel showed the general asking the man if he had any last requests. Panel three showed the man asking for a funny joke. Panel four showed the man clutching his stomach full of holes. He said, "Ha, ya got me."

At the mailbox on the end of the block, she said, "You sure you really a cartoonist? I didn't think comedians could be so sad."

At the front door, written on a Chicken Shack napkin, *When I was a kid, I thought heaven was a big mansion on the lake. I wish I knew back then I could just break in.*

Each house had the same combination: 3669. The inside of this one was clean of garbage and traces of human living. Dust covered the finely carved molding. I folded out my air mattress in the ballroom. We danced and drank the rest of the booze. She sang songs. We fell over. She landed on top and kissed me soft, then harder. Her breath smelled of vile liquor and offensive tobacco. An intoxicating aroma.

Luchi said, "I want to believe in the mercy of the world." A chill swirled around the large window we slept under. But with her wrapped in my arms and me wrapped in her legs, we felt warm enough. I tried to match my rasping breath with hers. In no time my lights went out.

The moan of a tugboat whistle pulling a barge into harbor woke me. I opened my eyes, and I realized they had been closed for a long time. The bright light of a new morning blasted my face. My head seemed to be splitting. My skin, a frozen shell. The threads of my thrift store suit came undone. A note I didn't recall writing was written on my hand. *Please don't leave. I love you.*

I rolled over and didn't see Luchi. I got up and took a piss in the winterized toilet. I looked at the front yard from the second-story bedroom window. The mailman tossed paper, and the school bus scooped up children. I checked the rest of the rooms.

On the back door in big bright green handwriting was the word *Sorry*.

I flung the door open. My dirty shoes crunched the plush grass cut evenly as carpet. I tried calling out, but my destroyed voice box sounded like a dying animal. There was no fence. A dirt path led out to a long dock. Luchi's yellow sundress was snagged on a pole at the edge, snapping in the breeze. Out on the street, cars drove by obliviously. My heart exploded. I ran, jumped. The endless tears of the lake rushed toward me. I landed foot first in the cold, cold water. The shock to my senses made me feel like a new person. Into the ferocious riptide, I would not return to the surface without her.

BIKE

Bryan Howie

At the beginning of summer, painting a dirt bike flame red suddenly became very important. My wife, Jen, said it was because flame red was the in color this year, and Tim had to have a red bike if he was going to be cool.

"A few years and he won't want to be cool," I said.

"That's fine in a few years, but he's ten," she said. "For now, he needs a red bike."

Tim picked out the paint. Using my father's old sand-blaster, I removed the old uncool color. First, I applied two coats of primer to make sure the paint stuck. Next, a base layer of white so the primer wouldn't bleed through, before putting on the red. I used spray paint and brushed in long stripes in a darker shade by hand. Then a clear coat to seal it and make it shine.

Tim couldn't ride for a week, and from the way he talked you would have thought we had cut off food and water. If he couldn't ride his bike, he couldn't do anything. Even video games and TV were only distractions from his main purpose in life: riding his bike. But we knew that when the paint was dry, he wouldn't care for biking again. Then it would just be another thing to occasionally distract him from video games and TV.

The bike looked good. It wasn't a professional job, a few drips and runs, but it didn't look like a dad-garage job.

My father used to do these things for me too. He painted out of necessity. My bike would be beautiful at the beginning of each spring and colorless by fall. We had different paint back then, and I guess Tim didn't like the mud and forest hills. A good tree, taken at the right speed, can strip the paint from your bike faster than ants strip the skin from a fried chicken leg.

The morning Tim could ride his bike again, he rushed down the stairs before the sun was fully in the sky. Jen and I were sitting at the breakfast table. I was drinking my morning pot of coffee while Jen sipped a diet milkshake drink. She always dieted even though she was thin. Maybe that's why she was thin, or maybe she felt paranoid of what she might eat later in the day.

"Dad?" Tim asked. He didn't need to finish the sentence. "Sure," I said.

"The paint might rub off for a few days, so wear some dark shorts," Jen said. "And make sure you wear your helmet."

"Helmets make me look gay," Tim said.

I nodded, but Jen told him not to say things like that because homosexuals deserved the same respect as everyone else. Tim wasn't discouraged. He fidgeted through the mini-lecture, looking to the window and the day beyond while Jen talked about human rights and the rest. Jen taught history and art at the high school, so she was keen about human suffering.

"Okay, Mom. I won't say it no more. Can I go?"

"Fine. Go ahead. Just remember to be careful," she said.

"And have fun," I said, countering her. He was a kid and needed to be a kid. Soon enough he'd be thirteen, and then the fun would be over for five years. Let a kid ride his bike.

Tim ran upstairs.

The coffee had cooled, but I never did like hot coffee. My tongue burnt too easily. Jen finished her drink and started looking through a women's magazine that proclaimed to have the answer to every question about men and sex. I thought the magazine likely full of shit, but in the morning you can only read guesses. The Sunday paper was open in front of me, a picture of the president standing next to a CEO of an oil company. The article explained the various kickbacks and contributions the president's cabinet had gotten from the big industries: oil, tobacco, guns, and the rest.

"Tell him not to hang out with that bully," my wife said.

"The president?"

"No, your son. Tell him not to hang out with the red-haired kid—Mikey Hannison. Tell him to stay away from him."

"Why?" Cold coffee bittered my tongue.

"Because he'll get Tim in trouble."

"It's summer."

"So? He doesn't need to get in trouble. That Mikey is a bully and a bad influence."

"It's the red hair. Makes people crazy," I said. Jen frowned.

"He'll be fine. He's got to learn what's right anyway. A bully is the best teacher there is."

"Tim is too small. Mikey could get him hurt. Ms. Welch said that Mikey was throwing rocks at cars on the freeway. Do you want Tim doing that?"

I picked up the paper, folded it, and set it back down. Half the president grinned up at me. "How would Welch know? She's a shut-in."

"Well, that's what she told me. And I don't want Tim doing something like that."

From behind her, Tim said, "I won't, Mom. I know better."

She turned gently to her son. "I know. But you have to be careful. You might not think something is bad while you're doing it, but you have to think about what happens after you're done having fun. People could get hurt."

"I know," he said. He was already wearing his helmet, the straps cutting into his neck. He had on an old pair of leather driving gloves with padded palms that I'd given him. He called them his good-luck gloves. "Okay, I'm going," he said, waiting for us to give him permission.

"Don't ride on the road. Stay on the shoulder, and stop if a car is coming. Let it go past before you start riding again," Jen said.

"I know," he said.

"And don't ride on sidewalks. It's rude."

"I know," he said.

"And be good," Jen said.

"I know," he said. He looked to me.

"Have fun." I winked at him.

He smiled and ran out of the room. The door slammed shut. I downed the coffee and went for a refill. The garage door whined open. Running warm water in the sink, I picked at the last of the red paint from under my fingernails. Tim took off down the road, his pedals flying faster than his legs could pump—a damn nice-looking bike.

"He'll be fine," I told Jen.

She had her face down to the magazine, but her eyes weren't moving. She just stared past the page. "He's a kid."

"A new couple moved in down the street. They have a daughter, but she's only eight. She's really cute, though. And smart. I guess she gets straight As."

"Girls always get straight As at that age. Boys get Cs; girls get As," I said.

"Mrs. Benson said the girl can do algebra. They're from Ohio or Idaho or something."

"Why'd they move here?" I poured a new cup of coffee.

"Wouldn't you?" Jen said.

"I wouldn't think so. But who knows?" I swallowed a mouthful of coffee to emphasize my point, burning the hell out of my tongue.

"Put milk in it," Jen said without looking up.

I stood against the sink, the warm sun on my back, not putting milk in my coffee. It'd cool down in time. Testing my tongue against the roof of my mouth, I felt very little sensation. But when the coffee cooled, I sipped at it. Burnt tongue taste to everything now.

"Can you see Tim still?" Jen said.

The street was barely alive. Mr. Crawler pushed his heavy old lawn mower through the dewed grass and cut the tips off, leaving most of the grass only bent. A blue station wagon with a smashed-in fender crept by. Our cat stalked to the tree in our lawn, watching the ravens that snapped dry branches and threw them at her. The cat's tail twitched as she formulated a plan for attack.

"Nope. He's long gone," I said.

"I think I'll start the garden again. It's been so long since we had fresh vegetables."

"Might be a little late in the season." I sat down in my chair. "But it'll give you something to do during the vacation."

"I still have a lot of lesson plans to do. And what would you know about gardens? You don't know," she said and turned back to her magazine.

I looked up to see her scanning the page in front of her, a makeup ad.

The next half hour passed in calm silence. Summer was here for her and Tim, but I only had a day off before I'd have to return to the shop. A town full of SUVs to work on, most of them having never touched four-wheel drive but with stereo systems that could end an FBI standoff.

The sun crawled up through the window, spotlighting the table, and I changed chairs to avoid the glare. The sounds of summer began: sprinklers, dogs, kids, Weed Eaters, and motorcycles. It was like music for the reptile brain, a tuneless drone about being alive.

When the phone rang, Jen jumped. She took a deep breath and got up and walked into the living room to answer it.

I turned an ear to the living room, trying to guess who it was. Her nosey mom, my boss, or Ms. Welch?

After a few moments of silence, I called out, "Jen? What is it?"

And then summer ended.

HEAVIER PETTING

Brien Piechos

Gentlemen, put your hands together for Diamond. Give a warm welcome for Mercedes. For Cristal. Show some appreciation for Freedom.

The club DJ introduces every girl that takes the brass pole as some big-ticket luxury item. It never fails. Strippers always choose their stage name after some object, some symbol they probably believe obtaining will signify their salvation. And who can blame them? Whether it's fantasizing about a promotion or losing that extra weight, everyone finds a way to cope with the reality that we're never rich enough, never slim enough, never quite happy or content. But we could be if we just had this one thing.

Next up, welcome Fantasy.

These girls need inspiration to encourage a believable smile. A smile that seduces you into believing you want them as desperately as they want to embody their stage name. Hearing that word, being called that object keeps them focused. Sort of like an incantation or a prayer, as if repeating it enough will make their wish come true.

Diamond will sparkle forever.

Mercedes don't cruise ghettos.

Crystal is the hallmark of taste and class. The entire world wants Freedom.

Welcome Destiny to the stage.

It's an old saying that everyone has a price, and nowadays it's a buyer's market.

My on-again-off-again girlfriend and I, we're off-again. It was an argument about getting a pet together. A dog. Bigger than the one she currently has. I said no. She says I'm afraid of commitment. That's not the problem. It's far, far worse than that. If I were a stripper, my stage name would be Selective Amnesia.

We have our issues. Everyone does. It's a constant tug-of-war. But one perk of a fickle relationship is during these off phases I can get away with almost anything guilt free. Almost anything. So I'm exploiting the opportunity to hack up this tale about her best friend without worry of ending up in the doghouse. It's been gnawing at my bones for months. And just in case we end up on-again, names have been changed to protect the guilty.

Considering the mess of this best friend's life, I'll keep with the theme and call her Redemption. Besides, what's in a name?

Actually, a lot.

Whether taken from a parent or grandparent, some saint, or even the late great Elvis, your name insists another person's dream of what you should have been. The portrait of some ancestral ideal lingers through heirloom names. Gender specific names imply all sorts of expectations. More than just a signifier used to summon, instruct, address, accuse, sometimes praise us, our names define and thereby limit us. They put us in a cage.

By definition that's what definitions do.

Rover will. Furry is. Sleepy, Dopey, and Grumpy were.

Speaking of playmates, consider how much a pet's name says about the owner's hopes and insecurities, their aspirations and fears. People name their pets after traits they wish they possessed themselves. Lucky. Butch. King. Or we name pets to stand in for everything we can't find in another human. Pet names are a confession the same way dancer names share a dream.

According to the baby name book, mine represents trustworthiness and virtue. Nice try, Mom and Dad.

By the same token, calling Redemption an eager bitch is accurate in the worst way. But Redemption wasn't always a bitch. What happened was her mom won some raffle or sweepstakes or bingo because that's the sort of mom she is. Her stripper name could be Jackpot. The payout was a trip to Vegas.

Ever heard that urban myth where a turkey ends up in the high chair and the baby in the oven? Redemption's mom makes that stoned babysitter look like Mary Poppins. Her daughter simply wasn't a priority until her mere existence was going to spoil big plans. The girl couldn't be trusted alone for a weekend let alone a week. Tickets in hand, mom realized she couldn't undo seventeen years of neglect overnight—but what about four days and three nights at the fabulous Luxor?

Now forced to deal with the inconvenience of her wild child jailbait daughter, she drew on personal experience, figured a seventeen-year-old girl with a detention record like Redemption's should learn the ropes before hanging from one. And where better to start an aspiring harlot's education than Sin City? So she toted Redemption along like luggage except she put it differently. Mom said it was making up for years of missed birthdays and gymnastics meets and all that.

They touched down with hours of desert sunshine left
and hit the Strip. Vegas wasted no time doing what Vegas
does, and mom slipped away to indulge in what Vegas offers
with an enthusiastic and friendly dancer—they're never
strippers, always dancers—leaving Redemption in the care of
a few women barely older than herself.

This scenario was so common, Redemption had taken to
calling it "funbandonment," but maybe this time her mom
was being ironic. Maybe this was one of those reverse psy-
chology scare-you-straight lessons like when sitcom fathers
catch their sitcom kids with cigarettes and force them to
smoke the entire pack—an outdated behavioral modifica-
tion technique like a smack on the snout with a rolled-up
newspaper.

Or maybe not. Maybe that's just me looking for goodness
in humanity, however misguided. But at least she didn't name
Redemption after the extra baggage she treated her like.

Redemption's mom peeled her off a few twenties and
told her to have fun before skipping away into the nether
regions of the club where her already thin guardian respon-
sibilities vanished faster than the first line off the mirror.

One of these platinum-haired Champagnes or tarted-up
Porsches or overinflated Barbies who swore to watch over
Redemption whisked her away to a place no seventeen-year-
old girl wearing matching cherry-red lipstick, heart-shaped
shades, and baby doll dress could resist. The dancer said, "My
boyfriend works part-time as a limo driver. Wanna go cruise?"

Stretched out in the backseat, mixing Redemption
another stiff vodka cranberry before she could empty the
first, and buffering each with a shot, she was even more generous with pills. "You like to party?" She set the scene with a

Nine Inch Nails CD and asked, "You wanna get fucked like an animal?"

To Redemption it was like this chatty spandex-wrapped fairy godmother had been her best friend forever—like sisters of the same litter. Like she could read Redemption's mind when Starlet or Collagen or whatever stumbled upon the young girl's price. Tripped over it, you could say, it was so low.

Vodka, check. E, check. Attention . . .

The stripper waved around a video camera and said, "You wanna be a girl gone wild?"

Check.

Frisky with booze, already posing for the lens, puckering up for all comers, Redemption flashed her perky seventeen-year-old nipples, the ones her ubercool mom signed a waiver to get pierced, and growled, "I'm savage."

Clawing the air with her French manicure and Hello Kitty decals, the stripper played along, a mewling minx in heat. With Redemption spread-eagle in the back of the limo, licking the gloss off her lips and sucking on a straw, the stripper asked if Redemption had ever considered her options besides boys.

And Redemption, being silly and sloppy, low on self-esteem and high on everything else, she shared a secret she never dared share before. And this confidante, this mind-reading gypsy pole dancer, she was so cool. She understood.

As if responding to a silent cue, the boyfriend dude swung the limo into a residential neighborhood. The wish-granting stripper pulled the magic wand out of her nostril and pointed it at various yards. At cruising speed she complimented the coat of a German shepherd barking

valiantly from behind a chain-link fence. Said how Dober-
mans and Staffordshire terriers are muscular, and muscles
are sexy.

Mute behind the wheel, Ecstasy or Fantasy or Fashion
Designer or whatever's chauffer boyfriend flexed his bicep.
The edges of the name Satan spread beneath a tattoo of a pit
bull, the letters sharpened like bared black fangs.

And Redemption, eager to need redeeming, she agreed.
This didn't weird her out at all. She'd considered this before,
all on her own.

The Doberman, maybe, she said. A pit bull would do in a
pinch. But she's into larger breeds. She thinks.

Big. Powerful, well-hung studs.

A Russian wolfhound or a mastiff.

And the stripper who renamed herself after some trinket
she believes will bring her happiness—I think her name was
Fame or Talent or Associate's Degree in Massage Therapy—
she so totally could empathize. She had this great idea. She
must have caught something special about Redemption's
scent. My on-again-off-again girlfriend owns a Chihuahua.
A female. That little cock-warmer has been our saving grace.
I'm the jealous type.

When the limo dumped Redemption off at the club, her
mom, twitching and sniffling with all things Vegas, what she
saw sobered her up faster than a defibrillator shock.

Running her fingers over the scratches trailing out from
her daughter's sleeves, the thick swollen red trio of claw
marks dug into her arm, the rips in her empire waist summer dress that somehow make girls look pregnant and preteen at the same time, mom didn't have to ask. She must've

had a similar conversation about her own future in the film industry over the mirror that didn't pan out.

She gripped the raised gashes of her daughter's shoulders and shook. "What. Have. You. Done?"

Eyes twinkling like coins in sockets made into muddy wishing wells by smeared mascara, Redemption, disoriented and sleepy with her hair all feral, more than a little drunk and twice as worn-out, she looked away and said, "Nothing." She said, "Chill out. We went to watch some guys skate." She told her mom, "Calm down, Suzy." She said, "I'm just tired." She tried to shake free but was too weak and gave up. "Jeez. Maybe I'm a tiny bit stoned. So what?"

She wiped a tissue beneath her mom's running nose and said, "Like you have room to talk."

Right about now her mom's stripper name might be

Responsibility or Alcoholics Anonymous. Maybe even Birth Control. Her eyes were big as exit wounds and just as wet. She repeated herself over and over. She wasn't saying the words to her daughter anymore. She was admonishing her own reflection in those camera-hungry, mascara-splattered eyes. Eyes that echoed like a mirror.

What have you done?

And when they finally broke from this definitive mother-daughter moment, Redemption and her mom were alone.

The high-buck strippers, gone. The chauffeur who moonlights as a filmmaker, gone. The vodka, gone. The blow, long gone. Only this mother and daughter, their crimes, four days and three nights at the Luxor, and an angry waitress holding a hefty tab.

This is so illegal that even in Vegas it's illegal.

Some people simply shouldn't breed. They don't have the dedication it takes to train a child, and their kids always end up doing as they do instead of as they say. Chewing up the furniture and running wild, so to speak. Their poor pedigree holds them back no matter what. Redemption was left to learn from example.

And just because this is always the first thing people ask, yes, she's extremely cute. Feature-stripper-in-training-with-pigtails cute. Most-likely-to-be-found-dead-in-a-hotel-bathtub cute. That big-eyed, pouty-lipped innocent cute you can talk into anything.

And that maxim about things that happen in Vegas staying in Vegas, like everything else in Vegas, it's a sham.

Redemption's Vegas secret followed her home, and she kept it. Before this story usually begins, when she tells it herself, this Redemption bitch uses vodka to purge her soul the way a criminal might try to burn evidence by pouring more gas on a pyre. Feed her any 80 proof bottle, and it'll howl all night long. When the flame gets too hot to handle she belches it out like every open ear is attached to her personal clergy. Reliable as menses and just as easy to see coming, she seeks solace in the pack. Her cuteness lures them in, and Redemption cuddles up to tell the tale. But she isn't sorry. She isn't ashamed. No one consoles her. No one attempts to understand. No one says much of anything.

No one ever really forgets about Redemption. But they certainly act that way.

Her confessions stick to your soul like tar. Even after the goop dries and cracks away, a dark stain lingers.

I don't know if she's trying to own the pain or seek out a kindred spirit or what.

And because this is always the second thing people ask, yeah, I threw her a bone. She's my on-again-off-again girlfriend's alcoholic best friend, so accidents happen. It only happened that once. And I was really, really drunk. Hank Williams Sr. drunk. Homer Simpson drunk.

But keep that to yourself. It's our secret.

And just because this is the third thing people always ask, yes, before Vegas. Although she often makes me wonder if size really does matter.

When Redemption tells this story there are more details I won't get into. Words I can't say with a straight face like *spurt* and *orgasm* and *thrust*. Words like *pain* and *hot, sticky mess*. When she tells it her way, with all the graphic finery and ruined upholstery and crawling and bucket of generic lube, half the room empties before the part where she straps on the spiked collar.

The folks who leave have heard it before, and once is one time too many. The rest, like you, well, that saying, "Once bitten, twice shy," will make a whole new kind of sense in a moment.

For the virgin listeners, when they're thoroughly shaking their heads and looking in every direction but Redemption's, holding their lover's hand tighter than tight, their buzzes not merely worn off but blown clear away, like a tornado scalping a trailer park, Redemption says she's worried the FBI are going to show up at her door one day. That the driver dude got busted or something, she thinks. Because they promised to send her a copy of the video but never did, the liars.

And that's the real issue, she says, being used. Being cheated like that. Otherwise she's really excited about

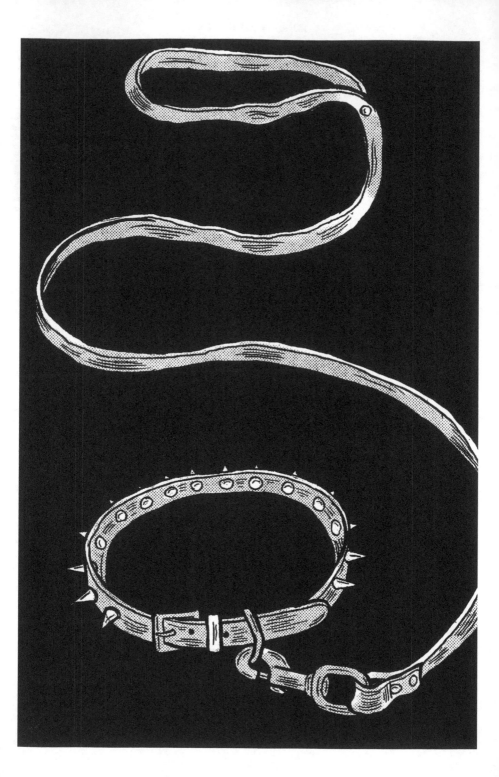

graduating from aesthetician school and getting her own place. Something with a big yard. Because she's been keeping her eyes open.

This is so twisted that even at the Freaky Fetish Fest, doms and subs were seeing eye to eye on how twisted it was.

Even at the Rubber Ball, the veteran dominatrix who struts around in the gestapo cap appeared a little upset.

The fat accountant who thinks it's "wicked cool" to show up in nothing but strands of electrical tape, even his pasty ass thought Redemption was in bad taste.

The last time I heard her tell it there was this torso guy listening in—just a head and rib cage. He'll lie on the floor at goth/industrial nightclubs and pay gals to walk across his chest in stiletto heels. Pinned down, he looked up Redemption's skirt and said, "Now that's twisted."

With each telling of her story, she drops a new detail. The second time it was the breed. After that, his name. Once she described the finer points of a certain position. Complained about the harshness of the lighting. With each rendition, the scene sharpens into focus. With every close-up, the room gets emptier.

After a few public showings with less than positive reviews, Redemption armed herself with a preemptive defense. Rationalizing it as a natural relationship. Citing historical precedent way back to ancient Greece. She uses the word *love*. The same word she used to describe how she felt about volunteering at the humane society and Dark Eyes vodka.

Redemption's current boyfriend and I don't hang out. I'm not what you'd call husky, but no way can I squeeze past the elephant in our room. There isn't enough cotton in the Deep South to weave a skirt big enough for this issue. But our girlfriends are best friends. I can't exactly avoid the guy.

At one party we ditched out to avoid the looks while Redemption told her tale. He told me that contrary to popular belief the human egg can actually be impregnated by canine sperm. The female miscarries before the abomination gets too far along. It doesn't look like anything, he said, no tiny fingers or toes or nothing. Nothing a Republican law would force you to keep. You won't have to raise some Anubis Minotaur thing in your attic. Just flush a squashed tomato. Claims he did some research on the internet. He said, considering . . . who wouldn't?

Around the bars they call Redemption lots of names, behind her back mostly, and Redemption isn't one of them. None of her nicknames are accurate. None of them are specific the way kids earn titles like Stinky or Fatso or Dicknose or Dogfucker. People in the know use common pejoratives in place of what we're all really thinking. To create a cushion of distance, they call her sicko, pervert, slut. That tramp. They flat-out refuse to use their imagination.

No one uses the B word.

You can tell a lot about people by the names they call others when they aren't around.

After her relationships inevitably fizzle, you don't see those guys bonding over the shared experience. They don't high-five and pound beers on the rebound while comparing fish stories. They sit at opposite sides of the bar. At parties they stand with their backs to one another at all times.

When she's all buckled knees wobbling on heels with one palm planted to the wall and the other swinging a big plastic bottle, starting in with, "So, tell me if you think this is really perverted . . . ," those guys dip out first.

The last party she bid everyone gather round, the buddy I brought along got too drunk and freaked out to let himself ignore the telltale signs. He'd recently moved in with his long-time girl. They'd always wanted a puppy. To test the long-term potential of the relationship before taking the next step, he said. A trial run. But after hearing Redemption's confession, he's having second thoughts.

You see, he found some stuff on her computer.

Knowing the internet is a jungle of pitfalls and vipers coiled to strike, he reasoned it away as spyware. A web surfing accident. Browsing history isn't conclusive the way your email address is. But the things Redemption said that night got him thinking maybe beastfuck.com showing up in the search history wasn't the side effect of innocent browsing.

Maybe that essay in the cache about safely training your pet for coital partnership he was compelled to read wasn't the byproduct of clicking a pop-up ad promising 50 percent off Vera Wang pumps.

On the ride home he explained how once the dog is all the way in, there's no returning him. Dogs have this joint, this knot in the middle of their dick that swells up as big and hard as an onion and traps the pair together until he's finished bucking and shooting his load.

He told me about cases where women have gotten trapped with the dog inside them. That knot thing engorged with blood, swollen to the size of a softball, wouldn't come out. And someone had to call 911.

Dogs don't tire out like us, he said. Their money shot isn't a few spurts before it's time to roll over and think about a sandwich. You might say they're the Warren Buffett of money shots. Imagine a fire hose of glue. They cum and cum and cum. It can surge for like forty-five minutes while the female is attached, locked in with him pounding away. And when Rex or Rocky or Bruiser finally deflates and pulls out, this bucketload of mess gushes, and I don't want to repeat how he described that.

My friend was like, Imagine bringing your friends over after the bars for a few beers to find your wife mounted on all fours, manicure shredded by the new linoleum, demanding five, ten, maybe twenty more minutes, who knows, 'cause Buddy isn't quite satisfied.

It's funny, right? Right?

Going green around the gills, he complained the keg beer wasn't sitting so well, and on this message board he discovered while snooping, the women posters confessed that semen is integral to their overall sexual experience. That their dogs fill them in a way no man has ever come close. And etymology aside, they really do have a bone in their boner.

This is so taboo that even the internet doesn't have a slang term for it.

They're called zoophiles, technically speaking. If you want to be politically correct about it. They call their lifestyle "animal husbandry" instead of, you know, the B word.

They argue the qualifying difference is consent. Judge all you want, but you can't prove the animal isn't having a blast. Head out the passenger side window to barf, my buddy said these "zoosexual" videos have popped up all over the place. People are going to prison. The dogs are up for adoption, but they're tough to retrain once they get a taste of the good life, and no one wants them. Well, no family. Especially not with daughters. He said go ahead, Google it. Some old queen was sodomized to death by a horse, and you can check it out if you're so inclined. Gives a new meaning to the term *horsepower.*

Google it. Do it.

I dare you.

And, yeah, this is so illegal that even on the internet it's illegal.

Except for in Denmark. And Hungary.

Brazil is a major exporter of these films. In the Netherlands there's a Great Dane named Hector that's considered a legit star. For a small fee you can meet Hector.

And to be fair, we all know anything goes in the Land of the Rising Sun.

"There are pay websites with videos," he said. "Hundreds of them."

Not just dogs and horses but goats too. And, yeah, your obligatory Tijuana donkeys. And some of these women are hot. You'd take them home without a second thought. If you didn't know any better.

Women with loyalty issues who equate love to dependence. It makes sense in a twisted man's best friend sort of way.

With his girlfriend asleep in the other room, my friend was free to roam the wild of the World Wide Web. One thing led to another, and he ended up browsing an info site listing average penis lengths separated by breed. The forum had hundreds of personal experience testimonials. Explicit directions. Positions, tips, pragmatic preemptive measures you wouldn't think of until the damage is done, like socks over paws.

Along with asserting articulate defenses against abuse allegations, the website's author claims a dog's cock is three times cleaner than a human male's. Her veterinarian said so. She alludes to psychological studies that report 80 percent of women have fantasies about being taken by an animal. The source is not attributed. And since it's no longer an analogy she never uses the term "doggy style."

She called it "making love."

When my friend's confession was interrupted by him puking out the window and down the side of my car, my on-again girlfriend's little teacup dog started going nuts in the backseat, forcing its golf ball–sized rat head through the smoking crack in the window, trying to lap up the foamy stream of vomit trailing toward the trunk.

My sometimes girlfriend brings the damn thing with her everywhere. She's even got a patent leather carrying purse with its name in rhinestones. It cost her well over a grand. The Chihuahua, not the purse.

Wiping his mouth with napkins from the glove compartment, apologizing and such, my buddy started in with details about what happens when that fist-sized knot is pushed in all the way and gets stuck in the vaginal cavity.

How zoophiles call it a "tie," and this is supposed to be the best, most intense part, he was saying, when that heart-clenching burble of a police siren announced the red and blue lights in my rearview mirror, ending the discussion.

In the backseat my on-again girlfriend got all excited, the dog yipping along as it burrowed between her legs. Looking back at the police cruiser, she said, "Ooh! He's got a Rin Tin Tin."

I said, "Face forward and shut up."

In my rearview the hood of the squad said K-9.

My friend said, "Chew on a penny. I heard that fucks up the Breathalyzer. Got any peanut butter?"

"No," I said, "that's an urban myth. Some shit people tell you so you go through life believing in bullshit."

His story must have sobered my face to a point beyond speculation because the cop just poked his head in and said, "Next time he does that, pull over."

"And you"—he knocked on the back window, the little dog wagging its ass at his face, its head buried in the junction of my on-again's legs—"restrain your pet and fasten your seat belt, miss."

Knowledge can be a real curse. Short of a serious concussion or a lobotomy, you can't undo it. Many a drunk have tried. And with the internet, knowledge is now as fast and cheap as any girl who names herself after a European car. I liked it better when you couldn't be so sure. When terrifying rumors were distant enough to be a UFO at the bottom of Loch Ness. When the horribly compelling train-wreck tragedies of less fortunate people's lives were only as real as you let them be.

Just a cover of a magazine, a black-and-white photo on some late-night commercial for a charity. Now confirmation is just a mouse click away. Pedophiles and violent felons live on every block. They bag your groceries and ring up your gas.

And any private problem that's been tearing you up inside, whatever deranged deviancy you've been hiding, someone else out there shares it. You're not so weird. You're not alone. You're not sick. And because misery loves company they'll encourage you. These people on the internet message boards. Lessening their burden, diluting the potency of their agony by sharing the load through a network. Others spreading their gospel like a virus.

The administrator for the advocacy page, she posted a ten-thousand word essay on fellatio technique. A first timers FAQ. She delves into the biological minutia of the slick scum coating a dog's penis, except she calls smegma "natural secretion," and expounds on the many benefits of bathing your dog before giving him a blow job.

This is probably the last time you'll laughingly refer to a dog's pecker as "lipstick."

She explains the three stages of secretion, the final being a highly alkaline "prostate fluid." And she says not to worry; you won't become ill, so go ahead and swallow.

When priming the aspiring zoophile, she outlines the biological composition of leaking milky fluids that will stretch and droop as sticky as webs of molasses. Her essays employ the technical word for every ingredient: 20 percent water, ash, protein, lipids, potassium, sodium, calcium, magnesium, phosphorus, iron, chlorides, sulphur, amino acids, albumins, proteoses, nucleoproteins, mucin, albumoses, fat globules, thiamin, riboflavin, pantothenic acid, niacin, ascorbic acid, enzymes, and fructose. As if any degree of distancing academic jargon could make a dog's dick taste like anything else.

Put the thing in a bun and cover it in chocolate syrup with marshmallow sprinkles, but a dog dick is a dog dick.

These zoophiles, they frown upon use of the word *beast*.

As if some Pavlovian retraining could suppress the gag reflex and divorce our humanity.

As I pulled up to his apartment, my buddy asked me for advice. "Should I confront her? Or just play dead?"

All I wanted to do was crawl into bed and forget, but he wouldn't leave.

"I mean, if it's consensual," he said, "who are we to judge?"
He looked to me for justification, his hand hesitating on the
door handle, the question hanging in the air between us.

I said enough is enough, dude. Thanks but no thanks.
We breached the line of decency a long time ago. I have zero
desire to know what comes next. My stage name could be
Ignorant Bliss.

But I lied. I found the web page. Don't judge. You will too.

The B word advocate, she describes dogs as passionate,
fiery, and enthusiastic lovers. Her "relationship" with dogs
started at age nine. She "docked" with her first male that
same year.

She argues that a true animal abuser is one who doesn't
help their poor pet achieve release. She asks how you'd feel
if you couldn't jack off. If you couldn't click away on your
little keyboard to sate all your secret, shameful desires,
dirty-typing strangers safely anonymized behind your internet identity, while you think your girlfriend or wife or kids or
whoever is sound asleep in the next room.

She asks what sort of world we'd have with everyone
pent up and frustrated all the time, living a lie, unable or
unwilling to say the words that need to be said and do the
things they're naturally programmed to do. Too neutered on
pharmaceuticals or tranquilized on booze to find what they
really need.

It didn't go over well, but this is why I disconnected our
Wi-Fi.

I'm too young to ruin a good thing. Legal sex is still fun.
Right?

One night while my girlfriend is quarantined in her
triage of chocolate bonbons and *Sex and the City* reruns

suffering through the feminine curse, I might accidentally take a wrong turn at Free streaming vids of sexy Maya Hills fucked doggy style, and the next thing you know it'll require no less than a dozen Asian preteen amputees in plush costumes gorging on human fecal matter hot from the tap and stomping hamsters bloody with scuba flippers just to get me interested.

Sounds interesting, but no thanks. Not again, anyway.

I'm too old to learn any new tricks.

When my friend got out of the car, he still couldn't wrap his mind around it. Redemption had to be a victim, he said. Maybe all this shows is Redemption trying to face her demons, ready to either be burnt at the stake by the court of public opinion or exonerated and move on with her life.

I said maybe she's just starved for attention. Someone should give her a treat.

That night my sometimes girlfriend's itsy-bitsy runt-of-the-litter-worth-its-weight-in-gold Chihuahua did what it always does at bedtime—it mined under the sheets like the rodent it is, fidgeting until it found its way in, and nestled between my girlfriend's thighs. Coiled up like a perfect cartoon shit. And for the first time I wondered, How did the dog learn to do that?

My sometimes girlfriend, she's always in heat. Disturbing story or no, near arrest or no, she's a total nympho and starts caressing my neck and teasing her fingers between my legs, between her own legs, the dog there, and now isn't a good time.

I have a lot on my mind.

Like the fact that my on-again-off-again girlfriend's best friend fucked a Staffordshire terrier. And who knows what else.

And liked it.

Because Redemption shares this skeleton, I refuse to imagine the bones she's burying.

When I shrunk away and didn't touch my girl for a month, we ended up off-again. Which brings you and I up to date.

So consider this story a favor and a warning. But I don't recommend spreading this around too generously. And whatever you do, don't mention you heard it from me. There's still a chance we'll be on-again. I forgive easy. I'm loyal like that.

Tell a priest or something. Get online. Being the guy who knows the guy who fucked the girl who fucked a dog will ruin your name in the party scene. Guilty by association. Same reason kids named Adolf or Osama might have trouble making friends.

And don't think I'm passing judgment here. But I'm not condoning anything, either. I'm just an imperfect man making sense of an imperfect world.

If this were a perfect world, girls could have all the sprawling luxury sedans, angular sports cars, top-shelf booze, and sparkling rocks they think will fill the hole in their heart instead of changing their names to objects. In a perfect world, who we are would be enough. We wouldn't need to masquerade behind leather masks and net handles in search of self-actualization.

People wouldn't exploit one another, and there would be enough happiness for all. There would be a home for every puppy.

But ours isn't a perfect world.

This story, her unloved mutt, I can't care for it any longer and have left it in a box marked free.

And you can swear to anyone who'll listen—hope to die, stick a needle in your eye—that this is a true story.

Because it is.

And now it's yours.

ENGINES, O-RINGS, AND ASTRONAUTS

Jason M. Fylan

That day we passed a lot of coded notes, our plans for Freddy.

Early the next morning, Mrs. Alphabet spent the first ten minutes of class staring at his empty desk.

I didn't kill Mrs. Alphabet, but I helped. We all did.

When she snapped out of it, she said, "Okay, then. How about a nice class picture?"

We helped Mrs. Alphabet set up the automatic camera on the tripod, and she lined us all up against the chalkboard. Third guy from the left, back row, Terence, check out the expression on his face. Everyone else stands squared up straight and smiling at the camera, but T captures something else to the side, his eyes wide, mouth open. The same expression Mrs. Alphabet had a month earlier when we'd watched the space shuttle *Challenger* explode live, throwing engines, O-rings, and astronauts all over the sky and into the ocean.

Mrs. Alphabet's real name had too many consonants for a class that could barely add two plus two. Our parents didn't like her on account of her being a "camel-riding AY-RAB" from "out there in the holy shit-hole desert."

But she was a place to dump us, their high-maintenance SpEd class kids, while they used their eight unburdened hours make-believing lives without special children.

The red fiery burst of shotgun found Mrs. Alphabet first, like a big stick of Acme cartoon dynamite blowing up inside her stomach.

Every year there's a candlelight vigil, and the few survivors, we all say we'll be there. This year it's just me and Terence. Afterward we meet up at the Barley House on the west side of town and take the booth way in the back, away from the bohemian hipster jack offs and college kids. We get a couple pitchers, joke around, look at photos of each other's kids, high-five about all the girls we've fucked, and part ways. I won't see or speak to T until the same time next year, if even.

T's mom died right before his seventh birthday, and by the sixth grade the poor kid broke down if you looked at him sideways. On Freddy's first day, T tried playing ambassador and introduced himself to Freddy, who responded by calling him a "retarded, penis-haired, chocolate faggot-faced nigger." Little Terence Moore, in his tan corduroys and striped JCPenney dress shirt, burst into tears, stomped his feet, ran over to a tree, and sat down with his face in his hands, little huffy shoulders bouncing up and down.

That same recess, Freddy pulled down Monica Jordan's pants, spat in Erica Veneer's hair, broke Sam Gifford's Pac-Man watch, and shoved this pathetic fat kid Herman Wesley face-first down some stairs.

As we walked inside, Mrs. Alphabet passed us in the hall, marching Freddy down to Principal Gathers's office. Freddy flailed around, kicked, screamed, shot milky green snot bubbles out his nostrils as foam fell from his mouth and a dark stain ran down his left pant leg.

After they went by, Colin Sterling said he had a feeling the new kid's soul was darker than the bottom of an empty pop can, and he pretty much nailed it.

When Mrs. Alphabet came back without Freddy, she told us we had to be nice to him on account of his hard, sad life and his daddy dying a couple of months back.

"Children," she said, "what do we do for people who are sad?"

We all responded in unison, ever the obedient cult: "Happy words make happy hearts!"

A little later, Freddy returned, sat down, and dropped his head on his desk.

Right before the buses came, when everyone was trying to make nice with him, Freddy told us he'd scored high on a "QI" test at his old school and didn't belong in a "fat, faggot, retard, spazzy SpEd class" like ours. And that him and his daddy used to shoot guns at birds and listen to Judas Priest, he set off a stink bomb at his daddy's funeral, and he'd once seen a magazine where two naked women were squeezing each other's tits and eating one another "down there."

Two days before the class photo, we'd pushed Mrs. Alphabet's love and tolerance all the way to the edge. The lines on her face creased deeply, the spaces beneath her eyes red and splotchy as she fondled a framed photo of some people standing together in the desert. After Matilda drew the shortest straw and asked her why she was sad, Mrs. Alphabet said when holy people take up arms against one another, good and bad fades, leaving only "hip-o-crits" betraying God by killing in his name.

"When you do something very bad," she said, "then the Devil made you do it."

She'd told us twice to settle down. Normally the third strike meant her piercing, scary "Palestinian scream" and deleted recess. But that day, she just got up and walked out. When she came back fifteen minutes later, everyone shut up and stopped jerking around, sat in their seats, and went back to reading. Except Freddy and me.

While Mrs. Alphabet took her walk, Freddy had tied a thin wire between our desks and told me he'd kill my mom if I said anything.

He raised his hand, and Mrs. Alphabet, her eyes dead and distant, shuffled over to him. Her foot caught the wire, whipped her to the floor, and smashed our desks together right on top of her. She sat up screaming, her dress yanked up to her chest, her hands scraped and filthy, lines of blood like black firecrackers exploding across her face. Some other teachers ran in and helped her, and we finished the day with Mrs. Adonis, the weird librarian who smelled like roses and cheese.

The next day Mrs. Alphabet hobbled in with a cane and burst out crying when she saw the flowers and get-well cards we'd left on her desk. She didn't say much but gave us the morning to paint and draw while she sat at her desk and cried.

Freddy rolled in right before lunch, swinging his Dukes of Hazzard lunch box and whistling the theme song from the show.

At recess we made war.

Me, Terence, Bo, Colin, Justin, and Sabrina cornered Freddy behind the monkey bars, past the wood-chip pile, just before the Big Toy. We huddled tight around him, thrusting him back into our circle as he shoved to get out.

"This is for Mrs. Alphabet," Bo said and popped Freddy in the face.

A wad of blood flew sideways out the corner of his mouth in slow motion.

Sabrina followed with an uppercut that blew Freddy off his feet. "That's for the puppy you hit with a rock."

Somehow she caught him again in midair before he hit the ground. "And that's for the second grader you kicked in the face."

Terence unloaded, all hyper and spastic and out of breath, crying his eyes out as usual, on top of Freddy, slapping the shit out of him while yelling, "I ain't no nigger, ain't no nigger, ain't no nigger. My daddy says I ain't no nigger!"

Colin and Justin used the moves they'd learned on *Saturday Night's Main Event*, throwing each other tag-team style into simultaneous flying elbows and dropped knees on Freddy's stomach and chest.

"That's for peeing on my backpack."

"And this one is for saying Jesus sucks the dick."

Freddy gagged and coughed as the wind sucked out of his lungs.

Sabrina shoved me forward. "Now you. Christ, already. Come on!"

I told Freddy to say he was sorry. "No," he yelled. "Piss off!"

I squeezed my hands into hot, tight little fists. "Say you're sorry for what you did to Mrs. Alphabet."

"No," he yelled. "Your momma fucks donkeys!"

"Beg us to forgive you."

"No," he yelled. "No! No! No! No! Your daddy fucks sheep and horses!"

"Say you're sorry for all the horrible, mean shit you do to everyone, Freddy, all the mean and horrible stuff you've done since you got here."

"No," he yelled. "Mrs. Alphabet is a sand nigger! A filthy, dirty, desert-dwelling, camel-fucking whore, and she's got the nasty pussy puke disease!"

I dropped to my knees beside him, busted him in the face, sat on his chest, and told him his mommy had been making babies with someone else and his dead, rotting daddy was six feet under getting munched on by worms and roaches. My fists were dry, swollen wrecking balls—swinging in to separate Freddy's head from his torso.

He bawled, his face breaking down further into a soaking crimson mask every time my knuckles cracked his head.

I told him his mommy and daddy hated him, and it was his fault he'd be going to live with the scary old home-less people we always saw when our bus passed Maple and Third. The ones Freddy said no one loved—not even God. The ones Freddy said ate kittens, raped little kids, and gave them AIDS. I stopped hitting Freddy when Freddy quit screaming.

Mrs. Alphabet limped over, dropped her cane, fell down next to Freddy, and dragged his still body into her arms. She glared at each of us through the stiff drapery of her black hair and said, "What did you do? What did all of you just do?"

Freddy came to, crying and bleeding all over. It smelled like he'd shit himself.

We didn't see Freddy the rest of the day—and the hammer of justice we were so goddamned afraid of never came.

The next morning we took our class picture.

And Freddy came to class twenty minutes late, his daddy's old shotgun swinging at his side. He didn't even aim, just raised his arm and threw fire around the room. In seconds we became bulletins, breaking news, headlines, sound bites, statistics, the interruption of your daytime soap just before the doctor gets the girl and the woman's life is saved at the last second by her evil twin.

Today I woke up before the sun, kissed my wife and daughter, sat in the basement, and looked at our class photo. There's this old urban legend that says the camera Mrs. Alphabet used jammed up and took three more pictures only a couple people have seen.

In the first, Mrs. Alphabet is falling backward, her guts blasting out of her and going airborne as we all stand there in the order she placed us.

In the second, Mrs. Alphabet's intestines and blood rain down on us as our expressions catch up with the action.

In the third, we're screaming as the side of Sabrina's face gets blown clean off.

I pack the photo away for another year and check my watch. It's Freddy's birthday, and someone has to lay flowers on his stone.

Mrs. Alphabet would say the Devil made me do it.

LEMMING

Terence James Eeles

In the creepy dark of a dying autumn, the tiniest light will live for miles.

And still waiting on this ghost tour to start, stealing warmth from the strangers I'm huddled with outside this pub—The 8 Lives of 9—I don't mean to offend, scare, or bore you with yet another ghost story . . .

. . . About living, about dying—or being stuck somewhere in between—but it was around Hallowe'en years ago when he first experimented doing this. Quarking about. Offing himself.

My brother—the Tremendous Dodo Head.

I lick snot water trickling at my nose and count the loose change of attendees: tonight's turnout poor compared to other ghost tours I've suffered through in other towns on other nights, stalking my sib—the Enigmatic Corner Dunce.

By a jack-o'-lantern's glow, dog walkers heel their mutts and Gore-Texed tourists wait poised with cameras. Behind them, a teenage couple—Ghoulfriend and boyFiend—hold hands, camouflaged in figure-hugging black.

I blow on a chestnut and then toss it into my mouth. Tongue folding steaming pulp, I mull over the remaining tour weirdo who belongs here even less than I do. He's fancy dressed in vertical black-and-white stripes, face ashtray dirty, his eye sockets charcoal-painted pits. Swigging from a can, peroxide hair flapping erratically in the wind, he looks like Beetlejuice on parole. Or Kurt Cobain's zombie corpse.

Popping another hot chestnut into my mouth—tasting if they taste right—I watch the amber haze behind Beetle-Kurt stretch out into the darkness. Stray beyond the jack-o'-lantern's grin, and you'll trek across rural Echmond all night, squinting in the dark with a headache behind your eyes and arms heavy from feeling out into nothing in front of you.

As kids, my brother couldn't carve a pumpkin to save his life. Like that half term he tried sabotaging mine but instead put a kitchen knife through his hand—somehow missing the artery on the finger he'd flip me off with. He just patiently observed his blood tear into his own gutted pumpkin, like candle wax beading down an old-school candelabra.

"Good All Hallows' Eve."

We turn to face the pub's entrance. There, a thick door closes behind the silhouette of a heavily cloaked shadow that lifts the nearby jack-o'-lantern by its rope handle.

"All alive and well, I pray," he booms, lifting the lantern higher with fingerless gloves, his coat's brushed leather shoulder flaps tolling level with his chest.

"I am your guide for this evening." He carefully cherishes each word like the next might be his last: this, a lifetime of community theater wasted. "Jack"—his am-dram histrionics boast—"the Day-Tripper."

He then checks his notepad against the lantern light, and his long, gray sideburns tint orange as he soundlessly counts off the name of each paying nobody, making sure—doubly sure—there aren't any freeloaders, any fare dodgers, any pikey hangers-on . . .

"Polterguests," he says and rallies a chorus of polite laughter from the tour group.

I roll my eyes into their warm sockets.

"Get on with it," says the striped loner BeetleKurt, slurring a stink of rotten toffee apples into his cider can. "I've somewhere to be . . ."

Tonguing my gums, I think, Me too—wherever the hell my brother, the Grand Bogey Eater, might be, if I ever find him—and I pop another chestnut.

"Somewhere, yeah," a voice snipes—the gothy Ghoul-friend of the teen couple—"like an AA meeting . . ."

Eyes rolling again, I instead turn to Echmond's village green. There—the trees wasted to just bones of bare bark with leaves dead at their feet, protected by some blah, blah Woodland Trust—is one tree in particular.

The lowest branch an outstretched arm on tippy-toes too high, shaped like an inverted *L*, it stands taller than the rest. Its branches are the color of wooden stocks and spread out like scabbed-up veins.

Despite tonight being Hallowe'en, this tree is the reason why mini fairies, goblins, and witches aren't running the streets and door-knocking for treats. Flower bouquets pile up against the trunk; Do Not Cross police tape cordons off the area, the material sighing like a lazily tied birthday present—the kind of gift my brother probably would've been ungrateful for.

Another uninvited birthday party the Outstanding Eejit surely would've ruined.

"The jack-o'-lantern," the guide says, raising his voice, "is a spooky light—*ignis fatuus*, the will-o'-the-wisp—that hovers over bogs or by distance at twilight. Meaning 'night

watchman' or 'man with lantern,' it is a tale of light surviving in the dark." I stifle a yawn. This tale I know already—where the tiniest light will live for miles. Like most oral stories there are variations, but the myth goes, a traveler on his journeys called Jack—a different Jack—tricks 'n' traps the Devil, ultimately stripping him of his powers.

"To release him, Jack made the Devil vow to never take his soul." The guide puts a hand on his heart. "And so when Jack passed away many years later, he found himself stuck. Helpless, just like the Devil was before him. Too sinful to go to God's heaven and barred from the Devil's hell, he became lost in the darkness . . ."

Then the Devil mockingly threw him an ember from the fires of hell—this I know—a spark that would never burn out—blah, blah—an ember Jack put inside a carved-out turnip to use as a makeshift lantern, to lead him across purgatory.

Toward a final resting place that would never come. "'Jack of the Lantern' is the story of your unpurified sins against God." My lips mime his words verbatim. "Exempt from punishment and damnation, from forgiveness and redemption, it is the story of your soul being led across the darkness of purgatory with the Devil as your light."

This feeling, I know, is like being turned away by the worst nightclub in town.

Such a waster, you couldn't even get into hell. And for your trouble all you got was a twinkly turnip.

What. The. F%k.

"Stay close," Jack says, the camp Hammer Horror actor dying inside him. "But not too close." He fumbles inside his murder mac.

There's a chunky click, then high-pitched scribbling. Faces in the tour group knot up in confusion as the audio of cartoon chipmunks erupts from Jack's cloak.

"One moment." He whips something out—something like an airplane's black box recorder but travel size.

Bringing it close to the grinning jack-o'-lantern, Jack spanks the relic cassette player once—like the time our parents smacked my brother after he dared me to poke a power socket with a walkie-talkie aerial. Twice—for the bang that blew it from my hand, tripping the house lights, toasting the fuse box. Thrice—for the black starburst it left around the socket pips and faceplate, for the indefinite grounding he was slapped with, as well as a raw arse—and I juggle another hot chestnut on my tongue.

"Those tea lights cooking smells of pumpkin pie." Jack nods toward the residential lanes, buying himself time. "Those lights burning brightest also burn the shortest."

He says, fingers clambering all over the junk player, "It's those lights that also make the scariest pumpkins."

My brother was always the kind to burn the candle at both ends—up to no good, since time immemorial—and when Jack finally thumbs the right button, uncrittered music rings out to soundtrack his narration.

"Wow," the Ghoulfriend deadpans. Over the naff chills and mediocre thrills of scratchy organ music, she huffs, "Lame." Tourists always love a stunt, something kitsch. Even if tour intros boil your blood, strangers will follow you to the end of the strangest places if you attach a gimmick. Before rain washes away chalk outlines or tribute wreaths begin to rot at crime scenes, already queuing at your service are a cluster of leisure and tourism mercenaries, dying to help you relive the grotesque.

Even after death you can visit hot spots like the cobbled streets of Whitechapel where Jack the Ripper disembowelled prostitutes in 1888. Or the claustrophobic Pont de l'Alma tunnel where Princess Diana's chauffeur-driven Mercedes-Benz wiped out in Paris in 1997. Or outside übercool LA nightclub The Viper Room where actor and teen heartthrob River Phoenix collapsed after fatally ODing Hallowe'en morning in 1993.

Not so much exploiting death as it is catering to a niche market.

"So let us reveal tonight." Jack turns and smiles through clenched teeth, patching the veneer of his eroding performance. "And revel"—he takes tentative steps toward the dark of town, his cheap eerie music playing—"in the ghosts of Echmond . . ."

"To Echmond!" BeetleKurt, his makeup running, pupils massive like open urns, toasts up high, startling the dog walkers' mutts into barking. He sloshes cider onto the tourists flinching beside him, inviting a host of WTF stares.

The thing is, on a tourist trap of morbid fascination like a ghost walk, you have to perish first before you become interesting. Before anybody cares. That's what excursionists through hearse-tinted spectacles really long for: where someone died, how it ended, where it all went wrong—begging you to dress it with backstory, build expectation, and deliver a payoff.

To Pied Piper punters around on hokey ghost tours at Hallowe'en.

"And ghosts!" BeetleKurt toasts again, wet landing on my neck as he crumples the can in his fist, but before Jack can turn to berate—tourees barging, shunting, and kicking the heels of those in front—BeetleKurt's already gone.

Already he's walking across the village green alone. With the collar up, his outfit's vertical stripes evaporate the farther he gets from the amber of Jack's lantern.

And just before he disappears for good, his breath an ignited cloud left floating overhead, he pitches his can into the darkness.

"Weirdo," the Ghoulfriend says, unSamaritan-like, triggering a moronic chortle from the group. I roll my eyes, then pop another chestnut.

"Let us endeavor once more," says Jack, winding his routine back up to torture me—but I'm losing focus and blah, blah zoning out.

Already I'm looking around, where I am and who I'm with—but not because I'm lazy. My brother's the half-arsed one. Such a bad liar, like the time he pushed me on a park swing, double daring me to go 360 and not to worry because gravity and science will take care of me. It's because I've heard it too many times:

Death.

Eyeing the ghost tour attendees surrounding me, I consider too many kooky scenarios, too much apparatus, too many fancy names for it, like foaming canine gums . . . savage dog walker petting bite . . . hydrophobia rabies . . . blah, blah, blah . . .

The tightrope between rehearsed tour anecdote and recent town fatality blurs. The old and the new. So I forget which death was what. How I know it. And what town I'm in. Looking around the group, wishful thinking, such as

murdered boyFiend . . . jealous Ghoulfriend . . . victim pre-
cipitated police homicide . . . blah, blah, blah . . .

Muddled tour or tragedy tales, such as packed tourist
coach . . . icy midnight motorway . . . multiple-lane collision
. . . blah, blah, blah . . .

I have to block out the morbid and remind myself how
I got here. Live to the end of every ghost walk just to con
guides like Jack out of rumo about my brother, the Amazing
Dipstick—who isn't dead dead.

Not exactly.

Only in a magician's sawn-in-half-, impaled-, drowned-
assistant kinda way.

Magicians with monikers such as the Outstanding Klutz
or Magnificent Spazmo. Specialising in hocus-pocus stunts
such as conniving apostle stitch up . . . sturdy wooden cross
. . . public crucifixion . . . blah, blah, blah . . .

So switching off—a habit bullied in from tramping
through dozens of these tours in the cold, wishing winter
was warmer, so I could then at least treat this like a holiday—I follow the tour into the Echmond dark, who themselves follow Jack and his lantern's amber safety.

Blindly, like lemmings.

Before the addictive computer game and celebrated false
myth, lemmings gained a reputation for killing themselves—
ironically—because of a natural instinct to survive.

When their population reaches a certain boom point, a
crux in overcrowding, hundreds and thousands of the furry
Indiana Joneses migrate in search of food and shelter, questing in all directions and coastlines, not full of death and
suicide, but life and optimism.

Hope.

Norwegian lemmings' reproduction oscillates so violently, so severely, that every four years they expand from overpopulation and shrink to near extinction, and no one knows why.

Every four years, the Lemming Leap Year of Death.

". . . Noncustodial father . . . cliff-parked car . . . coastal drowning . . . blah, blah . . ." Jack's maybe droning on his walk, I'm not sure, still occasionally thumping his cassette player, still flogging his tragic tour theme. Leading us down residential lanes and past houses with lobotomised jack-o'-lanterns glowing beside welcome mats, the candles melting grins into grotesque gurns that flicker up onto brickwork, he's possibly boring. ". . . Cold turkey quit alcoholic . . . top-floor council flat . . . defenestration . . . blah, blah, blah . . ."

If everybody else jumped off a bridge or a cliff, would you do it too?

Or would you rather be the first lemming—the infamous martyr who started it all? Because among my bungee cord–fastened tour notes you'll find suicide's a dangerously popular pastime: the most common fatality of teenagers in the UK.

At Beachy Head, the highest sea cliff in Britain, around twenty people a year plummet to their deaths. The same figure goes for The Gap in Watsons Bay, Sydney, Australia.

Late noughties in the small town of Bridgend, Wales, twenty-five youngsters committed suicide in a little over two years, up from the annual average of three.

The majority by hanging.

And most having known each other.

All through junior school, there were party invites I got that my brother didn't. Where the birthday peep would rather cancel than invite him. It wouldn't have hurt him during high school to dress better, talk to girls, but his popularity's boomed since then. These days, the Great Anti-Socialite is quite the unsocial networker.

Now it's never him that misses the party.

". . . Bullied transvestite . . . loft-beam noose . . . asphyxia . . . blah, blah . . ." Jack might be chivvying us, his lit pumpkin leading us into dodgy cul-de-sacs and down dark alleyways. Shuffling behind like some zombie chain gang, wearing the shadows of those in front the same way those behind wear ours, he could be goading, ". . . Bedroom tax repossession . . . industrial pesticide . . . toxic poisoning . . . blah, blah, blah . . ."

Yet these suicide cliques are nothing new. They're really just the modern story of Werther—from Goethe's *The Sorrows of Young Werther*—where the failed "hero," plagued by unrequited love, commits suicide by pistol. Except his suicide became so de rigueur for other losers sucker punched by love that back then as many as two thousand young men took their lives in the exact same way.

As nonfiction. For real.

So much so that shortly after publication the book became banned—one of the first examples of copycat suicide. In what became known as the Werther effect, young men even began to dress like Goethe's "hero" out of Werther-Fieber: Werther Fever. The same trend of misery back then that we see in the Ghoulfriend's boy-Fiend imitating right now: black eyeliner, tight jeans, and high-maintenance hair, sucker punched by love until panda-eyed, maybe misunderstood, seeking attention and a way out, like Werther.

Fashion sells, but death sells more.

Even Napoleon was down with the kids. The young Bonaparte writing Goethe-style monologues during his war campaigns, *The Sorrows* tucked in the back pocket of the fashionable Werther threads of his day.

Trying to conquer Europe, looking like a girl.

". . . All-girls' school . . . body dysmorphic disorder . . . hunger apocarteresis . . . blah, blah . . ." Jack could be yadaing as buildings become sparser. Tarmac losing out to dirt track, tall grass more frequent than brick wall, he maybe badgers, ". . . Job redundancy . . . railway platform . . . train decapitation . . . blah, blah, blah . . ."

In the late 1940s America, right after a front-page suicide story was run, around fifty more people would kill themselves. Simultaneously car-crash fatalities would also spike. And unproven suicides by auto wreck became a trend in US journalism for over two decades until new codes of ethics were introduced to stop influencing incidents. This also being why self-death can't be promoted. Why your Sky+ box set doesn't have a Suicide Channel—yet. Probably. Coming soon—terminal reality television.

Then at the Golden Gate Bridge in San Francisco, USA, like clockwork, one person jumps and dies every fortnight.

At the base of Mount Fuji in the forest of Aokigahara, seventy-eight suicides were found in 2002 alone.

Throughout the rest of Japan, online and group suicide pacts have tripled since police started keeping records in 2003. I bite into another tepid, rubbery chestnut. All this info is catalogued in my tour notes—from following

my brother, the Excellent Numbskull. And the ghost walk
before tonight's, an ambulance response call away in nearby
Brichford, so far fourteen teenagers have thrown themselves
off the town's coastal pier and drowned. All because they
heard about some new urban legend, some new prank-stunt
myth. Some new adolescent choking game they thought
they could get their teenage kicks from, get away with.

A game and faux cries for help that snowballed and went
viral from one Brichford victim to the next. Each casualty
also hearing of the Fantastic Phlegm Head who did it and
somehow survived. So maybe to those kids this just seemed
like a harmless game to play. A safe way to stop being
ignored and invisible and make others pay attention.

But naïve to think this wouldn't be permanent. The consequences terminal.

My brother, always excelling at trouble as a way to win
recognition in my shadow, him and these cluster victims,
their motives aren't so different really.

But when the exit methods echo those that were used
before, the experts in my ghost walk folder of newspaper
clippings call that a copycat suicide. The Werther effect.

These copycat suicides cumulatively bumped together
with a quick knock-on effect, like a line of falling dominoes,
they call that a suicide cluster.

The same repeated cluster location, they call that a suicide hot spot—and whether it's lemmings overpopulating,
then disappearing to near extinction, or young men idolizing
Werther like Kurt Cobain before throwing themselves off
bridges, like clockwork, there are these patterns and trends
that appear and disappear.

Then pop up somewhere else.

And then pop up somewhere else again.

"... Fled war refugee ... visa refusal ... self-immolation ... blah, blah ..." Jack might be hounding while I snack on another lukewarm chestnut, leading us over hilly bumps past decaying barns and skeletal ruins. Past hedgerows spiked with thorns and nettles flickered with lantern orange, he could be irking. "... Adolescent teen angst ... safety razor blades ... exsanguination ... blah, blah, blah ..."

Trending patterns that pop up somewhere else like here in Echmond and recent as only last week: The 8 Lives of 9 pub where we met on this one-night stand gimmick of All Hallows' Eve tonight. That stocks-colored tree on the village green opposite.

The one shaped like an inverted *L*—which witness statements in the *Echmond Guardian* are calling the "hangman tree": the word game where careless wrong guesses score gallows frame pieces.

Where so far five teens—each somehow knowing the previous—have snuck under and knotted yachting rope around their throats.

Then hanged themselves from the lowermost branch. And no one knows why.

Police cordon sighing in the wind, flower bouquets stacked below, ever since Echmond DIY and haberdashery stores have put an ID restriction on buying rope, sheets, and curtains.

All summer, it's been easier for the GhoulFiends to stockpile underage booze than to buy a ball of heavy-duty string.

Yet if any of the names dedicated on the floral tributes placed beneath that tree had held on for just one more day, for just one more night—they just might've felt different in the morning.

Happier.

With the noose-thick stack of notes I've accumulated across these tours, because of my brother—the Super TombstoneLicker, I've made their loss my loss.

The thing I carry heaviest is the weight of his guilt trip.

It's because of him and the Werther effect why parents won't let their kids trick-or-treat tonight along the streets of Echmond copycat dressed as tiny devils, vampires, and warlocks. Let them chase each other as teeny ghosts, revenants, and zombies back from the dead haunting Boo instead of Boo hoo.

". . . Crippling arthritis . . . accidental painkiller overdose . . . acute renal failure . . . blah, blah . . ." Jack possibly bangs on in the near dark, traipsing along until my feet are numbed into stumps. The squelch and smell of damp sod and earth the only proof there's any ground below—ruining my trainers, staining my jeans—he maybe pesters, ". . . Inoperable bowel cancer . . . disposable BBQ . . . carbon monoxide euthanasia . . . blah, blah, blah . . ."

Even without iconic Werther threads, my brother still fancies himself a rock star these days, a Cult of Personality.

Leader of an existential popularity contest, the Incredible Plebeian thinks everyone's dying to be him—literally, because this lemming Russian roulette is now his idea of fun.

But continually pit stopping, forever day tripping, eternally chasing him as a constant tourist isn't mine. Because it's not as simple as walking into a travel agent and taking a brochure. Bad taste or not, it's illegal to promote suicide—ethics, morals, journalism codes, blah, blah, blah—so local tourist boards won't help you.

Some small towns—Brichford, Echmond—don't even have a tourist board.

But every dead-end town with a population big enough for a cluster invariably has a ghost walk. Some spooky village tour with secrets and skeletons in its community closet that nobody wants to talk about.

Apart from me—schlepping county to county, town to town, my red Sharpie ringing round clues inside local newspapers. The ink-blotting stories of shady deaths near the front, and ghost walks at the back. Ads no bigger than postage stamps, jammed beside clairvoyants and house clearances.

From bereaving families. Moving town. Trying to start again. ". . . Postnatal depression . . . electrical appliance . . . filled bath electrocution . . . blah, blah . . ." Jack perhaps nags as we pass frost-glazed fields, my ears stinging with cold, and turn—welcome'd—back into the jack-o'-lanterned veins of residential streets. My nose numb and dripping snot, pumpkins gurning with the smiles kicked out, he arguably bugs. ". . . Spurned lover . . . 12-bore shotgun . . . severe ballistic trauma . . . blah, blah, blah . . ."

Death lives longer underground. Obituaries may be filed and forgotten, but I've learned the failed-actor ghost guides placing these ads are the unsung heroes of local folklore.

Heroic Pied Pipers like Jack—my light in the dark—chronicling and regurgitating creepy facts to flesh out their tour narrative, glossing over years of wasted am-dram theater, thinking limelight and an audience—like reality television—will solve their amphitheatre of self-esteem issues.

My brother and Jack, they're maybe not so different really.

And even though my Sharpie's fading and clippings are tattering, I know I can't be that far behind.

Always a step off the pace on this suicide tourism, this damage-control duty, I frisk the ghosts of yesterday for just enough info to foil him inspiring another copycat. Triggering another cluster. Defining another hot spot that somewhere ruins another community.

Wearing silly tight jeans, the Majestic Nincompoop, looking like a girl.

And I pop another heatless chestnut.

The last I saw my brother were the gap years we took before the unis we never went to. As we sat facing each other on our old garden seesaw, he said he didn't hate me.

With his packed duffel bag waiting on the grass, he held up his hand's Hallowe'en jack-o'-lantern carving scar. The same flesh hyphen burned onto mine from melted walkie-talkie plastic.

Mirrored, like the back of our scarred heads—his double dare to me vaulting off swing sets, my triple dare to him backflipping off seesaws.

Twinned, like our February 29 leap year birthdays.

"I just wish this was mine," he said, making his raised scar a fist.

He was fed up of living in my shadow; now it's me that lives in his. If you can call it living: my days now spent gorging on humble pumpkin pie on this morbid road trip, where the ultimate day trip is dying, and the greatest five-star package is death.

All piss and vinegar, my brother used to punch kids to leave dead arms. Now it's dead bodies the Astounding Jackass leaves as he jumps ship from one cluster to the next . . .

Repeating stunts at the next location hot spot . . .
Decreeing himself the first outlier, the trailblazer—the
Exceptional Copycat . . .

It's then I—we—suddenly stutter to a halt, tripping, kicking the heels in front.

The Ghoulfriend turns around to glare. "Watch out," she
says.

We're now nearly full circle, back at The 8 Lives of 9, feet
muddied stiff and hands numbed dead. Before I can reply,
Jack interrupts me to thank everyone for coming.

My eyes roll up into their sockets when he mentions souvenirs. He then asks, "Any last requests?"

I throw my hand up—like I'm back at school and all
teacher me-me-first against my brother. Back when we were
fighting to be each other's first accident.

Overpranking to be each other's Patient Zero. On over-
kill, dying to be the first lemming.

"Yeah," I say, pointing across to that cordoned-off tree on
the village green. "What do you know about the first victim?"

In the silence the tour group scowls at me and heads
shake, like somehow I'm the bad guy.

Jack holds my gaze, his eyes narrowing, searching mine.
Tour guides always get uppity when asked about the latest
copycat, cluster, or hot spot affecting their route. My modus
operandi is to wait for Q&A at the end of walks on blah, blah
autopilot, hoping they'll trust me and not tip off the police
about my curiosity.

Looking to The 8 Lives of 9 pub—with its beaten
kitty-cat signage hanging overhead—we all know what
happened to that cat.

And Schrödinger's.

"How about for a chestnut?" I prompt, popping another cold one into my mouth, jiggling the withered paper bag at him.

Jack smiles at me like an old friend. Wanting to borrow money. "Not even for a chestnut."

I tell the epic letdown it's important. "It's about my brother. He likes starting tours." I point to his jack-o'-lantern still grinning in the dark. "Like yours."

When we were growing up, most kids guessed through the alphabet to remember my brother's name. We were a double-edged seppuku sword to our parents, our teachers— celebrating and praising present me, mourning and ignoring invisible him, sweeping any talent of his under the carpet, locking any achievement away inside a box.

Sealed, like a Copenhagen coffin.

If I've learned anything, it's that bucking a trend is impossible when everybody else is doing it.

Like Werther, to just stop copycatting.

"Competition?" Jack swaggers toward me, rubbing the lid of his black box player, his irises flickering with lantern orange. "Nonsense. I have merchandise and a foolproof gimmick."

What if this is preemptive karma? Me, my brother, two sides of the same coin. Entangled. With the sins committed in this life—the trouble caused, the pain inflicted—coming back to haunt us.

Trap us. A bizarre Brothers Grimm fairy tale acted out, jinxed or punished by God.

Jack leans in kiss close to whisper, "Purchase a souvenir, and perhaps I'll remember something."

"Something you're dying to know." I smell Jack's sinusy stink, feel his murder mac's brushed leather touch my leg, as he taps his nose in poor pantomime and winks.

Yet what if that sin, jinx, or punishment turned out
to be a talent, which was not dying? You'd probably shit a
brick—a cassette brick, playing hokey horror music.

"Something you'd kill to keep quiet." Jack hushes his
cracked lips with a finger.

"About this dear brother of yours," he trails off, waltzing
away, taking the tour group with him.

It's not until my teeth stab with ache that I realize I've
stopped chewing.

That my jaw's dropped, my mouth fallen open to Echmond's icy Hallowe'en night.

As I follow Jack over to The 8 Lives of 9's amber safety,
it's now I really pay attention to his tour.

And toss another plasticky chestnut.

To understand this talent I share with my brother,
imagine a coin tossed ten times. And with every coin toss
it always lands tails. Ten consecutive tails will take nine
hours of trying—a day bored trying to make sense of this
limbo. But with every toss, time also branches and divides
itself between two paths—an alternate outcome, lifetime,
or universe you're unaware of where the coin landed
on heads.

Because all you've ever known in life is tails—and tails
never fails.

"Buy your souvenirs!" Jack whips open his mac, the lin-
ing teeming, tinkling with amber from dozens of cassettes.
"Buy your narrated ghost tour tapes here!" he booms.

And let's just get this straight: I'm not a ghost. I don't
see dead people.

But instead of coin tossing for just nine hours, consider your whole life. Those toss outcomes instead being

dangerous games of chance, life-or-death decisions, like stabbing arteries in your hand or power socket pips.

Scenarios with fifty-fifty chances of survival—like somersaulting off seesaws or loop-the-looping from swing sets onto your skull, accidentally taking your own life as some banal illusionist—the Brilliant Nappy Face. For every incident you probably didn't survive, there'd be as many alternate lives where you improbably did.

Like branches of a tree—shaped like an inverted L—each twig an outcome dividing into a forest of scabbed-up veins. That one branch destined for tails forever, no matter how hard you try in many worlds—or the Copenhagen interpretation—to change it.

Pretty impossible but possible.

What mathematics experts with letters after their names will call probability—or improbability.

What science geniuses with more letters after their names than in them—like scary statistical witch doctors—will call quantum suicide.

And by extension—like dreaded decimal voodoo priests—quantum immortality.

So what if a Hallowe'eny thought experiment then turned out to be true, instead of a far-fetched ghost story?

What if you were destined to survive death with only a quark of maths on your side—always surviving when you least expect it, when you least accept it—all because your life is that tossed coin, forever landing tails side up?

"Relive the experience!" Jack flaunts the drama haunting his bones deeper than just am-dram theater. "In this life or the next!" he blahs, his grin matching the jack-o'-lantern's.

The Christian belief is that to take your own life is a sin against God, and for it you walk the earth eternally cursed.

Cursed and unable to die. Never dead dead—like me or my brother, resurrected Zombie Jesus, that Jack-of-the-Lantern trickster.

Maybe even Jack the Day-Tripper, and I nom another chestnut.

"Are those roast chestnuts?" the Ghoulfriend says, looking to the bag I can't feel. "Or horse chestnuts?" Horse chestnuts being the conker kind, the kind me and my brother would rap each other's knuckles with until welted purple, before we started dying.

Why? I toss another into my mouth and offer her the bag bought from a street vendor who doesn't know his suicide from his soufflé, his quantum from his quiche. I ask, "Do you want to play conkers?"

"My mum's a doctor." Her bunched cleavage heaves proud. "Horse chestnuts are poisonous. Hemolysis." The toxins that rupture and destroy red blood cells or erythrocytes. "They might kill you," she boasts.

Staring at her chest, masticating another cold chestnut, I say, "I doubt it."

My tongue probes my gums and teeth for nutty shards and pulp. Even if they are horse chestnuts, it'd be just another miracle stunt to add to mine and that Wicked Dullard 's growing list of party tricks.

"Weirdo," she huffs, dragging her boyFiend with her. I shrug.

Even though that Spectacular Bastard's up to no good, he's still my brother. How quantum quick guilt catalyses hatred, it's no wonder families become so f%ked up.

The real curse is being flesh and blood.

"Be the first to scare your family and friends to death!" booms Jack, as tourists hang on his coattails, scrambling to get their picture with him and The 8 Lives of 9. His plastic audio wares rattling like imitation ghost chains shoo them away, the dog walkers unleash their mutts across Echmond's village green, and the GhoulFiends head back toward the residential jack-o'-lanterns. What if purgatory wasn't fire in your veins and creepy endless dark but instead something equally punishing? Like a family day out or a caravan holiday away.

Chasing your brother over mediocre towns in a lame limbo of tourism—forced to live when you want to die—still chasing the Astonishing Deviant years later across village greens . . . through Woodland Trust trees . . . via quantum suicide . . . blah, blah, blah . . .

And what if you were just lucky all along? This maths-science mumbo jumbo nothing more than a miscalculated belief system. A flawed religion. Fortunate and stupid, when one day my brother's luck might run out, and I won't have to stalk the Terrific Dicksplat out of sibling rivalry . . . at Hallowe'en . . . questing for quantum immortality . . . blah, blah, bl—

It's then there's a piercing scream—sharp like a knife wound. Then barking.

Way too much barking.

I turn like everyone else to the village green, where one of the dog walkers covers her mouth in front of the hangman tree, her eyes wide and white.

Above her a deadweight hangs from the lowest scabbed branch. Fancy dressed in black-and-white stripes, peroxide hair flapping, the jacket's upturned collar hiding the slipknot.

Another tragic hero, another wannabe Werther.

Another lemming: Echmond's sixth. After Brichford—another copycat, cluster, and hot spot CV credit for my brother.

This time I don't roll my eyes. This time I just close them. Three incantations of BeetleKurt won't bring him back.

It won't bring any of them back. And I'm such a hypocrite, but if I do catch my brother, I really will brain the Glorious Coward Weasel.

This time I swear, I really will give him something to die about.

But out here in the creepy dark of this dying autumn—suicide tourists or accidental lemmings—some of us were born to live forever.

THE ROUTINE

Keith Buie

At eight thirty a man drags his three sons back to the pharmacy, slams three prescriptions down on the counter, and says to make it quick.

"We've been at the emergency room for four hours." He smacks a pack of bubble gum out of the youngest son's hand. "I have to get home. The play-offs start at nine."

Amoxicillin, rubber-stamped in large black letters, lines the center of each prescription. The doctors at Huron Hospital all keep fill-in-your-name antibiotic prescription pads in their lab coat pockets.

The father scratches at red bumps on his neck. It could be a rash, but my guess is razor burn. Razor burn that he shaves over every day and only makes worse.

He keeps scratching his neck. "I told that nurse we needed three amoxicillin prescriptions. Same as last time. But we still had to wait four hours and pay a hundred dollars just for some doctor to look in their ears for five seconds."

When I ask how often the boys get ear infections, the father spanks the middle son for jamming cotton balls in his mouth and says, "This is their third ear infection this year."

Seventy-five percent of all children develop an ear infection by age three, their shorter Eustachian tubes between the ear and throat allowing easy entry for bacteria and viruses.

When I ask whether his sons have a runny nose or a cough, or more importantly if they have a fever, he smacks his oldest son for ripping pages from the *Sports Illustrated Swimsuit* issue and says, "Just fill the prescriptions and stop asking so many questions."

Viruses cause the majority of ear infections. However, a fever indicates infecting bacteria such as *Streptococcus pneumoniae* or *Haemophilus influenzae*, which can lead to mastoiditis, perforation of the eardrum, and in rare cases spread to meningitis.

After typing each prescription, slapping on labels, and mixing three bottles of bubble-gum-flavored amoxicillin, I walk over to the cash register, put my head down, and ask if he has any questions.

He points to the forty-five-dollar total on the register. "Yeah, why does it cost so much?" Then he dumps a pocketful of change onto the counter and lights up a cigarette.

"You can't smoke in here," I tell him.

"Try and stop me," he says, blowing smoke in my face.

Risk factors for children developing ear infections include upper respiratory infections, being bottle-fed instead of breast-fed, and exposure to cigarette smoke.

The father snatches the bag out of my hands and dumps two bottles onto the counter. "I'm only buying one. The boys can share."

I want to look him in the eyes and say each child needs the full ten-day treatment to completely kill any infecting bacteria, or else he'll be back in two weeks complaining about their fourth ear infection this year.

Instead I keep my head down and say he should probably buy all three, that maybe it would be best to follow the doctor's instructions.

He slides fifteen dollars in quarters, dimes, and nickels toward me. "Where's the other pharmacist? He always keeps his mouth shut." Then he scratches his neck again.

In rare cases infected razor burn can induce a fever and swell into pus-filled carbuncles deep in the skin that cause bacteremia.

But his three sons have finally finished ransacking the pharmacy, so I don't say anything that might keep him here any longer.

"Kids. Car. Now," he yells, smacking each one on the back of the head as they knock over a Kleenex display on their way out the front door. "If I miss the first pitch, I swear I'm going to beat . . ."

Abusive, chain-smoking fathers are always in a hurry.

I'm a pharmacist, but most nights, I'm also a verbal punching bag.

I walk over to the sink and turn on the water. I push down on the soap dispenser three times, vigorously rubbing the glob of orange antibacterial soap over every inch of my hands. My skin dries, and my knuckles crack with the constant washing.

After drying my hands, I sit down on the stool, open up my Pharmacology 101 textbook, and resume studying.

Side effects of amoxicillin overdose are hallucinations, seizures, and encephalopathy.

The clock on the wall says it is 8:45. Only seven hours and fifteen minutes to go.

Because at four o'clock all of this comes to an end.

In a twenty-four-hour pharmacy one of two pharmacists works the graveyard shift. This starts at eight o'clock at night and runs to eight in the morning. It lasts for seven straight days, followed by seven days off. Twenty-six guaranteed weeks of vacation every year.

At least that's what it says in my contract.

This is my sixteenth straight week without a day off. One hundred and twelve days. Twelve hours every day. Eighty-four hours each week.

All here in this pharmacy. My home away from home. Two pharmacists normally rotate the weekly shifts. But Ron, the other night pharmacist, the tan, blond, fresh-out-of-college heartthrob who looks more suited for a lifetime of modeling, hasn't been able to work for months.

Ron swims laps at the rec center every morning after his shift. He shaves his legs to speed up his lap time or maybe just to relive his Junior Olympic swimming days. One day he shaved too deep and cut a gash in his leg. He got in the pool, and whatever bacteria were floating in that chlorinated water found their way into his cut. A week later boils formed around the cut. After another week the boils grew into carbuncles, popped open, and started oozing thick, yellow pus. Two weeks after that he couldn't stand on his leg. The day he fell down clutching his chest and gasping for air is when the ambulance took him to the hospital. He spent the first month in intensive care, hooked up to intravenous antibiotics, before falling into a coma.

Doctors diagnosed it as a coma produced from pneumonia caused by a blood staph infection triggered by a laceration in his leg.

The dirty, white lab coat Ron wore every night and never washed still hangs on the wall in the back of the pharmacy. The brownish-green splotches on the sleeves almost look like tiny bacteria chewing their way up the coat, one strand of cotton at a time.

My district manager asked me to help out the company and work a little overtime. He said I owed them anyway since what happened last year. And it was fine, he said, because I was still legally available to work.

I asked if having me work more was in the company's best interests since my little . . . incident.

He said to just keep showing up and he'd let me know when I could have a day off. That was four months ago.

That was the last time I remember sleeping.

Customers see the four months of insomnia screaming out of my bloodshot eyes. They see it in the uncombed hair and perpetual five o'clock shadow. They see it in my pale, hollowed-out face from skipping two out of three meals each day.

And they have no problem letting me know about it.

"You look drunk."

"You look like death."

"Where's the real pharmacist?"

I keep my head down and don't say anything as they walk away shaking their heads.

Then I sit back down and study old college textbooks, read medical journals, and scroll through package inserts attached to each prescription bottle, memorizing every mechanism of action, bioavailability, contraindication, drug interaction, and adverse effect.

I study all night long, waiting for the next customer to walk up with a prescription, a question, or a disease. Then I do one thing. I follow the routine.

Until four o'clock.

At 10:45 a brunette with bloodshot eyes and a pink-studded tongue ring slides over a prescription for clarithromycin, opens a bottle of Diet Coke before paying for it, and tells me she got strep throat from kissing her boyfriend, Jake.

"And he got it from kissing that slut Joanna Jenkins." She jams her bar-stamped hand into her purse, pulling out a flask and pouring some kind of brown liquor into her soda bottle. Then she rips open a bag of potato chips off the shelf and stuffs a handful into her mouth.

No physician signed the prescription, so I call the City College Med Center to verify which doctor wrote it.

Red splotches wrap around her collarbone. It could be hickeys from her boyfriend, but my medical opinion says they're spider bites. They run down her chest, disappearing into a mountain of braless cleavage and a see-through white tank top. She scratches above her collarbone. "It's like I have Joanna's DNA inside of me now."

When different doctors keep putting me on hold, no one remembering writing the prescription, she says, "I didn't even see a doctor. I just sat in the waiting room for an hour, and a nurse brought me a prescription."

Strep accounts for only 10 percent of all sore throats in adults. Viruses cause the other 90 percent and produce coughing, sneezing, and nasal congestion—all symptoms of the common cold.

When I ask if the doctor stuck a long Q-tip down the back of her throat, she says, "I don't let anyone stick anything down my throat. Unless, that is, he's really cute."

Doctors swab a sample of cells from the back of the throat, add the sample to sodium nitrate and acetic acid, and within minutes they can locate a specific protein found in *Streptococcus pyogenes* bacterium.

Finally, after a resident tells me to fill the prescription and stop tying up his phone line, I walk to the register, put my head down, and ask if she has any questions.

"Can you get strep throat from oral sex?" She stuffs another handful of chips into her mouth, washing them down with the last of her Diet Coke. "Giving oral, not receiving it. Does that make a difference?"

I scan the empty pop bottle and empty bag of chips into the register, pushing them into a pile of mixed amoxicillin suspensions, cigarette butts, ripped magazines, and every other piece of trash my customers dump on my counter each night. "Because then maybe I got strep from Ryan," she says.

"Or Bruce."

I want to look this girl in the eyes and say the 10 percent who have strep throat wouldn't be able to eat potato chips, drink soda, and talk without pain, how they'd be sipping hot tea, sucking lozenges, and wondering why it felt like they were swallowing razor blades.

Instead I keep my head down and say she probably doesn't need the medicine, that maybe an anti-inflammatory would work better.

She swipes her credit card and leans over the counter, looking around the pharmacy. "Where's the other pharmacist? The cute one with the hot swimmer's body. I wanted to ask him out tonight." Then she scratches her collarbone again.

Hickeys go away on their own within a week, while severe cases of spider bites can lead to a staph infection in the bloodstream, causing headaches, stomach cramps, and loss of consciousness.

But since she starts stumbling down the first aid aisle—
now chugging directly from her flask—there is a good chance
she will experience each of these effects before morning.

She drops the empty flask into her purse and pulls out a
cell phone.

I wonder which lucky guy it will be tonight.

Jake. Ryan. Bruce.

"Hey, Steve, it's me. I'm heading back to the bar. Want to
hook up later?" She pops two pills into her mouth and stag-
gers down the aisle. "No, don't go out with Joanna Jenkins.
She's such a slut."

Drunken, horny college girls are always entertaining.

I'm a pharmacist, but on ladies' night, I'm also a temporary babysitter.

I walk over to the sink and wash my hands, rubbing the
antibacterial soap over still-bleeding cracks in my knuckles.
Then I sit down, open up my Microbiology 100 textbook,
and resume studying.

Side effects of clarithromycin overdose are vomiting,
vertigo, and pancreatitis.

Only six more hours until four o'clock.

Third shift in a pharmacy means fewer customers. It brings
fewer prescriptions and even fewer questions. And it provides more emergency room prescriptions for sore throats,
ear infections, and runny noses.

It means more antibiotics.

Doctors cannot run tests on every patient with an infection. Government regulations force cutbacks on throat cul-
tures and blood work, tests that require longer patient stays
and cost hospitals more money.

So doctors overprescribe antibiotics for colds and viral infections. Or they prescribe broad-spectrum antibiotics that treat a large array of different bacteria.

If doctors don't know what's causing the infection, then they have to guess how to treat it.

Over 130 million prescriptions for antibiotics are given out each year. And half of them are for the common cold.

People demand amoxicillin for ear infections. They think every sore throat is strep. They don't believe they will get better by drinking fluids, getting plenty of rest, and letting the virus die on its own after seven days.

Prescription medications go through years of clinical trials. During these trials, some patients unknowingly take sugar pills as opposed to the actual medication. Up to 50 percent of these patients drop out of each study because they claim the sugar pills cause unbearable side effects.

If you believe you are taking medicine, then your body reacts like it is getting medicine.

This is the placebo effect.

We can make ourselves believe anything.

As a pharmacist, I see all the potential diseases floating around. Every red splotch above a collarbone could be a minor case of hickeys, or it might be spider bites that eventually spread to a deadly blood infection.

But if no one directly asks me a question about it, I keep my head down and let them believe whatever they want.

It's better to be a ghost than to try and be a savior. It's all part of the nightly routine. Until four o'clock. Until right now.

At four in the morning the world stops. For one hour.

The phone forgets to ring. The front door stays closed.

The soft buzzing from the fluorescent lights fades away.

For one hour between four and five, no one is sick. No one needs a prescription filled. No one has any questions.

Three o'clock is late. Bars close by two thirty, leaving stragglers swinging in for cigarettes and condoms and Doritos.

Five o'clock is early, people turning off their alarms and getting up for work.

But at four o'clock, for one free hour every night, I am completely alone. And that's when I scan the 9,516 drugs surrounding me on the shelves.

I could walk over to the shelf and make a meal out of a heaping handful of Vicodin, and within twenty minutes those tablets would plummet my heart rate, make my muscles go limp, and turn my skin cold, clammy, and blue, all while chewing a hole in my liver and pushing me into a full-blown coma.

I could take thirty of those chalky white potassium chloride tablets used to treat hypokalemia, and the potassium would paralyze my muscles and scramble my heart rhythm, not stopping until finally giving me a heart attack.

Then there's zolpidem—the quick-acting imidazopyridine—and a bottleful of those would let me drift off to sleep, escorting me into a pillowy coma as my heart slowly stops beating.

Any drug can be a poison, depending on the dose.

Especially the drug erythromycin, an antibiotic used to treat bronchitis and pneumonia. I should have learned that it doubles your chances of sudden cardiac death due to ventricular arrhythmias. And if it's taken with a blood pressure drug like diltiazem, which inhibits the CYP3A enzyme used to metabolize erythromycin, this increases erythromycin's concentration in the bloodstream, trapping salt inside heart muscle cells, prolonging the time in between heartbeats, and triggering fatal, abnormal heart rhythms, which eventually cause the heart to stop beating altogether.

I was supposed to remember learning this in school. But I will never forget it now.

Side effects of dispensing erythromycin are insomnia, endless bouts of guilt, and the nightly urge at four o'clock to swallow an entire pharmacy and drop dead on the floor between the birth control and asthma inhalers.

I look down at yesterday's newspaper. The obituary says Edith Reddy passed away at home alongside her loving husband. It doesn't mention my name. Or the word *murder*. But I know the cold truth.

Pharmacists can kill anyone at any time, just by handing them a bottle of pills.

The only admirable thing to do now is take one final dose of my own medicine.

SURVIVED

Gus Moreno

Four summers ago I stopped waking up to watch *X-Men* and slept the extra two hours until *Saved by the Bell: The New Class*. And during that summer—when Jordan came out of retirement for the first time and six hundred people died from the city's heat wave—a man collapsed in my grandmother's building. When she woke up that morning I was sitting in the living room, inches from the TV with a bowl of cereal resting in my lap, my legs wrapped Indian style. Instead of telling me to move back, she asked why I never wore the pajamas she bought for my birthday.

"The one with the footsies?"

She didn't answer and walked toward the kitchen. Then the phone rang a full Zack Morris monologue before she finally picked up. Grandma walked back into the living room, the phone nestled between her left ear and shoulder. "Take the bowl and go outside."

"Why?"

Her eyeglasses slid down the bridge of her nose. "Go outside and wait for your *tio*."

My shorts snagged on the front steps. The paleta man wheeled his mobile freezer to the curb, but I told him no thanks. He pedaled on past me and jingled the bells along his handlebars.

Tio Raúl double-parked in front of the house and rushed to the door. "Are you okay?"

"I'm fine. Can I go back in?"

"No." He traded glances between the second floor windows and me. "The light guy collapsed upstairs."

"No way."

"Yes way. Where's Grandma?"

From what she had said, Doña Rosa paid a visit to the electrician working in the empty apartment next to her. She knocked twice with no answer. When she leaned against the door it creaked open, and there the man lay, facedown with his body collapsed on his arms. Doña Rosa dropped her pitcher of rice water and called my grandmother.

Outside, two men dressed in oil-stained jumpers walked past the stoop. They talked in Spanish and way too fast for me to understand. One guy pointed to his crotch, and the other one laughed. When the two were almost down the block, I could still hear them calling each other guey which sounds exactly like *way*.

Way. Way. Way. Way. Way.

From inside the house, my uncle yelled into the phone, "Damn it, just go back in and check his pulse."

The electrician's pulse.

Across the street, a woman stepped out of her car to make sure she didn't hit the curb.

Upstairs, the rice water pooled around the electrician's body, soaking into the carpet, seeping between the cheap clip-together floorboards. Already dripping onto the drywall below, my grandmother's ceiling. Moisture and time would turn the rice water into a moldy outline of the electrician's body. It would be months before it showed through the ceiling, another few weeks before my grandmother noticed it. Something like a man's shadow hovering above us in the living room until my uncle replaced the drywall.

Paulina lived on the third floor. Every tenant had to walk down my grandmother's stoop to exit the building, and as I turned around, Paulina was walking down the steps that led to the rest of the apartment floors. She stopped next to me and said, "Don't go upstairs." Her purple lips turned yellow when they pushed against each other to make words.

Even with only bums and churchgoers roaming the streets this early, an ambulance would take some time.

The running joke was that out of the six hundred deaths that summer, Latinos only accounted for 2 percent of the heat-related fatalities. The people stereotyped as overloading cars and living in cramped spaces like ants in the wall, they were outliving the rest of the city. Everybody laugh.

Grandpa died that April, which ruled him out as a casualty to the heat. A cousin who wasn't really related to me recorded the entire wake and funeral to send to relatives in Mexico, but after he passed around a bottle of mescal with my uncles, the tape went missing.

Grandpa's funeral came and went, and summer vacation meant a whole season flipping through cable channels with a blank tape inside the VCR, the TV set up to record anything with sexual content or brief nudity. Anything with Demi Moore would do. I sat alone at home while my mom waited tables. Never answer the door, she would tell me, but answer the phone because the answering machine had stopped working. One day the phone rang, and the caller ID read my grandfather's name.

My dead grandfather's name.

He couldn't hold a job so my grandmother paid the bills. She put everything in her name. Every ring created a new explanation for how this could be happening. He was calling to me as I raised the phone to my ear. His cold voice freezing the side of my face, his throat coarse and dry from the soil buried over him, he called me *mijo*. He asked his *mijo* how he was doing.

"*Qué pasa?*"

It's hazy whether the phone dropped from my hand or if I hung up on my grandfather. The one thing that sticks out, I wish I forgot: running out the front door and crying to no one but myself. The moment you hear the voice of someone who should be lying in a satin-lined time capsule, your mind starts to gather all the rules you've learned from zombie flicks. Only old enough to think masturbation is something you invented, you ponder whether you could take a crowbar to the back of your grandfather's head if he really is part of the undead. But mostly you're just plain confused.

Five minutes later my cousins called back laughing. The phone in my grandfather's room was a separate line.

Under his name. And still in service.

My uncle peeked out from behind the doorway. "Paramedics show up?"

"Nope." I handed him my empty bowl to take into the house. He set the bowl on the floor and headed upstairs.

I could see the park from our stoop, it being only a block away. Three Asian women practiced karate moves in slow motion. A stray dog limped past me. Tio Raúl checked the electrician's pulse while two boys from across the street

clapped to get the dog's attention. They were wrestling in
the baseball field, and beige dust created a cloud around
their heads as they clapped and howled. Doña Rosa was
somewhere sprawled in her apartment, sobbing.

Nothing went unnoticed, especially in a neighborhood
clustered with buildings so close together. A family in one
building could smell dinner from a family in another building. It's the reason the heat stayed concentrated. So many
buildings and pavement to absorb the rising temperatures.
You stayed trapped inside your neighborhood, your own
private frying pan, and things remained hot and only got
hotter. The county coroner had to call in refrigerated trucks
to store all the bodies that came in during those months. So
it was nice to have the morning air slip through my shirt-
sleeves, though I told myself the goose bumps came from
spotting Maria across the street. Maria's mom called out
to her as she walked along the sidewalk with laundry bags
slung over her shoulder, and I broke eye contact.

The elote man deflated the silence of parked cars with
the static from his stereo hanging off his cart of corn. Butter, lime juice, and hot pepper clogged my nose.

I turned my head toward the door and asked my grandmother, anyone, if I could get a corn on the cob.

And a voice echoed back to me. "Sit outside and wait
for the goddamn ambulance."

Grandma never swore. She sneered and squinted
four-letter words. The curse came from Lucia who lived
three floors up. Her apartment came with no bathroom.
She had to use the toilet in the hallway. She always got a
pass for the attitude. The ambulance pulled up without the
siren on, only the lights above the truck flashing, barely

making a difference through the sunlight. An entire block
of curtains opened like fans doing the wave in a baseball
stadium. I saw people sliding away hanging fabric to push
their faces against the window screen. *Comadre* Vicky lived
in the white building that turned rust at the edges. She
pointed out her open window, and Don Juan poked his
head out. The paramedics brought out a gurney, and my
uncle met them at the door. People opened their front doors
and pretended they had left something outside. I couldn't
hear anything Tío Raúl said to the paramedics. His shaking
body and clenched fists told the whole story. I caught the
words *badge number* and *supervisor* before they followed
him upstairs. The four señoras who went to church every
day slowly trailed off their usual path and gravitated toward
our building.

Letí and Isabel both lived two houses to our right.
When an ambulance parked outside, it seemed like the
best time to sweep their share of the sidewalk. The church
señoras were the first to start loitering around our building. Their palms were interlocked with rosaries. Wrinkles
hugged whatever life was left in their faces.

The señoras approached our stoop like the altar, bow-
ing their heads with their eyes still focused upward. "What
happened?"

And Doña Rosa screamed from her window, "He's dead,
Díos mío."

Letí and Isabel walked toward me with faulty brooms,
saying, "Who?"

Who? Who? Who? Who? Who?

The dust brothers from before, the ones playing with
the dog, they showed up with purple Popsicles in each

hand, a woman with a firm grip on their collars. Whatever traffic passed through the street slowed down to a crawl. The speed to catch every bit of what was going on.

More people joined the crowd. More people began to forget why they were standing there and started talking about their own business.

Isabel made a public announcement about a Tupperware party she was hosting.

Irv, the owner of the corner store, asked Compadre Mundo about the vacant lot he owned.

Comadre Vicky wanted to get together with Patricia and Leticia to make tamales like they used to.

Lucia left my grandmother and stood outside now, her hips leaning to one side, and asked Victor if his fingers were broken. How come he can't call anyone?

Grandma was in the living room with her neck craned toward the ceiling, listening to what was the tap, tap, tap of rice water on the other side.

The elote and paleta men fought for attention using rattling bells.

He wasn't my real *tio*, but Tio Pepe asked if my grandmother had made anything to eat.

Fausto yelled from his slowly passing car about what was going on.

Norma wanted to know why Fausto wasn't at work.

Through the group sway of people droning to one another, I spotted my mom in her waitress gown, walking to the front of the crowd.

"Are you okay?" she said to me. "Raúl called and told me what happened."

"What did he say? Did he tell you if the man died?"

Grandma stepped behind me with my book bag in her hand. "I'll see you tomorrow, *mijo*."

We weaved through the crowd to her car. Mom would tug on my arm and I'd continue walking, and with her back facing me, she said she found the videotape of Grandpa's funeral in the VCR. "What were you watching that for?"

The tape I'd used to record the first half of *Disclosure*. I thought that tape was blank.

Doña Rosa went down the steps first, and everyone crowded even closer, making it impossible for us to leave. We both stopped as the neighborhood closed us in—stuck inside the surrounding conversations of job searches and upcoming parties.

Church bells rang across the alleyway. The sound made its way through the streets every Sunday, and from any point in the neighborhood you could hear the calling sound pulsing from our block. Everyone knew it was no use to try to talk over it. They pulled out cigarettes, stared off at the passing cars. The bells sat in the air like the humidity, and using the opportunity, Mom pulled on my arm until I bent my knees and stumbled after her.

We would soon get home, and I would have to snatch the tape from the VCR before my mom ever had the chance to see what I had done, which was snub out her dad's funeral with milky white tits, perky pink nipples.

My mom was already a fragile woman to live with. She took Grandpa's death real hard. Months before all this happened, Mom changed our phones. Real fancy phones, the cordless kind that wouldn't drop calls and had caller ID already installed. Trouble was, once we got the phones our answering machine stopped working. A few weeks passed as she tried to figure out what the problem was. A man came to our home and said the phones worked fine. He checked the answering machine, and that was fine too.

Then Grandpa died.

Voice mail is a funny little invention. Because when you have the voice mail option already activated on your phone there is no need for an answering machine. A company operator explained this to my mother. After receiving the password, Ma sifted through messages a month old. Then she heard from someone she wasn't expecting. Her father. She sniffed and clenched her eyes shut when my grandfather's voice came on the line and asked where the hell she was. He'd been waiting at the DMV for half an hour. Mom buried her head into her chest after she heard my grandfather's old message, asking for a ride to church on Sunday.

In another message, my *abuelito*, talking from the grave, wanted to know if there were any plans for my birthday. She leaned against the wall, eased herself down to the floor. A month's worth of her father leaving messages no one knew existed.

The paramedics tried swinging the gurney down to the first floor, the weight of the body causing the gurney to shift from side to side, smashing each paramedic's fingers against the walls. You heard the wheels banging against the steps before they appeared.

Mom tried to haul me into the car by pulling my arm, but she paused, too, to watch the men shimmy through the doorway and stabilize the gurney on the cracked sidewalk. One paramedic opened both ambulance doors while my uncle and the other medic held the body steady.

Crowds congested the sidewalk, but no one spoke. They all stood still, observers for the first time—witnesses to the man on the gurney. The white sheet, draped over the electrician's head, changed his face into landscape.

My mom's hand grazed through my hair, over my shoulder, and down my elbow, feeling for my hand again without looking. I looked up at her, but she was somewhere else. I fitted my hand inside hers, and she gripped tight, like she was bringing me back to life.

ZOMBIE WHOREHOUSE

Daniel W. Broallt

Answering yes would be a lie. And I can't lie without sweating. Answering no could create suspicions as to how I found this place.

The doctor repeats his question. "You ever fuck a zombie before?"

Lesson learned from eight years of marriage—when you don't know how to answer, it's better to grin and shrug.

"Well," the doctor says, "I'm legally obligated to warn you that it's not like fucking the living."

"There are laws about this?" I say.

The question hovers between us and my microphone wristwatch. With luck it will capture every syllable of this potentially Pulitzer Prize–winning investigation.

The doctor has a blond moustache and long hair. He smiles at me like I'm an old friend and says, "You ever hear about how you could cut a hole in a small watermelon and microwave it and it'd feel like a real pussy? Well, fucking a zombie is like that without the microwave. Of course, the quicker you move, the less you notice."

"Is this a problem for a lot of clients?" I say.

Making a note on his clipboard before double clicking his pen for emphasis, the doctor replies, "Most folks are more interested in the sensation of being smothered by ten or so naked girls. Half our clients never get to stick it in."

"Half is how many, exactly?" I say.

The doctor licks his sandy moustache and says, "If you think it'll bother you, the red dispensers are filled with warm sensation lube."

I slide my wedding band into my back pocket and feel a little better about explaining to my wife how I got this talk show circuit earning story. "It's not cheating if she's dead" becomes "It's not–cheating if I didn't get to stick it in." I wipe the sweat off my forehead and remind myself that concerning my career, my wife has always said, "Success requires sacrifice."

In 1887, Nellie Bly shocked the world with her exposé on the miserable conditions and abusive treatment of inmates in New York City's Bellevue Hospital's Asylum for the Insane. The facts she documented came from her personal experience, faking mental instability to become the world's first undercover journalist.

A little over a hundred years later and my editor tells me it's time to revive this laudable profession. After the Food Lion fiasco, most television networks and print media began calculating the cost of undercover investigation against the potential legal fees and lawsuit fines. The days of white men painting their skin black, feminists posing as Playboy Bunnies, or either sex cross-dressing to get a good story faded amidst accusations of misleading job applications, failure to perform the tasks assigned, and trespassing.

"You'll need to sign here." The doctor hands me a separate clipboard of twelve single-spaced pages. "Just initial the bottom of each page, and fully sign the last page. You're agreeing any disease or injury you acquire during your visit is your responsibility. Also, while referrals are encouraged, it's best to consider what happens in the playroom to stay in the playroom. We reserve the right to release video to ruin your life if you try to ruin our operation."

"How important is secrecy to the daily operation of Anchor Playhouse?" I say. "Have there been incidents of attempts to expose this place?"

"In the playroom, there're condoms available for your protection. Lord knows the girls don't have to worry about getting pregnant."

The last notable work of undercover television journalism ended in allegations of entrapment and a scandal involving an internet video of an alleged pedophile being routinely raped by baseball bats wielded by several self-proclaimed neighborhood protectors inspired to proactively defend their children after the episode aired.

"You acknowledge you have been informed that the red dispensers are filled with warming lubricant and the yellow are filled with flavored syrup."

"What is the flavor?" I ask.

"It changes. I believe it is maple at the moment."

I ask if the flavor changes per customer request. I ask if there are many repeat customers.

The doctor informs me that the blue dispensers are filled with evaporating antibacterial disinfectant. He informs me rose oil is used to soften the skin of the girls and ensure a pleasing odor.

When an editor suggests an assignment, there is always an option to refuse. When the editor starts offering story suggestions to other reporters, the only option is to complain and seek a new profession. When the editor has limited resources and the other reporters have the ability to flirt their way into receiving more assignments, it's best to seize the opportunities men naturally have an advantage to report. Like meatpacking plant contamination. Illegal whaling. Migrants exploited in the construction industry. Underground zombie fucking.

The doctor continues to check boxes on his clipboard. "You agree that you are aware of the consequences of attempting to remove the mouth guards."

"What are the consequences?" I ask.

"Don't remove the mouth guards." He says, "You declare that your initial physical has discovered no disqualifying conditions and that after your time in the playroom you will submit to a follow-up physical before clearance that may last up to six hours. You have indicated you desire thirty minutes alone in the playroom with our most popular option, the Maximum Variety, Maximum Amount package."

I say, "That's correct. How many is the maximum?"

Nellie Bly exposed herself to ten days of uncomfortable concrete quarters, being forced to wash under buckets of frigid water, subsisting on rotting meat and stiff bread, pushed into and out of rooms for contemptuous medical examinations, all while being continually yelled at and demeaned by the sanitarium staff. Her exposé initiated a public outcry that led to the improvement of the lives of thousands of the mentally ill and increased scrutiny on the unfortunate cases of women being declared insane when often they were only being women.

"When your time is complete, the bell will ring three times. You will have five minutes to free yourself from the girls and exit through the gold door. There are several ways to reach this door; you can choose which will be easiest. Remember, zombies are slow and dumb. However, if you cannot remove yourself or choose not to leave at your appointed time, our staff will enter to assist your exit. Please sign the liability release forms."

The handwriting is mine. The name is not. Sweat wets my forehead. "Do your staff have to assist many of your clients?"

He says, "Don't worry. As the oldest and largest operating zombie brothel, we have established the standards all the others aspire to imitate."

I ask how many other operations exist. He assures me I will be satisfied.

The doctor walks out as two men in white coats enter and motion for me to follow. We descend a long, cream-colored hallway. The orderlies ignore my inquiries about working hours and wages. They ask what option I've chosen. "Maximum Variety, Maximum Amount," I say.

The one on my right suggests choosing one of the specialty packages next time, like Arabian Tights or End of the Rainbow.

He says, "They've painted all the girls, so it's like this crazy interactive art museum."

Questions for the article: Does man's ability to personalize his deviation make it less repulsive? Easier to pursue? More likely to be shared?

We walk toward a pink door. The man on the left says he can no longer enjoy sex with living women. The one to my right nods. The men stop at the entrance, which opens, and another doctor asks me to join him in the locker-lined room. He's heavier than the first doctor, and his hair is darker. He looks like my local grocer.

"Welcome, welcome," he says. "Leave your personal belongings in this room, and when you are ready, the play-room is through that door at the end."

"Can I keep my watch on? To keep track of the time?"

"It's not recommended," he replies. "The girls can be rather grabby. The doctors who observe your playtime will announce how much time remains."

"It's a gift from my wife," I say. Sweat collects on my fore-arms. "I never take it off."

The doctor shrugs. "It's your choice. But we are not responsible if it gets broken. And if you tear one of the girls, you lose your deposit."

I ask how often a girl is torn.

He informs me that they have a large reserve. I store my clothes in a spotless locker.

"We will release one girl to start. The first five minutes you can play with her however you see fit. Another couple will be released every few minutes. You'll hear a bell to announce their entry. For thirty minutes, you can expect to see ten to twelve girls, but remember you can request as many as you like. There's a two-way microphone on the ceiling by the observation window. But speak loud. After five girls it's hard to hear over the moaning. It's best to signal how many more you want with your fingers." He laughs and says, "In my opinion, five girls is the perfect number if you want to stay in control."

Another doctor, portly and freckled, sticks his head in to say they're ready. He suggests next time to try Hairy Ferry. "Nothing is shaved," he says, whistling for emphasis before disappearing.

"What's it like?" I ask, hoping to gather as many first-hand accounts as I can for the article.

The doctor who watched me undress says, "When I was younger I used to lay in the shallow part of the lake and hump the sand while watching my sister's friends tan on the shore. It's kind of like that without the water."

Note for the article: Does facilitating zombie sex remove one's sense of shame?

"How many people work here?" I ask, completely naked except for my microphone wristwatch.

"Oh, I don't know," the doctor replies. "Fifteen medical professionals, maybe. Twenty or so of general help. Sixty to seventy girls, I think."

He laughs again and adds, "And counting."

One of the more disturbing discoveries Nellie Bly uncovered was the presence of sane women in the insane asylum. One girl claimed she was put there by a jealous husband who assumed her refusal to satisfy his nightly wishes was proof of adultery. Another insisted her family had her locked away over an inheritance dispute. Still others found themselves declared mentally insane for possessing traits applauded in men but inappropriate for women. Assertiveness. Questioning authority. Self-dependence. My father could have had my sister put away for flirting with the paper delivery boy from the poor side of town. I could have committed my wife to avoid the inevitable accusations she'll raise when this story runs.

The playroom is the size of a half-court for basketball, with padded surfaces in the same cream color as the hallway. Waist-high geometric shapes interrupt the clinical flatness of the floor. Raised ovals. Circles. Rectangles. It's like being in a giant, white miniature golf challenge. A grated drain covers the center of the floor.

In each corner sits a large bucket of condoms. Along each wall hang the different-colored lube and flavor dispensers. Before me, two shut doors stand on either side of a steep ramp that rises to a golden door set halfway up the wall. A narrow ledge begins at the foot of the door and wraps around the room to the midway point where it is met on both sides by small ladders.

I see myself small, naked, and sweating in the reflection of the observation window in the ceiling. Two large vents whir beside the mirror window and fill the room with cool air. With my armpits moist, I tell myself, Success requires sacrifice.

A loudspeaker beside the window transmits the voice of the first doctor, which echoes throughout the chamber. "Enjoy yourself."

A bell rings, the door to the left opens, and the first girl stumbles out.

In the reflection, I see myself move in the opposite direction.

My editor shut the door when he called me in about this story. He handed me a folded-up piece of paper and said, "Look at this."

Scribbled at the top in blue ink was a note: *I was paid 500 dollars to translate this into Russian. Discreetly. I don't think it's a joke.*

No signature. No return address on the envelope.

Top 10 Questions Concerning Having Sex with a Zombie

The girl lumbering toward me is dark-skinned. Her black hair is pulled into two pigtails, high on her head. She wears movie star sunglasses. A plastic mouth guard covers the lower half of her face.

The first question was not about the source of the sex zombies. It was not about reassuring potential clients that innocent living girls were not being abducted and transformed into zombies for sexual purposes. It was not about reassuring husbands and fathers that their loved ones would not be remade into someone else's fantasy.

Potential follow-up piece to the article: Men, are you protecting your ladies from all the aftershocks of the zombie threat?

The padded floor whispers under my bare feet as I retreat to the condom bucket in the far corner.

The loudspeaker says, "Their eyesight is poor. You may want to make some noise to attract her attention."

The girl looks upward toward the sound. She waves her arms, catching air. Every one of her fingernails has been removed. I see her naked reflection in the two-way mirror of the observation window, and despite my disgust at this exploitation of the undead, I can't help but admire the curve of her dark back.

The first question was not about safety. Later questions and answers detailed the precautions taken to prevent the spread of the zombie contagion—the medical supervision, the careful cleaning after each use, the innovative solutions to prevent bites and scratches.

Except for the sunglasses and mouth guard, the girl shuffling toward me is completely naked. Her legs lack cellulite, her waist lacks rolls, and her breasts are perfect, the size of Florida oranges with round, purple nipples like eraser tips pointing in my direction, a little larger than the first breasts I ever felt and a little smaller than my wife's. Between her legs, her thick, dark patch has been shaped into the form of a star.

No, the first few questions and answers on that info ad read:

Are there visible signs of their death? Holes, teeth marks, etc. that would make them unattractive?

Only the most eye-pleasing, least damaged zombie victims are used at Anchor Playhouse. You will not notice any physical damage from their cause of infection.

The scent of roses fills my nose as the dark-skinned zombie reaches toward my neck. Raspy moans escape through her mouth guard. The moans like my wife makes when I sneak out of bed in the morning to read the paper.

Is it true their skin is gray?

Our girls are kept in top condition. Our patented intravenous solution provides the necessary vitamins and nutrients to keep the skin looking lifelike long after it has become undead. However, if gray skin is your thing, your desires can be easily accommodated.

I move around the raised rectangle, and the coffee-colored zombie girl reaches out like she's searching for a doorknob in a dark room. I hear the sticky sound of her oiled feet sliding along the floor.

A bell rings, the door to the left opens, and two more zombie girls enter. Both have pointy breasts. One of them, a blonde about four feet tall with an attractive athletic build, shares the mouth guard and sunglasses look. The other wears a giant mouse head with cartoon eyes, like a mascot mask or character at Disneyland. Her entire body has been painted a brownish red, and she drags a long tail. I move around the raised platform for a better view. The tail is attached above her large jiggling ass and swishes back and forth as she walks. The short one shuffles twice as fast to keep pace.

I wish I paid extra for a spy watch with video.

The voice from above announces, "Welcome to the Maximum Variety part of your package. The first girl we send in is usually as close to her state of change as possible. But now it's time to experience the miracles of science."

After the appearance questions and before the safety questions in the pamphlet my editor showed me, there read what might make another good follow-up article to the straightforward exposé:

Why come to the Anchor Playhouse when there are so many other brothel options available with living girls?

The first zombie girl released reaches for my arm, and I raise it away. Above me I see three naked zombies reaching toward my fleeing self and the fingers on my hand outstretched to their reflection.

"Five more? Your call, champ," the loudspeaker says.

"Whoops," I say and yank down my hand.

The bell rings, and the door to the left opens, revealing a brunette at least six feet tall with long, droopy breasts like socks on a clothesline. She shuffles in beside a girl with short blue hair and her entire body painted in hippie flower pastel designs. Yellow suns circle her sharp nipples. A black girl with a shaved head and covered in tribal tattoos everywhere except on her plum-sized breasts follows. The door shuts as two more stagger in, a pale-skinned girl with red hairs covering her long, freckled legs like a pair of pants and breasts like two large loaves of bread and a completely painted lavender-colored child.

Maximum Variety, Maximum Amount is breaking my heart. None of the pamphlets mentioned a child option. The apple vinegar taste of vomit collects in the back of my throat.

"You better get to work if you want to get in any of these lovely ladies," the loudspeaker suggests, "or are you waiting for the suffocating frottage action as these honeys cover and love you with the blanket of affection you so rightly deserve?"

Three naked zombies fumble over each other near one of the red dispensers on the wall. The child shuffles alone, pawing one of the raised shapes. The giraffe, the hair pants, the hippie, and the mouse stumble toward me as I slip across the drain grate.

I run around a raised oval. The gathering mass of naked, oiled undead follows as I yell, "Where were these girls infected?"

The bell rings, the door to the left opens, and two more girls enter. The newcomers are bald everywhere and wear angel wings on their backs. Their outstretched hands display peacock feather gloves, making their fingers seem to stretch out twice the length of their shapely legs. Except for the mouse and myself, everyone in here is wearing a pair of sunglasses and a matching mouth guard. When they get close, I can see liquid collecting under their chins.

Note for the article: Zombies drool.

The loudspeaker says, "The first touch can be a little shocking, but come on! Make your move! You're spending good money to experience the kind of free-for-all orgy that no girlfriend or wife will ever willingly give. Perhaps some mood music will help."

And adding to the overwhelming smell of rose oil and the constant noise of sliding footsteps, moans, and air conditioner whir, a soulful rendition of Gershwin's "Summertime" blends with the increasingly aggressive suggestions from the loudspeaker.

The tall one grabs my wrist. Its finger catches on my watch and tears with a squelching sound as I lunge onto a square to escape.

"There goes your deposit," the loudspeaker announces.

I shake my arm and fling the finger across the room. My watch flies off and slides along the floor, landing near the drain grate beside the feet of a group of the oiled and naked undead. I dive in. My fingers slip past cold, slimy ankles and the rough steel of the grate before grasping onto my watch band. A few more inches and my recordings would have fallen into the drain.

Before I can rise, cool, oiled, and soft skulls press against my neck and back. Weak fingers pull at my arms, my legs, my hair, and my ears. The sound of moaning drowns out the music. Flesh of different textures and firmness slides across my torso as I twist and turn, trying to break free. Slimy hands grip my dick. Hair tickles my exposed skin. With a forceful thrust, I shove the naked, slippery undead off my chest and pull myself from their clutching fingernail-less hands.

I climb on top of the oval, and their reaching hands leave oily smears near my feet.

"Seriously?" the speaker says. "Most men love that squished-under-tits-and-cooch feeling."

I raise both hands to signify I want out and recoil as a loud screech fills the room. The piercing wail disorients the girls, who stumble and flail in every direction.

"Was that feedback?" the loudspeaker asks. "Are you wearing a wire?"

The bell rings, the door to the left opens, and four more zombies enter.

The voice says, "Are you a cop?"

The bell rings, the door to the left opens, and six more zombies enter.

Around my ankles, oiled hands clutch for a hold. The squeezing scent of roses disorients my thoughts. A variety of breasts, a pair for every fruit in the produce section, taunts me with the possibility of kicking each one open.

Hopping on one foot to evade their reach, I shout, "I'm not a cop! That wasn't me!"

The loudspeaker says, "You want to play undercover hero, we'll help put you under."

The laughter of the second doctor fills the playroom.

One of the hands reaching for my ankle is missing a finger. My microphone watch is covered in oil. The bell rings, the door to the left opens, and eight more zombies enter. In a moment, they'll be able to climb over one another and onto the raised oval.

"You're making a mistake," I say. "I'm no cop! I want to fuck a zombie!"

Profuse sweat begins to rinse the liquid mix of rose oil and zombie drool from my glistening limbs and chest.

The bell rings, the door to the left opens, and before I can count how many zombies enter, three hands seize my leg and pull me into the mass of the naked living dead.

"Here's your chance to prove it, officer," the loudspeaker says.

I lose the reflection of the window under crowding wet chins. Everything is dark. It's difficult to breathe. I struggle against the pressing puzzle of zombie breasts, legs, and thighs. Against my bare skin, slippery nipples and the hard plastic of the mouth guards become indistinguishable from the increasing weight of the pressing undead.

Note for the article: There is no oxygen to be found under a pile of over twenty slippery naked zombies.

Also: Zombies taste like burnt fried potatoes.

I pray my editor is smart enough to drop the story. I pray there is enough of me for my wife to identify wherever they drop my body. I pray that when this place is exposed my name is remembered as the brave soul who sought to uncover truth for the betterment of mankind.

Success requires sacrifice.

I'm crushed, dizzy, and drowning when a surprisingly firm and warm hand seizes my arm and yanks me toward the light. Through the roar of the moans, a female voice says, "Outside the gold door is another long hallway where several doctors will easily catch and kill you if that watch really is a wire. Are you actually a cop?"

As I emerge from the pile of crushing, naked, oiled zombies, my rescuer stands over me wearing a pair of movie star sunglasses and a mouth guard. She's the four-foot athletic blonde who came out with the mouse.

"Help me," I say, grasping her arms. My grip slips as the naked undead tug at my legs.

The blonde pulls me up and pushes her mouth guard into my neck. She says, "I'm undercover to expose this blight on humanity. You won't believe the award-winning story I've got."

Note for the article: Even heavily rose-scented air is refreshing after emerging from a near flesh drowning.

I smile at my salvation and say, "Your name wouldn't happen to be Nellie, would it?"

She lunges at my neck. "Don't be an idiot. Through the door the girls come through are cages of zombies, most of which are now in the room. If we can make it through, there's a vent that leads out to where I parked my van. It's too high for me to reach alone, but with your help we can get out of here. And with your captured audio, I'll have credibility for my exposé."

She says, "Until then, treat me like I'm a zombie, you know, either push and run or give me a slight spanking, but don't get too far ahead until we're close enough to the door to make our escape. Then you can call your backup and I can call my editor."

I nod and toss her over the mass of undead so she lands on the rectangle near the slope. Sunglasses litter the floor near where I was rescued. The zombies stare as I jump over their outstretched oiled arms. Their dead glassy eyes seemingly imploring me to write about this injustice, expose this horror, get this award-winning story, and be the hero whose journalistic courage saves all the innocent women of the world from this outrageous fate.

The bell rings, the door to the left opens, and five more zombies enter. In the reflection of the observation window, the entire room is filled with naked and oiled zombie women, swirling around the geometric shapes.

The blonde and I stand alone on the rectangle island at the edge of the playroom. She lurches toward me, acting the part, her hands outstretched. I hold her head back and notice she's missing all her fingernails.

"Hey, pig, you got the goods. Can you use them?" the loudspeaker says. "I see you're finally cocked and loaded, so to speak."

The bell rings, the door to the left opens, and the blonde says, "Now may be our only chance before they realize we're faking and the door shuts. Hop over the crowd, and run through that door."

She starts her move, and I grab her wrist.

"Are you insane? I can only save your life once."

Holding her struggling arm, I feign a cough and pull my watch's memory card out with my teeth and toss the watch into the grate. It slides between a crack and disappears into the drain.

"I'm not so sure," I say, twisting her around and pushing down her head so her butt, like two small watermelons, faces me. "What are you doing?" she says. "Stop!"

"I think there's another way for me to get out of here," I say.

I hold the memory card under my tongue. Her moans are louder than the others.

"That's my guy," says the loudspeaker. Laughter echoes through the room. "Force it! No rubbers! No lube! Like a true man!"

The loudspeaker says, "Sometimes a guy just needs a little adrenaline rush to get his priorities straight. Next time don't wear a damn watch in the playroom."

Her sand-colored hair violently brushes the padded top of the elevated rectangle as several strong men in doctors' coats come through the door on the right with large net poles and begin ushering some of the mass of naked, oiled undead out of the playroom. She tries and fails to scratch me. Tears slip past her sunglasses to splatter on the surface as she whispers something I cannot hear over the moans.

Outside, I know I'll never buy my wife roses again.

BIOGRAPHIES

Daniel W. Broallt graduated from Southern Methodist University with a BA in creative writing in 2001. After graduation, he pursued a series of short-term job adventures, including AmeriCorps and Peace Corps. He currently lives with his wife in a residence hall near Washington, DC, and assists college students in making wise life choices.

Keith Buie lives in Cleveland, Ohio. His work has appeared in *Eleven Eleven*, *The MacGuffin*, *Natural Bridge*, *Quiddity International Literary Journal*, *Rio Grande Review*, *Willard & Maple*, and *Metal Scratches*. Keith recently finished his first novel, and he is represented by Elizabeth Winick Rubinstein of McIntosh & Otis, Inc. Literary Agency. Keith is currently working on his second novel.

Chris Lewis Carter has been featured in over two dozen publications from high school textbooks to award-winning magazines and podcasts, including *Nelson Literacy 8*, *Word Riot*, *Solarcide*, *Cast of Wonders*, *Niteblade*, and *Pseudopod*. He is a member of Kontrabida, an independent video game studio, and the creator of *Camp Myth*, a young adult book series with a supplementary tabletop role-playing game. Find out more at www.chrislewiscarter.com.

Michael De Vito Jr. began writing while attending the University of Maryland as a US Marine sergeant stationed in Okinawa, Japan. Finding an affinity for the recitation of poetry and short stories, he helped found the Eat Write Cafe/Traveling Poets' Society, where service members and civilians congregated weekly for spoken word expressions of original and classic works. Following eleven years on the Asian island, he moved back to his hometown of Staten Island, New York, and started working with a nonprofit foundation serving at-risk NYC high school students. Today he serves as program director for his borough office and is completing his certification to teach English in NYC public schools. Michael resides in Staten Island with his wife and daughter. He has penned dozens of poems and several short stories. This is his first published work.

Born in Croydon, South London, **Terence James Eeles** is an '80s child, underdog appreciator, library slut, and ex-window monkey. He has worked mostly in retail purgatory for his sins. In 2011 he was commended and short-listed in the Manchester Fiction and Bridport Short Story Prizes for his subversive, lyrical, and motif-driven fiction and in 2012 completed his MA in creative writing at Birkbeck, University of London. His piece "The Trojan Horse Mixtape" is the opening story in issue 9 of *The Mechanics' Institute Review*. He is currently developing several novel-in-stories collections (including a music festival coming-of-age disaster and a neo-noirmance), as well as drafting "Lemming" into a longer body of work. "Like" his author page www.facebook.com /terence.james.eeles for fiction updates.

Matt Egan is thirty-one and lives near Cambridge, England.

Jason M. Fylan is a college instructor in English and speech communications who resides in Oxford, Michigan, with his wife, Amanda. He earned his bachelor of arts in English at Siena Heights University and master of arts in English/literature at the University of Dayton. He is currently working on several writing projects, including short stories, novels, and screenplays.

Amanda Gowin lives in the foothills of Appalachia with her husband and son. She is currently completing her first novel, *Boxing Day*. Her first collection, *Radium Girls* (Thunderdome Press), is now available. She was guest fiction editor for the Spring 2013 issue of *Menacing Hedge*, did a run of unusual author interviews at *Curiouser and Curiouser*, and coedited the *Cipher Sisters* anthology from Thunderdome Press. Find her at lookatmissohio.wordpress.com. She has always written and always will.

Bryan Howie lives in the American Inland Northwest. He loves photography and motorcycle riding but has a hard time doing both simultaneously. His work has been included in the *Best of Carve Magazine* volume 6, *Solarcide Presents: Nova Parade, Flash Me! The Sinthology*, and *Aliens, Sex & Sociopaths*. Links to more of his work can be found at bryanhowie.com.

Tyler Jones started playing guitar at an early age and in 2002 was signed to an independent record label based out of Seattle. After recording their debut album, Tyler and his band toured the world for one year before breaking up. Since that time he has written five unpublished novels and numerous short stories.

He is currently writing material for a new album as well as studying with the acclaimed novelist Tom Spanbauer. He lives in Portland, Oregon.

Phil Jourdan is the author of *Praise of Motherhood* (Zero Books), *What Precision, Such Restraint* (Perfect Edge), and *John Gardner: A Tiny Eulogy* (Punctum Books). He fronts the award-winning rock band Paris and the Hiltons.

Neil Krolicki is a writer, illustrator, and expert lover who writes darkly humorous fiction from his hometown of Denver, Colorado. His most recent creative endeavor has been writing and illustrating a crime-noir comic book set in a futuristic metropolis whose most lucrative local trade is erasing the identities of ruthless criminals through radical reconstructive surgeries (120 Doses). He is also churning away at several other writing projects. He lives with his beautiful and intelligent wife, Alyssa, who will most definitely be reading this bio.

Richard Lemmer is a twentysomething English writer. He studied English literature and philosophy at the University of York. He was chosen by a Booker Prize judge to appear in the Oxbridge universities' student anthology—even though he was not studying at either Cambridge or Oxford. Aside from the anthology, his writing has appeared in the *Guardian* and the London literary magazine *Litro*. He has had a variety of jobs, from working with people with learning difficulties to interviewing The Killers.

Tony Liebhard has worked in the healthcare field for over a decade. He currently lives in the Midwest with his wife and is training to be a physician. In his spare time he likes to write and volunteer at the Humane Society. This is his first printed publication.

Gus Moreno maintains a residence on the south side of Chicago. He is currently working on a novel, has stories published in online journals *The Legendary* and *Bluestem Magazine*, and grinds his teeth in his sleep.

Chuck Palahniuk, editor, is the best-selling author of 15 novels, and his writing has appeared in *Playboy*, the *Los Angeles Times*, and *VICE*. The movie adaptation of *Fight Club* has become a cult classic, and his book tours draw large crowds.

Brien Piechos lives in Minneapolis, Minnesota, where he is currently working on a novel and a short story collection. He enjoys combat athletics, vintage British motorcycles, black T-shirts, thrift store hunting, Irish whiskey through the winter, and tequila all summer. His friends call him "Daego."

Adam Skorupskas was born on April 1, 1984, in Detroit, Michigan. The third of four children, Adam is often described as inescapably a writer. He can also be found working as a janitor, a taxi driver, and a carpenter.

Richard Thomas, editor, is the author of three books—
Transubstantiate, *Herniated Roots*, and *Staring into the
Abyss*. He has published over 100 stories, including work in
Shivers VI with Stephen King and Peter Straub, *Cemetery
Dance*, *PANK*, *Midwestern Gothic, Arcadia, Gargoyle*, and
Weird Fiction Review. In his spare time he is editor in chief
at Dark House Press, a columnist at LitReactor, and a book
critic at The Nervous Breakdown. His literary agent is Paula
Munier.

Brandon Tietz is the author of *Out of Touch* and *Good Sex,
Great Prayers*. His short stories have been widely published,
appearing in such anthologies as *Warmed and Bound*,
Amsterdamned If You Do, and *Spark* (volume II). He also
serves as a contributor for LitReactor.com. Visit him at
www.brandontietz.com.

Hailing from North Plains, Oregon, **Gayle Towell** is a writer,
a drummer, a teacher of physics, and a mother.

Fred Venturini grew up in Patoka, Illinois, where he survived being lit on fire by a bully, a neck-breaking car accident, and being chewed up by a pit bull. His first novel, *The
Heart Does Not Grow Back*, was published in 2014. His short
fiction has appeared in *Booked. Anthology, Surreal South
'13, The Death Panel, Sick Things*, and *Noir at the Bar 2*.
He lives in southern Illinois with his wife, Krissy, and their
daughter, Noelle.

Dennis Widmyer, editor, is the webmaster and creator
of ChuckPalahniuk.net and LitReactor.com. With partner

Kevin Kolsch, he founded Parallactic Pictures, a banner for all of their independent film projects. To date, they have directed two features, a number of shorts, and have penned over a dozen screenplays.